Designing for a Royal

THE UNEXPECTED ROYALS

BOOK THREE

TOMI TABB

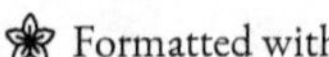 Formatted with Vellum

To JA. Thank you for inspiring me to begin my own writing journey.

Prologue

Clarissa Lee, owner of the Clarissa Lee Atelier boutique, woke up the shop's computer as the telephone rang. The petite-Asian woman—dressed in an emerald green, silk, cap-sleeve top, black ankle-length dress-trousers, and black pointed-toe ballet flats—swept her jet-black hair up into a sleek ponytail. Her manager, and good friend, Sonya, lingered in the doorway, but was waved off by Clarissa.

In a peppy tone Clarissa answered, "Hello, and thank you for calling the Clarissa Lee Atelier. Clarissa speaking, how may I assist you?"

A formal voice came on the line. "Good afternoon. My name is Abigail Martins, calling on behalf of Her Royal Highness, Princess Charlotte, the Princess Royal."

Clarissa sank down onto the stool behind her. Her eyes nearly bulged out of her head.

"We understand that it is terribly late notice; however, would you be able to accommodate a private shopping trip for Her Highness and one guest today?"

"Her Highness? Today?" Her voice jumped up an octave.

Ms. Martins patiently said, "That is correct. Her Highness is searching for a British designer who specializes in petite women's fashion."

Clarissa's fingers furiously punched the keyboard. She held her breath. There were no confirmed bookings for the rest of the day. "I'm certain we can clear our entire diary. May I place you on a brief hold?"

Clarissa received a yes and quickly ran over to the shop's front door to change the *open* sign to *closed*. The shop was deserted.

She took a moment to compose herself. Slightly out of breath, she picked up the phone. "Thank you for your patience. I have excellent news. We are fully available today. Do you have an estimate as to when the staff should expect you?"

Ms. Martins spoke. "Would one this afternoon be acceptable? I also must request you have a seamstress on site, please. If the guest of the Princess Royal selects a dress from your atelier, it must be ready to wear this evening."

Clarissa nodded. "Absolutely. I will personally be here to assist you in any way possible."

"Excellent. I'll pass the information along. Please look for Her Highness's security team to arrive twenty minutes to one."

"Thank you." Clarissa disconnected the phone. Placing it back on its receiver, she stared in disbelief. Clarissa's hands shook.

This was the break they had been waiting for.

The shop's front door opened as Sonya entered carrying a takeaway drink tray.

"Is there a reason the shop is now closed in the middle of the day?" Sonya raised an eyebrow.

Clarissa jumped out of her seat in delight. "All of our troubles are potentially over! You won't believe me when I tell you who just rang us." Clarissa accepted her strawberry boba bubble tea from Sonya. "I have one hint for you. It's a customer."

"After the lull in sales lately, we need *any* business." Sonya placed her bubble tea next to the register as she recycled the takeaway tray in the rubbish bin under the counter.

Sonya shrugged on the blazer hanging directly behind her and modeled it down an invisible catwalk. "It *is* only a matter of time until your designs are on the cover of *British Vogue* and you are the envy of every single wannabe fashionista in the world." As a tall, leggy, blonde of Russian descent, Sonya could have easily passed for a high-fashion model.

Clarissa laughed. "You are not the slightest bit curious as to who we have a booking with?" Her heart rate increased as the reality of the situation finally began to take hold. She sipped her drink.

Sonya chuckled. "You win. Who called?"

"The Royal Palace."

Sonya dropped her boba, spilling it behind the counter. The tapioca pearls splattered in every direction. Her eyes widened. "We received a call from a royal? Us? No!"

Clarissa yelped. Together they picked up the loose tapioca pearls and patted down the mess with paper towels.

Sonya apologized. "I'm so sorry I'm such a klutz! I just can't believe it."

"Princess Charlotte always favors the high designers. It seems too good to be true."

Sonya checked the floor for any contents they may have missed. "It's about time something amazing happens to us. You've earned it; somehow you managed to pop up on their radar. What time will they be here today?"

Clarissa checked her watch and exclaimed, "One! I can't

believe how late it is. We only have two hours!" She sprinted to the storage cupboard for more cleaning supplies. In record speed, they scrubbed the boutique from top to bottom.

"At least if I had to spill something, it was behind the counter," Sonya joked.

Clarissa, though stressed, broke into a bright smile. "Truer words were never spoken."

In the middle of vacuuming the carpet, Sonya abruptly stopped. "Are we going to be expected to provide refreshments for our royal guests? The last time I surveyed our snacks, we had only a few stale biscuits and tea bags."

Clarissa gasped. "I have no idea. We better be prepared just in case. Do you think some loose leaf-tea and nibbles from Cora's Bakery on the high street would do the trick?"

Sonya had her phone and wallet ready to go. "On it, boss!"

"What can I do to make this up to you?" Clarissa's shoulders sagged in relief.

"Make me employee of the month? Though, as I am the only employee at the shop, it isn't saying much." Sonya accepted her jacket from Clarissa's outstretched hands.

"I'll do you one better. If we nail this account, you can officially become the employee of the year. As my silent business partner, I'm certain you'll have no qualms at approving my request." The two sniggered. "Now off with you. We only have an hour left."

Sonya saluted Clarissa and skipped out the door. As she watched her best friend from uni leave the boutique, Clarissa was grateful she was about to share the impending experience of a lifetime with someone she considered family.

~

"Here we go!" Clarissa whispered as a black Range Rover pulled up alongside the shop's entrance on Portobello Road of

London's Notting Hill district. She shot a nervous glance to Sonya who held up her crossed fingers in a show of support. Clarissa ran to the front door to unlock it. She took a deep breath.

A short, salt-and-pepper-haired man with glasses and mustache entered the shop. He glanced around the sales floor of the boutique, finally sighting Clarissa who stood stiffly, holding the door open.

The stout man greeted Clarissa. "Hello, miss. My name is Sam. I am the head security officer to Her Royal Highness, Princess Charlotte." He shook hands with Clarissa and waved over to Sonya. He cleared his throat. "Her Highness will arrive shortly. Do you mind showing me around your shop? I need to perform a quick security sweep before she enters. All standard protocol, I promise you."

Clarissa nodded. "Go right ahead. Sonya, if you could, please show him through."

She examined the shop one last time to ensure everything was spotless for the arrival of their special guest as Sonya led Sam to the back area of the boutique. Sam spoke through his radio, indicating it was clear. A few minutes later, the Princess Royal entered. Clarissa's excitement rose ten-fold. A jolt of energy shot through her system as if she had consumed double the amount of caffeine as normal.

Clarissa soaked in the Princess Royal's outfit. Dressed from head to toe in a bright-pink tweed Chanel suit, Princess Charlotte carried herself with perfect posture and poise. The tailoring was immaculate.

Chanel Cruise Collection 20C. Someday I'll own a ready-to-wear piece like that.

Despite being in her late fifties, Princess Charlotte retained a youthful appearance. Accompanying her was a small lady with long brown hair, wearing a blue maxi dress. *That must be the guest of Princess Charlotte.*

Clarissa and Sonya deeply curtsied. Clarissa spoke first. "Your Royal Highness, it is an honor to have you in my humble shop."

Greetings exchanged; Princess Charlotte and her guest seated themselves on the two light pink sofas in the center of the room. A glass coffee table between the two sofas contained an afternoon tea service with a large assortment of sandwiches and confectioneries still warm from the oven. The strategic light-colored tones within the shop drew their clients' eyes to Clarissa's creations.

The Princess Royal poured herself a cup of tea and selected a cucumber sandwich to enjoy. She nonchalantly crossed her legs and drank her tea. "Now then, Clara will be attending the Westminster Ballet with me this evening and requires a suitable gown. My son will be wearing black-tie attire."

Clarissa relaxed, feeding off the easygoing nature of the Princess Royal. Her eyes roamed over Clara's figure, mentally taking her measurements.

She is so much like me. Flat, and in need of clothing that gives her a shape.

Many options ran through her head. Did Clara like colors, or was she a fan of neutral shades? What accessories would she be wearing? Clarissa spotted the cast on her leg.

Her dress needs to cover that and be hemmed so she won't trip over the skirt. No long trains.

Clarissa asked Clara, "Are you opposed to any particular styles or cuts? Do you have any specific requests you would like us to accommodate?"

Clara hesitated. "If it's not too much trouble, can you give me curves?"

Clarissa smirked. "If there is one task I am suited for, it is dressing a petite body. I can absolutely give you curves." Clarissa rubbed her hands together. Sonya positioned herself to gather the gowns Clarissa called for. "I think we should pull the purple, the aqua, and the pale yellow dresses."

Clara offered Clarissa a bright smile.

Just who is she to the Princess Royal? Princess Charlotte is spending so much of her own time assuring that Clara is properly attired for this evening. She even mentioned her son! I wish I could gossip with Sonya about her now. She's likely wondering about Clara too.

Clarissa took a few physical measurements from Clara to validate her mental calculations as Sonya reappeared. Clarissa scraped down a few notes on her favorite sketch pad.

Sonya cleared her throat. "Let's try on the purple first, please. If you'll follow me, I'll show you where the fitting room is. Then we can discuss any alterations with Clarissa."

Clarissa came to a halt. She had almost forgotten about the Princess Royal. Her face colored. "Please forgive me, Princess Charlotte. I should have consulted you first."

Princess Charlotte enjoyed her tea, blinked slowly, and waved her off. "I'm just a fly on the wall. Do whatever you need to do my dear."

The butterflies in her stomach began to abate. Perhaps this appointment would not be nearly as stressful as she had originally thought.

The moment they saw their clients off, Sonya and Clarissa high-fived one another. They locked the front door and pulled the shades across the large front display windows to block anyone from looking in. Sonya clicked on some quiet background music.

Sonya sank down onto one of the two client couches, placing her feet up onto the table. "Well that was one afternoon I will certainly *never* ever forget. Talk about a down-to-earth royal… Princess Charlotte was truly the opposite of everything I've read on social media."

Clarissa stepped into the back sewing area. She carefully packed Clara's selected gown into a garment bag before joining Sonya in the client area. "I agree. It went exceptionally smooth. I hardly have any alterations to do. The purple dress was perfect from the moment she slipped it on. It fit her like a glove. It's frightening. We were on such a similar wavelength." Clarissa sank down onto the couch opposite Sonya.

"This is going to change our lives, Clarissa. Just wait until that dress makes it onto the front page of every newspaper in London or even around the globe," Sonya said. The two enjoyed the leftover fruit tarts and tea.

Clarissa cracked her neck from side to side and released some of the built-up tension in her shoulders. Though mentally drained, her thoughts returned to her client. "The Princess Royal was so invested in Miss Little. Do you think there is more to the story than meets the eye? You're the one who notices details like that, Sonya."

Sonya helped herself to the last tea sandwich. She enthusiastically nodded. "Absolutely. She has to be important to have a member of the royal family personally take her on an outing."

Clarissa laughed. "Do you think she could be a romantic interest of the 'Boring Royal?'"

Sonya snorted. "No! Everyone always says he is the one royal who will *never* marry. He's too busy wrangling Prince Edmund's messes." Sonya sighed. "Now there is a handsome royal, Prince Edmund. He can take me out for a cozy date any time he pleases."

Clarissa nearly choked on the tea she was drinking. "You and Prince Edmund? Not very likely. He's much too wild for you. I highly doubt *anyone* is ever going to tame him." Clarissa gathered the dishes. "Come on. We had best do the washing up. I need to work on the hem of this dress in the next half hour. The courier taking the dress to Miss Little will be here before we know it."

Sonya pushed her away. "I'll take care of washing up, boss! Go ahead and work on that dress. Our future is literally in your hands."

Clarissa frowned. "Then I better not mess this up." She headed to the workroom.

Sonya yelled back, "You won't."

Just as Sonya had predicted, the newspapers went mad with photos of Clara once they confirmed her as the love interest of Prince David, the Duke of Leeds. The moment Clarissa was identified as the designer Clara wore to the ballet, she was immediately inundated with orders and requests for replicas of Clara Little's dress. It was a shock to their systems. In just a matter of days, the Clarissa Lee Atelier had sold through their entire inventory.

Within five months of the miracle appointment, the Clarissa Lee Atelier officially opened a second location in the more exclusive Bond Street area of London. For Clarissa and Sonya, two women who were only a handful of years removed from the London School of Fashion, and after months of struggling to make rent, it felt surreal to be able to hire a staff. Though Clara Little remained her highest-profile client, soon several other highly influential clients reached out to Clarissa.

To think that my label is now associated with a royal! If only Mama and Baba could understand I am a legitimate designer now.

At the age of twenty-seven, her career was one topic that continually came up every time she visited home. When would she stop designing and find a *real* job? Followed by her parents asking if she had a boyfriend, or her personal favorite, was she *ever* going to marry?

For Clarissa, dating and being in a relationship were the furthest topics from her mind. *Been there, done that.* For now, she concentrated on keeping up with demand for her creations and ensuring that her items continued to be affordably priced and not thousands of dollars.

Every woman should be able to look amazing and feel confident in what they wear.

"Clarissa? Are you still here with me?" Sonya asked one morning after their weekly huddle with the staff of the Bond Street location.

Sonya divided her time between the two shops, overseeing the needs of the staff these days and focused on the business needs of the Clarissa Lee Atelier. Seldom did both friends find themselves in the same location at the same time. Clarissa rarely strayed far from her dedicated design studio on Bond Street.

Clarissa turned her entire focus to Sonya. "I'm partially here. Just thinking about the fall collection. What's on your mind?"

Sonya poked her head out of her office to ensure the hallway was empty. Coast clear, she closed the office's door.

Sonya whispered, "I just set up a consultation with Clara for you."

That's nothing new. Why is Sonya whispering? It shouldn't come as a surprise to anyone.

"Okay?" Clarissa asked. "What's different about this time more than any other?"

Sonya grabbed hold of Clarissa's hands. "It's for a wedding dress consultation! You could be designing the royal wedding dress!"

Of all the news she could have been prepared to hear, it wasn't this. Her heart raced in excitement.

Clara is considering me for her dress?

"Wow. Just wow."

They jumped up and down in joy and hugged one another. After beginning their business in Clara's dodgy studio flat to now having two shops, their dreams were coming true. Clarissa's eyes teared up. Clara could ultimately select any designer in the world for such an important dress; to even be considered meant the world to Clarissa.

Chapter One

PATRICK

Lord Patrick Nelson, the Earl of Renbrook, leaned forward as he tightly gripped the reins of his favorite spirited stallion, Chester, urging him into a canter. His thighs squeezed the sides of the brown thoroughbred as he progressed through the wild fields into an all-out gallop. The wind whipped through his hair as he breathed in the crisp morning air.

"Come on, boy, punch it," he yelled into the ear of the horse who responded with gusto.

Chester's breathing increased; his hooves thundered against the hard ground with long powerful strides, snorting in exertion at the effort. After about two minutes, Patrick eased up and asked his mount to slow into a canter, trot, then walk. Horse and rider caught their breaths. It was Patrick's preferred way to begin his morning each time he was home.

The wind tousled Patrick's unruly and messy brown hair. He leaned forward and patted Chester on the side. "Well done, mate. We just might make a true racehorse out of you then. Your Dam and Sire were champion runners, and so you shall be as well. Walk on then. I promised you an extra helping of oats and carrots today." Chester snorted in reply.

The sun rose over the skyline of his Gloucestershire home, Rainridge Manor.

There is nothing more perfect than a sight like this.

Seeing the first rays of morning light touch the tips of the large manor home's angled roof from the ridge on the property's boundary warmed his heart. He soaked in the view from his saddle.

Rainridge Manor dated back to the nineteenth century and stood three stories tall. Cool, gray bricks covered in ivy with sash windows dominated the Victorian-era architecture. Natural light could be found at all hours of the day throughout the home's interior. With twenty rooms, Rainridge was smaller than the other great manor homes of the period; however, it cost just as much to maintain and run. The same struggle was shared with many of his fellow peers.

Losing his father two years ago had come as a shock. Patrick never expected to undertake the earldom's responsibilities until much later in life. Last night brought a second shock. The very idea of his mother snogging Lord Alistair Manners, the Earl of Greyston, in the very way she had once kissed his father made him enormously uncomfortable. He required several strong glasses of port after that.

Sleep evaded him as countless thoughts ran through his mind. Why had his mother hidden her relationship with Greyston? Patrick had been so upset upon seeing them kiss, yet could not fully comprehend as to why it bothered him so much.

Mother has known Alistair for close to forty years. He's widowed himself and a stand-up gent. He has assisted me so much over the past two years.

In his heart of hearts, he understood his mother might be lonely. It never dawned on Patrick that his mother would *ever* find a man to replace his father, let alone a close family friend despite being the father of his ex-girlfriend. Would he have reacted differently if they had informed him before the encounter? Likely not.

Today, however, dawned a new day. As his father once said, *everything is better in the morning.* Patrick pulled on Chester's reins and turned him back toward the stables. The estate demanded him. After all, today Rainridge Manor was hosting its first wedding of the season.

The dowager countess and Patrick's mother, Lady Lucy Nelson, greeted her son with a peck on the cheek upon his entering the modern kitchen, refreshed from his morning ride. Behind her trailed the ten-year-old family cocker spaniel, Guinevere. After a hot shower and a quick change of clothing, Patrick awaited the ensuing awkward conversation. He helped himself to a fresh cup of coffee from the stove top.

I really shouldn't be having coffee, but I need it.

"Mother. Good morning."

Patrick's mother, like her son, preferred to keep early hours. Lady Lucy's nostrils flared as she entered the kitchen. "Relieved now that you're present. I don't want to go anywhere near that imbecile mother of the bride again. She's been up and at me since six this morning. Can you believe she had the gumption to ask whether or not our fine china was hers to take home as a part of their wedding package? My own wedding china!"

Patrick sighed. *And so the wedding drama begins.*

There was always one problem or another. If weddings weren't so lucrative, he'd steer clear of the business altogether.

Tension began to build in the back of Patrick's neck. "I'll speak to our supervising wedding planner and have a word with the father of the bride. Mr. Brunner was rather calm when I explained why there was no more hot water after his daughter and her entire bridal party *all* took it upon themselves to prepare for the day at the same time yesterday. He should be able to smooth any ruffled feathers." Patrick finished his first cup of coffee and went in for a refill.

Patrick's mother crossed her arms. "See that he does."

She's scary when she is cross.

Now that his mother had joined him, Patrick served himself breakfast. They dined together whenever he was home in a tradition that began after his father's demise.

He was quite proud of how well-to-do their catering and events business was doing. Not only had it succeeded in bringing him and his mother closer together, but it gave them a renewed sense of purpose through the darker times. However, Patrick, unfulfilled by the business, required something different. Provided Patrick made himself available to assist as needed during the wedding season, his mother had been more than willing to take on the full responsibility of the business.

Patrick poured himself a simple bowl of cereal and a glass of orange juice to accompany his coffee. "Now, Mother, please play nice. They are spending a hefty sum on their wedding and have high expectations. We need to appease them so they can spread word about Rainridge as the perfect events venue. Our roof needs repairing, and in an old building, it doesn't come cheap."

As much as he loved his father, the man had failed to properly keep up with the repairs on the manor home. After a small ceiling collapse and a portion of the first-floor buckling, Patrick was stunned to discover the sheer extent of neglect. The preliminary repairs estimate exceeded the value of the house. Every extra bit of income they could spare was reinvested into Rainridge. Patrick would not give up on his ancestral home without a fight.

Lady Lucy muttered under her breath. Her attention shifted to Patrick's welfare as she made up a plate of eggs and toast. "You need more fuel. A man your size cannot sustain himself on just cereal. You are too thin. Don't you ever eat down in London? I have half a mind to visit your new flat and stock it myself with sufficient food. You haven't been nearly the same since your break-up with Mary." Lady Lucy bent over and scratched Guinevere's ears.

Patrick humored his mother and accepted the extra plate of food, placing it next to his cereal. "Thank you. I promise I am looking after myself. Better than well, to be exact. It's been more than a year."

That's the first time I've been able to hear Mary's name without so much as feeling a single thing.

He paused and cleared his throat. "Speaking of looking after ourselves, I need to address the elephant in the room. You and Lord Greyston?"

Lady Lucy gathered the dirty dishes and placed them near the sink. Her own toast, bacon, and eggs remained untouched. She didn't look at her son. "There isn't much to say. Alistair has been a loyal friend and confidant for a long time.."

Alright. Nothing that I didn't expect her to say.

Patrick squirmed in his seat. "Are his intentions with you... ahem... honorable?"

Lady Lucy stopped herself short of dropping the glass in her hands. "Paddy," her voice warned. Her eyes bulged.

Guinevere yelped.

His face flushed. "Forget I asked. It is not *any* of my business. So long as you are happy."

Lady Lucy's countenance immediately brightened. "If there is one thing you should be keenly aware of, it is that Alistair has *always* treated women as if they were queens. He was my first romantic interest." His mother's eyes sparkled. "In fact, Alistair and I are married."

Patrick spit out his coffee and began coughing.

What did Mother just say?

"You are what?"

Lady Lucy held out her left hand and revealed a princess-cut diamond and second gold wedding band. "We celebrated a quiet civil ceremony at Town Hall nearly three weeks ago. A spur of the moment decision on both our ends. We were going to tell you and his children soon. Mary is out of the country at present."

"I see."

That's the best I can manage? She's married?

He needed to congratulate her and Greyston, but Patrick had never felt so distanced from his mother.

She didn't even invite me to her civil ceremony.

More hurt than anything else, his mind slowly processed all the new information. Questions of self-worth and doubt lingered in the back of his mind. He forced himself to tread carefully to keep calm.

Lady Lucy stared out the window with a faraway look. "I'm normally not the spontaneous type. However, we are both getting on in our years and want to be able to enjoy one another's company as much as possible. We'll split time between here and his primary estate of Belshaw Hall. My dear, when you're my age, when a second chance at love comes to you, you take it and grasp it before it flies away." She turned to face Patrick, but still could not meet his eyes. She offered a small piece of bacon to the family cocker spaniel who greedily lapped it up.

Love. The enemy. He couldn't imagine even wanting a second chance. Patrick involuntarily shuddered at the thought of his own last relationship with Lord Greyston's daughter. Mary had been the perfect match for him in temperament and interests, or so he thought. Mary, a wicked smart barrister and avid polo player, had gotten on well with him. Then he introduced her to his former mate from Eton, Maxwell Longwood, the Marquess of Carnock. Reminiscing, Patrick had to admit he had been vacant and engrossed in learning how to manage and run the estate the last few months of their relationship.

The knife to the heart came when Mary informed him via text message that she had *never* harbored *any* romantic interest in him. Patrick's eyes had opened. What he thought was love had only been a way for Mary to pass the time until someone more appealing came along. Mary declared she was madly in love with Max who was fitter, richer, and a marquess.

Patrick hadn't pegged Mary as a title chaser, yet nothing shocked him much after the initial message. Mary and Max had been secretly dating for a year. Shortly after parting ways, Mary and Max married. Since then, what mattered was upholding his promise to his father of keeping Rainridge in proper order.

The wounds from Mary reopened. His thoughts returned back to the present moment. "I suppose congratulations are in order. I am very happy for you mother. Shocked, but very happy indeed." Patrick embraced his mother and kissed her on the cheek. Yet, internally, Patrick was drained, defeated, and stricken. He needed time alone. No longer in the right mood to finish his breakfast after the news, his appetite dissipated.

Lady Lucy tucked into her breakfast, sitting across from him. "Paddy, are you staying the rest of the day? I'm planning to prepare a Sunday roast."

His mobile phone rang, saving him from having to answer the question. He identified the caller as of a former Eton housemate, Prince David, the Duke of Leeds. "Sorry, Mother, I need to take this call. It's Leeds." His mother nodded in understanding as he stepped into the hallway and out of the earshot of his mother.

Patrick whispered into the phone, "David, before you tell me why you are calling, find any excuse for me come down to London and you'll be the best mate for life. I'll explain more later."

A dry, baritone voice chuckled on the other end. "In a spot of trouble with Lady Renbrook, are we?"

"David!" Patrick's voice was short.

Prince David laughed. "You're in a mood. You are lucky. I rang to ask if you might be interested in meeting with Uncle Reginald and me. He has a project you might be the perfect candidate to take charge of."

Patrick couldn't believe the timing. "Excellent. I'll be on the next train to London." Patrick examined his watch. "I can be there by two this afternoon."

David shot back, "Just because you are eager to work today doesn't mean I am. As an engaged man these days, my Clara says no work on Sundays unless she's dancing. You know the saying, happy wife, happy life."

Another love reference.

David continued. "I need to check with Uncle Reginald's secretary, but tentatively let's say half-past nine at his Buckingham Palace office."

"Fine then. I'll meet with you tomorrow." Patrick confirmed a few more details and disconnected the call.

Lady Lucy had finished her breakfast and was putting away some of the dishes.

Patrick hoped his voice would not come across as too phony. "So sorry, Mother, David has called me down to London. I'll be unable to stay late today. I truly wish I could."

Lady Lucy voiced her disappointment. "Right then. Better not miss a meeting with David. Please send my love to him and his mother. Ring me when you reach London, and I'll see you next week."

Patrick swallowed hard with guilt. Taking his mother's

hand, he looked into her eyes. "I promise I will. We shall celebrate your marriage to Greyston soon. I'll speak to Mr. Brunner before I leave." To appease his mother, he quickly finished his toast and eggs, but the cereal was too soggy to enjoy.

I'm a coward for running away to London. I just can't handle all of this happiness and these emotions right now. Too many memories.

He needed his own neutral space. He needed to leave as soon as possible, even if his meeting with David was not until tomorrow.

Chapter Two

CLARISSA

larissa snapped her sketch pad closed and pulled the earbuds out of her ears just in time to hear the cool female voice of the London's Underground automated system announce the arrival to her intended destination. "This is Kew Gardens. The next station is Richmond where this train terminates. Change here for service to the London Overground. This is a District line train with service to Richmond."

The forty-minute journey from central London passed all too quickly. Clarissa huffed and threw her pad and pencil unceremoniously into her lilac tote bag. Bounding out of her seat, Clarissa, in the nick of time, squeezed out of the train's doors as they closed.

She let out a deep breath. *I can't afford to get so distracted. Why am I such a mess right now?*

She only had two hours before the grounds closed. The weather didn't help her situation. Light mist fell from dark gray, almost black, clouds and threatened heavy rain at any moment.

Making her way to the fare gates, Clarissa tapped her

Oyster card on the sensors and briskly walked the five hundred meters to the Victoria Gate entrance to Kew Gardens.

So thankful I changed into my Converse before I left Portobello Road.

She followed the familiar path up to the member's entrance gates and soaked in the scents of the fresh foliage, wet earth, and rain, and instantly relaxed. To her body, the mixture of fresh floral, sweet, and earthy scents denoted a safe haven from the outside world. Nature provided the perfect balance of yin and yang as her mum liked to describe it.

"Do you need a map, miss?" one of the ticket booth workers inquired.

Clarissa politely declined. "No, thank you. I'm intimately familiar with the grounds."

She examined her surroundings. *I want shapes, textures, and structures.*

What could serve as her inspiration today? Clara Little was a fan of butterflies. Did she want to incorporate those into one of her sketches for tomorrow's wedding dress consultation? No. They had already played upon the butterfly theme in their first collaboration together.

Think outside of the box. Go beyond what you deem safe.

Clarissa stopped just short of the Waterlily House. She entered the Victorian glasshouse and headed toward the pond in the center of the exhibit. The Waterlily House earned its fame with the astronomically large Santa Cruz lily pads the gardeners attempted to grow each spring. They never failed to amaze the public. Although, if successful, the flowers only lasted forty-eight hours.

The wheels in her mind began to turn upon seeing the contrasting colors of fish within the pond. Picturing the fish with the water lily flowers, Clarissa immediately sat down on one of the benches inside the conservatory, flipped to a blank page of her sketchbook, and set to work.

She bit her lip as she attempted to capture the balance of softness and sharpness of the pink, purple, and white flowers, and the reds and oranges of the koi fish.

This is the perfect shape basis for the skirt. Maybe I can play on the asymmetry and develop an overskirt from it.

Reference drawings complete, Clarissa roughly sketched out two dress concepts. She delicately colored in the hues with her trusty pastel colored pencils. Clarissa focused all of her attention on the small nuances of the waterlilies and on finding a subtle way to incorporate them into the dresses. She blocked out all awareness of the outside world when at work, a trait that, as a fashion designer, could work in her favor.

Placing the last bit of color on her sketch, she carefully studied her work. *Not bad, but right now, there is no time to improve it. I will have to wait until I return home.* Clarissa checked how she was doing on time. *I have about forty minutes left before closing. What might serve as a contrast to this?*

She closed the drawing pad, stood, and took off from the Waterlily House at a jog. *I need darker hues and maybe something bolder with blues or reds.*

She examined the pathways, and she encountered a patch of woodland and blooms outside the Temple of Aeolus. *I'll settle for this lot.*

Kew Gardens closed promptly at sixteen hundred hours. With over three hundred acres of land, there was no chance Clarissa could cover much more ground and still have time to sketch.

Why did I procrastinate?

She knew the answer. Despite how many sketches she placed on paper, not a single one stood out to her as memorable, nor did it scream Clara's name. Forced designs never worked. Kew Gardens held many special memories for Clarissa.

As a fashion student, she'd wandered the grounds for hours, becoming lost in the world of plants. Kew Gardens *always* provided an answer to her problems. For the first time in a while, Clarissa fed upon the energy of the plants and harnessed the hope within a world full of possibilities.

I am almost done. Just a bit more shading.

Clarissa stuck her tongue out, a nervous habit she needed to someday conquer. All of a sudden, someone tapped her shoulder. She yelped, and her notebook went sailing into the air and into the grassy field of wildflowers. She jumped up from her crossed-legged position on the ground, her heart beating rapidly. Her breathing intensified.

"Miss, I am terribly sorry. I had no intention of frightening you, but we are twenty minutes past closing time. I need you to gather your belongings and depart the grounds. We will reopen tomorrow morning if you would like to enjoy our gardens at such time," a kindly older male worker informed her. He helped her stand. Clarissa noted the hint of fresh lavender on his person. He wore well-worn jeans, a long-sleeved navy jumper, and a gardener's apron filled with tools.

"Oh. I apologize. I became consumed by my work." Clarissa brushed the dirt off of her jeans.

She searched the perimeter for her sketchbook. *Where did it go? I can't afford to lose it! It has all my notes and work in it!*

The worker offered her a knowing smile, spotted the lost item, and retrieved it for her. "I understand. In a place such as this, it's easy to find oneself lost in awe." He scanned the open page of the book before handing it back to her. "You have some delightful renditions of the bluebell flowers and the heather. Are they for a school project?"

Clarissa packed away her art supplies into her almost

forgotten tote bag. "Thank you. The wild nature here truly is stunning. Kew Gardens is one of my favorite places in the world. My sketches are for a work project. Sometimes I wish I was still back at school. Life was so much simpler then."

The two surveyed the flowers carpeting the ground in an untamed fashion. They both enjoyed the silence for a moment. "I could get in a right spot of trouble for doing this, but why don't you take a sample with you since you haven't finished your work." The man pulled a pair of small pruning shears from his work apron and cut a cross section of flowers from a neat-looking patch, passing them to Clarissa.

Clarissa's eyes grew large as she looked on in appreciation. "Thank you so much." She let out a breath. "You have no idea how much this means to me. These flowers are going to be the center stone of my project." Clarissa accepted the flower clippings.

The worker repocketed his cutters. "I hope it goes well, miss. Best of luck to you. I hope we see you around these parts again soon. If you ever need anything, ask for old Jim. I best be heading out myself. Take care." Jim tipped his cap to Clarissa and left.

Clarissa watched him depart. *There are still kind people in the world. I'll return the favor to the next person who needs it. He was so thoughtful. I shall return.*

Clarissa was determined for her hard work to succeed. She sniffed the flowers and closed her eyes. The scent, as if by magic, evoked a vision within Clarissa.

This is the dress I am going to bring to life.

Clarissa's feet found the exit of the garden grounds. Outside the property, Clarissa opened her sketchbook and outlined the dress from her vision. Kissing the flower, Clarissa tenderly settled it inside her sketchbook and hugged it to her body. Kew Gardens once again provided Clarissa with exactly what she sought.

Chapter Three

PATRICK

En route to London, Patrick had lost count of how many times the train conductor had made this particular announcement: "We are sorry to inform you that due to a damaged trackway, this train service to London Paddington will be delayed. Thank you for your patience and understanding. We are working to resolve the situation as quickly as possible." He continued to type away in the word document detailing the breakdown of supplies and quoted estimates for Phase II of Rainridge's renovations.

He massaged his temples, recognizing the beginnings of a tension headache. *I've stared at this laptop screen for too long.*

Patrick took off the reading glasses he wore when working and placed them on the seat table tray near the computer. He rubbed his eyes. *I should have driven myself. But no. I had to be stubborn and save a few pounds.*

Truthfully, Patrick didn't exactly trust himself to drive in his current state nor did he trust the weather. *What time is it? I'm famished.* He opened his eyes and glanced at the silver Rolex watch on his right wrist. Half-past four.

No wonder the snacks from the dining car have worn off.

This trip should have taken two hours, not four! How had he failed to notice how much longer it was taking to reach London?

Patrick sighed and turned his attention back to the computer. With a few more keystrokes, he finished inputting the necessary data, saved his spreadsheet, and closed the program. He truly needed two full days off. The stress of having a large wedding at Rainridge always took a toll upon Patrick, but the additional emotional stress depleted his energy reserves.

His mood lightened somewhat knowing the cash reserves from the last round of repairs were finally replenished. Estate work completed, Patrick put the computer away and sat with his arms crossed, staring out into the dark afternoon. The rain pounded against the train's windows reflecting his mood.

There is no reason for me to work myself into a state. Reflect on the coping techniques you have learned. He shuddered. *I promised myself I would never go back to dangerous stress levels ever again.*

Wasn't that the entire reason why he left the corporate world? He'd also promised himself no more twelve- to fourteen-hour workdays.

Patrick's general practitioner had warned him to change his work habits and lifestyle. At twenty-nine, Patrick was already diagnosed with high blood pressure and high cholesterol. Combining those early onset risk factors with a family history of heart disease did not bode well for him. He'd implemented the advice and took the words to heart after one close call too many.

The overhaul of his diet and exercise were the easy bits. Learning to limit stress, anxiety, and forcing himself to sleep a minimum of eight hours a night proved much more difficult. Thus, a year ago, Patrick quit his job in finance and focused all of his efforts on being able to keep Rainridge Manor from having to forcibly sell off sections of the property. Estate management equated to a full-time job.

Patrick contemplated their foray into the world of fairy-tale-like weddings. There were so many unknown factors in the beginning. He laughed at the absurdity of just how many close calls and mistakes had plagued them throughout the beginning stages of the venture. The key had been to delegate and hire on a staff already knowledgeable in the event-planning business.

Their manager, Kelly—now his mother's right-hand woman—was irreplaceable. As Patrick had come to learn, those looking to marry could be hefty spenders. Between wedding bookings, Patrick allowed Kelly to organize high-teas and food-lovers weekends for anyone who wished to experience a small taste of how his ancestors had lived.

Those particular types of weekend events tended to attract a steady flow of single females looking for a single man with a title. On occasions such as these, Patrick made himself scarce and only available to Kelly and the staff.

The problem with these women is they want the grandeur they associate with an earl. They don't want me for me.

Should he consider dropping the use of his title altogether and only go by Patrick Nelson? Titles, in the modern-day era, mattered little. And still, his father would never have come to terms with Patrick dropping its use.

And then there are the questions about my behavior today. He had chosen to run away from the home that had once served as a refuge. Life was changing for all those around him.

The train conductor's voice returned to the loudspeaker system. "Attention passengers, we have a positive update for you. The trackway is clear and we shall begin to move momentarily. We are, however, forced to run at reduced speeds due to the inclement weather."

The passengers in the car around him cheered. Patrick

suddenly became aware of the two couples in front of him embracing and celebrating the conductor's happy news. Loneliness, jealousy, and resentment arose within him. All the sensations he had bottled up throughout the day. Couples were all around him on the train and in life. Patrick experienced an epiphany as the train began to move.

These past two years, he'd dwelled upon the past. *I've constantly had low self-worth and esteem. Try as I might, I have never fully accepted myself as good enough. This changes now.*

When Patrick was with Mary, he'd always felt the need to prove himself to her. He couldn't be anyone but himself.

The universe has not-so-subtly attempted to tell me love is in the cards for me. I have to be patient and wait for the right person to come into my life.

It was time to let go of the past and embrace change. It was his moment to make a fresh start, a new beginning. The call from David Leeds offering him an opportunity in London could not have come at a more opportune time. He felt lighter and, in a matter of moments, full of hope.

Chapter Four

CLARISSA

The journey from Kew Gardens to Clarissa's home in one of London's poshest areas, Holland Park, was uneventful. Success had brought the benefit of moving from a shared one-bedroom flat into a brand-new upscale one she could call her own.

Just as she stepped outside the Holland Park Tube station, the foreboding clouds finally opened up and released thick pellets of rain. Off in the distance, Clarissa heard a clap of thunder. Gusts of cold wind added to her misery. Her umbrella sat in the back room of her Portobello shop.

Walk quickly and you should be at the flat before long. The rain just needs to let up for five minutes.

Clarissa focused on protecting the irreplaceable contents in her tote. Tucking the bag in close to her body, she made a quick jaunt down the four blocks to her flat. Building in sight, Clarissa dodged the muddy puddles on the sidewalk and slipped into the lobby of her building slightly out of breath. She welcomed the lobby's warmth.

At least there wasn't a lorry driving past and submerging me with puddled water like in my uni days.

Stepping to the side of the entry doors, Clarissa shook the excess water off her drenched tan trench coat and placed her tote on the ground, away from the offending liquid. Water and leather never mixed. She gave a cursory glance in her bag to see if her efforts to protect her sketchbook were successful.

So far so good.

Clarissa's hands moved to her stringy, sopping wet hair. If it wasn't in a ponytail, it would've been flying about in who knew how many different directions. She didn't want to track more water inside the lift than necessary.

Ponytail in hand, Clarissa moved over to the rubbish bin and squeezed out any excess water she could. Clarissa mentally pictured herself in the bath with nice hot water, surrounded by scented candles.

She shivered as the cold from her damp clothing seeped through to her skin. Goosebumps formed on her neck and arms. Clarissa debated taking her coat off but ultimately concluded she should wait until she was inside her sitting room. With each step she took, her Converse shoes squeaked. Heading over to the lift, she stepped inside and selected the sixth floor.

Despite her current predicament, Clarissa was in an upbeat mood. Tomorrow morning, she would show Clara the three potential wedding dress sketches she'd completed on the ride home from Kew Gardens.

If she earned Clara's commission, Clarissa's plan was to immediately begin sourcing fabric, lace, and other required supplies. She debated the best way to expend the nervous energy radiating through her system as she reached her front door. Should she watch a film? Meditate? Maybe she'd just pick up one of the side sewing projects she had in her home studio.

Shifting her tote bag around on her shoulder, Clarissa scrounged through the large interior in search of her keys. She desperately needed to make herself an organizer. The bag was beautiful, yet a black hole for everything. She had some thick felt that would be perfect for an organizer. That's what she could spend her evening working on.

Clarissa knelt down and placed the bag on the wooden floor. *They have to be in here somewhere.* Finally, she spied the keys under the sketchbook. *Aha! Gotcha. Come to me!*

Hello Kitty key chain in hand; she stood, brushed off her jeans, and inserted the keys into her lock. It clicked; however, the door was stuck. She tugged at it, and to her utter shock, the door handle fell off into her hands. *Well that's rotten luck.*

Staring at the doorknob, Clarissa attempted to shove it back in its place. She frowned. *Maybe I can click it back in somehow.*

How hard could it be? Despite her best efforts, nothing worked. She sank to the floor in defeat, pulled her knees into her chest, and rested her forehead against them.

She closed her eyes. *Think, think. Would the building supervisor be available on a Sunday evening?* That was option number one. *Maybe I can find a video of how to fix it.* Option number two.

Clarissa scrambled to find her mobile. As she tapped the screen to bring it to life, the low battery display popped up. *Okay, I only need to have one percent to place a call to the maintenance manager.*

Her fingers tapped on the internet icon to look up the number that should have been stored within her contacts.

Unable to find signal? No! This cannot be happening to me right now!

The phone beeped twice and then died. She tossed the phone into her bag. She needed another plan of action.

She inspected the hole where the door handle was supposed to go. Clarissa was dismayed to be able to have a clear look inside the flat. She didn't want anyone knowing what she owned in case someone got it in their head to burglarize her home.

If I go down to the lobby, maybe I can find the night concierge or a charger to borrow.

She took the useless keys out of the lock, picked up the doorknob, and marched with determination back to the lift. She didn't have to wait long for it to return to her floor. *DING!*

The doors opened and a tall, brown-haired man stepped out, his eyes glued to his mobile. Clarissa attempted to side-step him. The floor was wet, and Clarissa slipped just as the man's shoes slid out from underneath him. Their bodies collided.

Chapter Five

CLARISSA

Clarissa fell and slid backward on the polished hardwood floors. She thrust her arm out to stop from sliding. The man fell smack against the lift's back wall. For a moment, there was only silence as they both breathed heavily. Neither one moved. Clarissa sat upright, grunted, and assessed her body.

She ached, or rather, the muscles in her neck ached. Her left wrist already revealed light discoloration and minor swelling. She was eternally grateful it wasn't her right wrist. Looking around her, Clarissa saw the contents of her bag spewed out around the floor.

The doorknob rolled and clattered down the empty hallway. The man she had clashed with groaned and remained slumped against the wall in an awkward half-upright sitting position. He breathed shallowly, eyes closed.

"Are you alright there?" she called out to him.

Clarissa stuck her foot inside the lift to prevent its doors from closing and rushed to offer her aid. *Did he fall that hard?* Hopefully he only had the wind knocked out of him. The doors slammed shut with a click. *This lift had better not move.*

Without regard for her purse, sketches, and other assorted belongings in the hallway, Clarissa pulled the red emergency knob. The lift jerked up and down, shaking its occupants within. Clarissa steadied herself.

As soon as it stopped moving, she repeated her question, kneeling beside the man. "Are you alright?"

His eyes were still closed. She smelled a light wooden, musky scent. Clarissa gently brushed a few of the man's stray curly brown hairs away from his forehead. A jolt of electricity pulsated through her body.

She quickly withdrew her hand. He moaned and took several deep breaths. Clarissa jumped up with a start. *Such a strong jawline.* His face didn't appear to harbor any cuts; however, dark indentations around his left eye indicated the beginnings of a black eye.

"S'alright," he managed to breathe out.

His eyes snapped open; he quickly sat up. "Hurt almost as bad as falling off Chester," he muttered to himself. His hands flew to his face. Clarissa cleared her throat. He squinted in her direction. "Are you alright, ma'am? You're gripping your wrist."

Those have to be the bluest blue eyes I have ever encountered. Were those flecks of gold? Against the bruising, the blue makes them look just like Van Gogh's Starry Night.

She shivered under his gaze and uncertainly said, "I'm fine. Just wet." Clarissa nervously dropped her aching limb. "What about your eye?"

The man was too tall to have collided with her. It suddenly dawned on Clarissa that the size of the bruise appeared eerily similar to the size and shape of the doorknob. She facepalmed. *It's all my fault.*

The man bestowed a ghost of a smile on Clarissa. "I'll survive. The only appendage truly injured is my pride." His eyes turned to the floor of the lift. "I have my reading glasses and mobile around here somewhere."

Off to his side, the man's black horn-rimmed glasses frame lay broken in two pieces, but the mobile was intact. "They took a worse tumble than either one of us." The man started laughing. "No surprise after the type of day I've had. From here, things can only go onward and upward."

Clarissa felt awkward. She wanted to stare at the man and learn more about him. His musical laugh drew her in. Just what type of day *had* he experienced? "Um. I can only imagine."

That's the best you can do? There isn't anything else you could have said?

She swallowed hard. Heat rushed to her cheeks; she flushed bright red. The man tilted his hand to the side. The more she looked at him, the more guilt set in.

Clarissa kept her head down and quickly pressed the button to open the lift's doors. She needed air. "I'm sorry to hear about your rotten day, and I am sorry for running into you. I hope it turns around. If you need an ice pack, I'm in flat 3C. Please excuse me. I have to find someone who works in maintenance."

Ding. The doors opened and she rushed back into the hallway. She began to unceremoniously throw whatever was on the ground into her bag. Her left wrist throbbed. She gripped it waiting for the pain to pass.

What he must think of me! He was rather good-looking too. Why was she thinking about a man at a time like this? *I'm letting the energy of Mama and Baba seep into my head.*

"Please. May I assist?" The man bent down as Clarissa nodded, not trusting herself to speak. His hand hovered over a few of the flowers from Old Jim. He sniffed them. "Nature's beauty. Lavender and wildflowers. Hm... these are truly wild, not from any shop. I'm surprised. It's getting late in the season for flowers like these."

How did he know that? Clarissa nearly swooned. "Yes, um from Kew Gardens."

His hand brushed over Clarissa's as he handed the flowers to her. His fingers were warm, surprisingly rough with callouses, and so much larger than her own. He obviously worked with his hands. Where did he earn those?

"You mentioned searching for someone who performs maintenance?" The man frowned. "Does it have anything to do with this doorknob? Or perhaps you always store one in your handbag for emergencies."

Clarissa's ears burned. "My flat's door is broken."

The man's face lit up in amusement. "You are making quite a unique first impression on me." He turned the door-knob over in his hands. He looked over to the gaping hole, then the door next to it, flat 3D. "It appears we are neighbors. I just recently moved into this building, two months ago, though I have hardly spent any time here. I sought change after my old flat finally sold. It's certainly convenient to be near central London."

The man attempted to wink and failed. The purple patch below his eye, like her wrist, was darkening. "I'll make you a deal. You are sopping wet and clearly in need of a strong cuppa. If you join me, I can go ahead and look into the problematic door. It would be much quicker than waiting for anyone to come out to fix it. I had to wait over an hour for the building supervisor to arrive on move-in day with the keys."

Clarissa suddenly grew aware of the water still dripping from her hair and coat, pooling around her feet. *It's only a cup of tea.*

Should she take him up on the offer? Clarissa shifted her legs back and forth in nervous anticipation. She hesitated, leery of trusting any man. Though Clarissa had overcome much of the past damage from her ex, she still found herself reluctant to trust anyone again.

She weighed the pros and cons. So far her new neighbor had been attentive to her, kind, and as a brownie point, held knowledge of wildflowers.

Don't get involved. Remember rule number one, focus on the goal. Clara Little's wedding dress designs. But what good will it do you if you catch a cold or are unable to get inside your own flat?

She was inclined to accept his offer. "I really do have to find someone to fix the door so I can get into my flat. I don't want to cause any more trouble to you."

He relaxed. "No trouble at all. I make household repairs all the time. My name is Patrick." The man picked up Clarissa's bag and extended his hand to her.

She bit her lip and looked up into his eyes. The azure, no, cornflower blue sang to her. His eyes changed colors from earlier.

They must reflect his mood.

Blue was Clarissa's gateway drug. They welcomed her in. Clarissa hesitated. Nothing appeared off in his body language.

"If you're certain. Thank you. I don't know what else I might do." They shook hands. His grip was strong.

Patrick's eyes danced in amusement. "Pardon me, but do you have a name?"

Clarissa stammered. "I'm Clarissa." Her dark hair fell in front of her face like a curtain hiding it. How had her hair escaped the ponytail?

Patrick signaled for Clarissa to follow him. "Well then, Clarissa, do you take milk or sugar? I have a proper service I just unpacked and possibly some lemon tarts, if my grocery order came through. I ordered it from the train."

Patrick was dressed in dark wash jeans, a white dress shirt, and a cashmere navy crew neck jumper. He carried a medium-sized duffle bag she hadn't noticed before. Clarissa's eyes examined his choice of fabrics. She noted a black overcoat, black umbrella, and plaid scarf in his arms. Patrick had a stocky build, but the clothing he wore was all too big for his body.

As a fashion designer, Clarissa knew everything screamed high-end, designer quality. *He shouldn't wear baggy clothing.* It didn't suit him. Why buy expensive things if he was going to procure the wrong sizes? *The high street shops would be a better value for money.*

They walked the three steps to his flat's front door, directly next to hers. Her shoes squeaked as she walked. She cringed. Patrick laughed. At this rate, her face was going to be permanently pinkish red. Patrick pulled out a set of keys and opened the door to his flat. Stooping down, he picked up a small bag of groceries without pausing to scan the contents.

The layout of his flat mirrored hers. They walked past the entryway and into the sitting area that opened to the kitchen. Fully packed boxes lay scattered about. The flat screamed unlived-in bachelor pad, with the black leather sofa and coffee table. A large-screen television dominated the common area's main feature wall that, consequently, was unadorned and bare white.

Patrick placed the box of groceries on the kitchen's island, took her coat, and hung it in the powder room near the entryway. He offered her a dry towel and told her to slip off her shoes.

She thanked him. He threw his belongings down by the couch and motioned for her to follow him through to his kitchen. A stainless-steel kettle and tea service layout on the counter. Again, there were no personal touches to this spartan space.

So far, everything appears normal but too sterile, almost cold.

With his knowledge of her flowers, she had expected to see

a few plants, based on the amount of time he had owned the flat. He had not been joking earlier about not spending much time here. Once he *did* settle in, what homey touches could she expect to see?

Patrick moved to the freezer and pulled out an ice pack for each of them. She said, "Thank you."

Next, Patrick opened his refrigerator, filled the kettle with water from the tap, and placed it on the stove to heat up. Clarissa sat on one of the three bar stools next to the kitchen island.

Patrick placed an apron over his jumper and jeans. "It's no trouble at all, but you never did answer my original question. Do you take cream, milk, sugar, or some other concoction in your tea?"

The apron pulled taut, giving Patrick a nice shape and making her want to tailor his clothing. Her fingers began to itch. Did he lack confidence? She didn't think so. After all, how many men would have worn an apron? He obviously wanted to protect his clothing. Or was he a chef? The apron appeared well-worn.

"I take my tea straight please." Clarissa took in the kitchen. Had he received those lemon bars? She loved lemon with her tea.

Clarissa detected Patrick's gaze on her. He met her questioning eyes. "My home is a mess of boxes. I've been to visit my mum for the last few days. The rail service delayed me nearly two hours today. The plan was to unpack a bit tonight. I've neglected this place since the boxes arrived from storage last week." Patrick checked the kettle and moved around the kitchen, pulling out some sugar and loose-leaf Earl Grey tea.

Clarissa timidly answered. "I'm impressed by your mind-reading ability. If I'm home, I am available if you need any assistance unpacking. It's a tricky challenge. I moved about a month ago. I only just finished placing the last of my belongings in their new homes."

It was nice to finally meet one of her new neighbors. These days, everyone in the world was always on a different schedule. Or if they were introverts, like Clarissa, they preferred their privacy.

Emboldened, Clarissa asked, "Do you have the skills of a magician or telepathy? What am I thinking now?"

Patrick's face remained neutral. "You should know that true magicians *never* reveal their secrets." He unpacked the grocery delivery and stopped upon reaching a pastry box. "Aha! Care for a lemon tart?"

Clarissa laughed. "Telepathy indeed. Lemon is one of my weaknesses."

Patrick chuckled. "No. If I dabbled in magic, my flat wouldn't be in a state such as this. As it is, I didn't have the foresight to label the contents of my boxes. It took a fair bit of time just to find my kettle, teapot, cups, and a few other utensils."

The kettle whistled. Patrick turned his attention to pouring the hot water into two white ceramic cups. He placed his ice pack on the counter.

If he's messy, he more than likely can't be a chef either. They prefer their kitchens to be pristine and orderly. Just as when I'm designing and creating.

Clarissa accepted a tea ball of loose-leaf tea from Patrick and placed it into the hot water. Patrick followed suit and added a cube of sugar. "So, Patrick, if you aren't a magician, what is your day job? By night, you must be studying to be a ninja."

"It's a little complicated, but the short answer is I work a variety of odd jobs. My most recent project will hopefully begin tomorrow. I have a meeting early in the morning." He turned the tables on Clarissa. "If you don't mind me asking, what line of work are *you* in?"

That's a decidedly vague answer. Must be the CEO or CFO of one of those big companies here in London. Investments? He appears to be the type who would spend all day in an office glued to his computer. He's too well dressed to be an underling. Two can play the vague game.

"I work in fashion."

Patrick said, "Excellent. Perchance you can recommend a tailoring service. Normally I'd pop down to Savile Row and see my man, but I'm in a spot of trouble. I understand it's after five on a Sunday; however, that meeting I mentioned earlier requires a clean, pressed, and polished suit. The only suit I have in my possession at present is not fit to wear."

Clarissa's eyes widened. Savile Row? So Patrick *did* invest in only the best. Clarissa's esteem for Patrick continued to grow. *I'm shocked he would trust a person he has just been introduced to for recommendations on alterations. What if I knew next to nothing about clothing? I could be a shop attendant for all he knows. Is he so desperate?*

Why would Savile Row not have taken care of everything when he purchased the suit? Bespoke menswear was supposed to be perfectly fit to the client. That's why men bought it, and why it came with a hefty price tag.

Patrick played with the rim of his teacup. "My dry cleaner wasn't open on my way here from the train station. He has the one suit I have that's passable and won't open until half-past ten tomorrow. The rest of my suits are in storage. I've been lucky enough, until recently, to work in jeans and wellies."

Patrick tapped his hands on the island's counter. "Of all the items to forget to have sent down from storage, you would think I would've remembered my workwear. There is your true proof I'm not a magician. Too late to worry about it now. At this rate I may just rely on sellotape and safety pins."

Clarissa shuddered. *No. Absolutely not. Sellotape? Safety*

pins? There is no way I am letting any piece of clothing be worn in such a manner! It's an insult to fashion!

Did he seriously think anyone was available to work on such short notice on a Sunday evening? Why didn't he just come out straightaway and ask her to fix the suits or ask if she knew how to sew? She'd do it in a heartbeat. *I'm obviously not a model. I am much too short for that.*

"You've been so wonderfully helpful to me. Let me return the favor to you. I'll do your alterations myself since you so kindly offered to fix my door handle. I have a sewing machine and all the supplies we need inside my workroom in my flat."

Should she mention she owned her own business? Not yet. It was slightly more information than she felt comfortable sharing.

Patrick's mouth turned into an "O" shape. He appeared stunned by her offer. "Oh no. That is too much. I really do just need a tailor." Clarissa, surprised to see him sounding so sincere, watched his shoulders hunch. "I do not want to take unfair advantage of you. It's my own fault I'm in this bind."

You are not getting out of it now, Mr. Patrick. Clarissa had fully invested herself in the project. *He looks dashing when he's worried, and maybe even more so in clothing that fits.* Where had that thought come from?

"It's no trouble at all. I was going to work on a side project tonight even if I hadn't encountered you. I promise I'm just as good, if not better, than any tailor. I've worked on menswear before. I'll have you sorted out straightaway," Clarissa promised.

His large eyes widened and revealed the depth of his gratitude. "As soon as we finish the tea, I'll set to work on your door."

Clarissa paused and suddenly remembered the emergency sewing kit in her tote. She tapped her head with her hand. "I have my travel sewing kit in my bag. I can pin and mark up the adjustments now and finish them when I have access to my machine. Was it only your trousers, or does your jacket also require alterations? What about the shirt you intend to pair with it?"

Patrick frowned in thought. "I'm confident the jacket and shirt are alright; however, I'd certainly appreciate a fashionista's opinion. I'm not so hot at picking out clothing. I understand the basics."

Patrick cleared his throat. "This is embarrassing, but my mother usually consults on my attire if I need a woman's opinion. Otherwise, I rely solely on my tailor. The suit was commissioned eight or nine months ago. I don't believe my body has changed too radically in that time frame." Patrick smiled and finished his tea.

We shall see.

What he considered to fit and what Clarissa considered appropriate might be on two entirely different levels.

Patrick stepped away to change while Clarissa finished her second lemon tart. The perfectly soft and flakey outside melted in her mouth. *This is so good.*

She needed to find out where these little slices of heaven came from. She might never go back to her Tesco ones again. Sonya must be converted to these. Could they justify them as a business expense?

Speaking of Sonya, she will never believe that I spent more time fraternizing with a member of the opposite sex than sketching!

Patrick came out from his bedroom almost comically holding up the trousers to keep them from falling down. "Here we are."

Clarissa tried and nearly failed at holding in her laughter.

She would never have believed this was a bespoke suit that belonged to him if he hadn't made mention of it earlier.

The jacket fit his shoulders, but the rest of the proportions were severely off-kilter. The same rang true of the shirt and trousers which, at first glance, appeared two to three sizes too large on him. The navy and white pinstripes matched nicely against his coloring, yet the question remained, why was the fit so horrid?

Patrick was silent as Clarissa directed him to stand under better lighting. She walked around him and pulled at the suit in a few places, and pinning back the seams of some of the baggy areas of fabric.

"This suit is definitely yours? This won't do at all. This fit does nothing for you. Forgive me, but even earlier I noticed your everyday clothing does not fit correctly to your body."

Clarissa took several measurements and made a few chalk marks on the jacket. *I did want something to work on this evening. Alterations might take up an hour. Bespoke suits are easy to adjust at least. Seems a shame to cut all these hand stitches.*

Patrick reaffirmed. "Yes. I had this suit made up by Andy. It was slightly loose and needed to be taken in when we did our final appointment, but he fixed all the issues."

Clarissa clucked. "I've got the jacket sorted. These trousers are barely staying on. Are you planning to wear a belt, braces, or should I add in some side tabs?"

Patrick considered the question. "I usually wear braces and a waistcoat. I can go get them for you."

Clarissa stopped him. "In a moment. First, I need to confirm where you want the waistband to sit. Unless you prefer a high-waisted look?"

"Just where you have it." Patrick crossed his arms to hold them out of Clarissa's way.

Clarissa finished marking up the trousers and reviewed the

fit of the shirt. Tucked in, they decided to make the minimal amount of adjustments.

Muuuuuuuuuuuch better. All easy fixes.

She had Patrick place the jacket on once more and checked over the alignment of the stripes on the fabric. "Take all your suits to your tailor. I have a suspicion they all need altering."

Patrick ran a hand through his hair. "I don't think it's Andy's fault. I suppose I've lost some weight from when this was created. I became a vegetarian this past year. My health wasn't the best."

Clarissa nodded. That made a lot of sense. "I hope everything is better now. No residual health issues?" As much as she desired to know more, now wasn't the time to pry for more personal information.

"Indeed, much better. Actually, that is one of the many reasons I moved here. I'm starting fresh in a new flat, and Holland Park is supposed to be a more relaxing area of London than other parts of the city. Did you know this area was once a Roman Road?" Patrick glanced down at the suit. "You do excellent work. I'm impressed."

"Thank you. And I didn't know this was once a Roman Road. There is a lot to Holland Park I still have yet to uncover. I've heard the gardens are exquisite."

Would Patrick be interested in exploring them with her?

She filed that thought away for later and asked, "You have so much first-rate knowledge of the area. What else can you tell me about Holland Park?"

Patrick spouted off, "Cope Castle, where the gardens are, was once a Jacobian castle. The grounds encompassed fifty-four acres of land. It was later renamed Holland House. Unfortunately, it took on extensive damage during World War II. Only a small terrace and one wing of the home survived."

A walking encyclopedia. He holds so much information in

his brain. Clarissa slowly put the last of her supplies in their case. She didn't want to end their conversation yet.

"If you change clothes, I'll be happy to finish this up. There are two places I prefer to work on by hand."

Patrick departed to change. *Stay professional.* She pushed aside the thoughts of what it had felt like to be able to run her hands over Patrick's body. He had a shape he shouldn't be so timid about revealing.

There is a reason I don't work with male clients; I might be much too distracted.

Additionally, while Clarissa could proficiently craft menswear, it never ignited her passion the way an evening gown did.

~

As Patrick described it, the door could easily be repaired. Clarissa had no understanding of how he did it, but she considered the experience enlightening. She watched him force the door open and expertly oil and replace the screws and mechanisms to get her inside the flat.

As promised, Clarissa set straight to work. "I need to use a machine for the stitching on the trousers. I'll be ready for you to try this on in about half an hour. I'm just in the back room. Holler if you need me."

Patrick wiped his brow. "I should be done in about the same amount of time."

It took Clarissa longer than she wished. Her left hand had begun to stiffen. Forty-five minutes passed. Clarissa surveyed the now whole door by testing the lock and handle. "This girl is impressed. Is this a world's record for how quickly you've worked?"

"Yes. In all fairness, I'm rather used to older hardware and repairs. My family home dates back to the nineteenth century.

I've become adept at small-scale repairs over the years. Mum has never trusted anyone else to work around her antiques." Patrick glanced down at his hands covered in oil.

I do need him to model the suit and check my work. Shall I take a chance? She also had no desire to see him leave just yet.

"Please come inside. My flat's layout is identical to yours. The powder room has a blue towel you can use to clean your hands off with. Meet me in the sitting room. Once you try this on, we can both celebrate with some dinner, if you'd like. I can order any takeaway in the city."

Clarissa left Patrick to his own devices as she stepped away to procure his altered clothing.

Chapter Six

PATRICK

Patrick studied Clarissa's flat. Framed photos lined the walls of the front entryway. *The smiling couple must be her parents. They have round faces like her. And is this one her brother?*

The photo revealed a younger Clarissa wrapping her arms around a boy of ten or eleven. He was holding up a tennis racquet and an oversized trophy.

Before reaching the area that opened to the sitting room, he noted her diploma from uni and a framed article about the Duke of Leeds's fiancée, Clara Little.

Why does she have that framed?

Patrick yawned and berated himself for rubbing his swollen eye. It began to pulse and send out several throbs. The fatigue from a long day was catching up with him. He searched for a place to sit.

The dove-gray sectional sofa framing the center of the sitting room appeared inviting. He placed his five-foot, eleven-inch frame onto the center of the sofa. He sagged in relief against the soft cushions.

Where a television set was mounted to the wall in his flat,

Patrick spied a large tropical fish tank in Clarissa's. The lights highlighted several brightly colored fish and seahorses swimming around a coral seascape.

He found himself moving closer and staring at the aquarium. The seahorses drifted back and forth with the flow of the water, their tiny tails gripped to the arms of the corals. Their fins flickered as they swam closer to the glass.

Patrick spoke to the fish tank. "I may need to ask your owner about getting a school of you lot for myself. You are handsome fellows indeed." It greatly relaxed him.

Simple decorations adorned the rest of Clarissa's sitting room. From the white rugs to the mahogany bookcases, the room, though sparse, proved tasteful. Vases of cheerful flowers complemented the gray, white, and gold color scheme.

Patrick enjoyed browsing over Clarissa's Dior, Chanel, and Louis Vuitton coffee table book selection. *From the look of this room, it's easy to see fashion consumes a large part of her life. What exactly was Clarissa's occupation?*

Clarissa returned to the sitting room. "Well, certainly not my usual standard, but this should do for tomorrow. Go on. Use the powder room to try this on." She impatiently pushed his altered suit into his outstretched hands.

Patrick understood the hint. *Feisty thing, isn't she.* Patrick chuckled to himself. He returned to the powder room. As he changed, Patrick couldn't believe the transformation in the mirror. *Is this me?*

Normally, he didn't care to study his reflection unless he was shaving. *Clarissa, you are a miracle worker.* Truly looking at himself, he could see how his body had changed. For the first time since his childhood, Patrick had a defined chest and waistline. His body was now healthy. He felt himself glowing at all the hard work he'd put in.

What a difference it makes to have a suit feel like a second skin.

He pulled at the trousers and jacket. "Fits better than it should," he offered and stepped out of the powder room.

"Take this and this and stand straight." Clarissa handed him a cool glass of water and an aspirin. "In case your face feels as sore as my wrist does."

Patrick happily accepted the medicine and swallowed the cool water. "Thank you, but you shouldn't have worked on the suit if your wrist was aching. I feel so guilty." He shoved his hands into his pockets. "Now that I think about it, I never apologized to you earlier. I wasn't looking where I was going in the lift."

"The fault is also mine, but it's all in the past. Now, please, stand straight. I have to ensure the pinstripes line up correctly and check on the seams of the garment." Clarissa didn't look up. She inspected the fabric up close. "Hmm. Yes, this should do for now."

How do I properly thank her? This was a lot more work than fixing a door. Dinner? I bet she's as nippy as I am. It must be near seven.

"I am so pleased with my turnout. I am a new man. You've literally saved my hide for tomorrow." Patrick paused. "Please don't take this the wrong way, but would you consider having dinner with me? Instead of ordering takeaway, that is. I was planning to make eggplant Parmesan. I have plenty of ingredients for two."

Clarissa considered his offer. "I've already taken up so much of your night. I hate to impose myself upon you."

"I would love to have company. Plus, maybe you could assist me with recommending what I should add to the nonexistent decor in my flat. I love the elegance of your decor and the fish tank. How long have you had seahorses? I am keen on adding a fish tank to the flat now that I have seen how it can brighten up a space like this."

*I need to find out more about who you are Clarissa —
fashion worker extraordinaire.*

It would be nice to have a friend to dine with instead of being alone. Eggplant Parmesan for two sounded much better than for one. Patrick missed having another person to interact with outside of his family.

Now that his mother was newly married, he truly felt alone. For the two short hours he'd been in Clarissa's presence, he had fed off her energy and infectious inner radiance.

Clarissa let out a breath she was holding. "I can't promise that I'm that decent of a conversation partner; however, be forewarned that once I start in on my little seahorses, I may never be able to stop. They are extraordinary sea creatures."

Patrick smiled. "Brilliant. I want to hear everything about them. We can walk back to my flat together."

Clarissa locked her door behind her before they traveled the short distance to the flat next door. "I have to admit, I'm absolutely thrilled to have a home-cooked meal tonight. I always order takeaway. Someday I wouldn't mind learning how to make beans on toast or a pasta dish."

Patrick rubbed his hands together in delight. "I can offer you a module on kitchen basics, should you so desire. It may even have to become a nightly tradition. I always have recipes I enjoy experimenting with. I learned a lot from my mum. It was our way of bonding. I was a hit at uni. My flatmates had me do all the food preparation. Having company would be a boon to me."

Clarissa laughed. "If only you were serious. I would love to have a personal chef. Please knock on my door whenever you need someone to sample your culinary delights! I'm always available, especially with lemon!"

Little does she know, I am quite serious. Patrick held the door open for Clarissa as she entered. His heart beat wildly in excitement. Here was his fresh start.

Chapter Seven

CLARISSA

Clarissa groaned as the morning sunlight awoke her. *Too bright. Too early. Need sleep.*

She lay in bed, berating herself for staying up so late chatting with Patrick. Only after they'd exhausted the merits of caring for saltwater fish over freshwater ones did she leave Patrick's flat.

It must have been two in the morning. Time quickly passed before either of them had noticed. Spending time with a man who was the complete opposite of her ex-boyfriend provided an entirely new experience.

Patrick had invested himself in *her* and asked for nothing in return, just company and conversation. It had been a novel experience. Clarissa wished the night could have lasted longer.

The alarm on her mobile went off, angrily blaring at her. Eventually, she managed to stagger out from underneath the warm covers to dress for the day. Puffy bags under her eyes greeted her in the mirror.

She yelped upon seeing the time. *Of all days to have a lie-in, it happens to be today! I am going to be late!*

She threw her hair into a simple French braid. After

rummaging around her closet, Clarissa tossed several outfits onto her bed and stared them down. She could wear all black, but it was not her lucky color. The jewel-tone sapphire blue reminded her of Patrick's eyes. She paired it with knee-high boots, a white belt, and a blazer. *That should work out lovely.*

Hurriedly, she sprinted out the door and hailed a black cab for the one-kilometer ride over to Portobello Road. She could do her makeup upon arrival at the shop. Under normal circumstances, she preferred to walk. She entered the building to find Sonya already preparing the tea service and showroom for their V.I.P. clients.

"Sonya, what would I do without you?" Clarissa hugged her friend and placed her coat and purse in her back office. "I owe you boba today."

"Here's your coffee. When I arrived before you, I thought you might need something extra strong." Sonya's knowing eyes raked over Clarissa's less-than-perfect appearance. "You appear to have enjoyed yourself last night. I don't remember you warning me you were planning on an evening out. I would have joined you. Are you still sloshed?"

Clarissa colored. She couldn't hold more than one glass of wine. *How much did I indulge in last night? Two or three glasses? I never should have agreed to a wine pairing demonstration.*

She had been intrigued by Patrick's explanation of how wine could enhance subtle flavors within their dinner and completely change her outlook on flavors she *thought* she knew. She could still taste the seasonings on her taste buds. She'd wanted to step outside her comfort zone and try something new.

Clarissa's cheeks flushed deep red. "No comment for now. I um… need to finish preparing myself. As you can tell, I awoke late." Flustered, Clarissa walked into the back room.

Her hands shook with nervous energy as she gripped the edge of her desk.

Sonya followed her. "So that's code for yes." Sonya shook her head at Clarissa. "Come on. You are obviously in no fit state to do your own makeup. Hand me your kit, and I'll have you ready in three minutes. Tell me, did you find a *man* to take home? Was he handsome? Details, please."

Clarissa daydreamed as she reflected on Patrick's attributes. From the corners of his mouth upturning into a bright smile to the way he sensually sliced up an eggplant with a chef's precision, for the first time in a long time, Clarissa had enjoyed having dinner with a male companion.

How is Patrick getting on this morning? Does he harbor the same curiosity as me? She had never connected with someone like this.

With steady hands, Sonya worked on Clarissa's foundation. She pouted. "I'm waiting. Was he Asian?"

Clarissa sighed. "I have a new neighbor on my floor. We bumped into one another, exchanged favors, and dined together. There isn't much to tell. No he isn't Asian. I won't limit who I date to fulfill my parents' wishes. Not that it was a date. Just dinner."

"You exchanged favors... hmm. What kind of favors?" Sonya baited Clarissa.

"Nothing like that. My door handle fell off and Patrick fixed it, but he also needed a few minor alterations on his suit for this morning. A Savile Row suit, nonetheless. You should have seen the fit. It was all out of sorts." Clarissa grimaced.

"A likely story. You stayed up late and volunteered to fix a Savile Row suit? You will most definitely need to come up with a better excuse than that. Everyone knows Savile Row suits are cut to perfection." Sonya laughed. "All done. You're presentable. I'll ask you for the *real* story about Patrick as soon as our guests depart."

Clarissa glanced into the compact mirror and hugged Sonya again. "Deal. Now let's score this account!" They performed their lucky handshake.

~

Clarissa anxiously paced the store. Her hands gripped the rose-quartz charm on her necklace tightly. Today could potentially be the defining moment of her career. Her mind played out the many different scenarios that could occur when Clara Little and her entourage arrived. Then there was Patrick. Could she afford to have a man in her life right now? Meeting him had been unexpected and caused Clarissa to cautiously lower her barriers.

What are the odds that I will encounter him tonight? I have no idea what working hours he keeps. Had he enjoyed himself last night?

Clarissa pictured herself assisting Patrick with finding aquarium supplies and other decor for his flat. What would a decorated flat reveal about his personality and his interests?

The front bell to the shop rang out. They were early! Clarissa's hands shook. She took a nervous breath and carefully showed the two personal protection officers from the team of Prince David, the Duke of Leeds, inside.

"We'll conduct our standard security sweep, if that is alright with you, Miss Lee."

Clarissa didn't trust herself to speak, and nodded. She wasn't this much of a mess the last two times Clara visited. Today, however, there was so much more at stake. The men surveyed the perimeter and checked the entrance and exits.

"Thank you." Given the all clear, they escorted their charges inside.

The chatter of three excited ladies trailed off as they entered the room. "Welcome back to my shop, Miss Little. It is an honor to have you here today." Clarissa winced as her voice pitch jumped. *Don't be so nervous!*

"Clarissa, it is so good to see you! I am sorry we're rather early today." Clara smiled as Clarissa showed Clara and her two associates to the twin, light pink sofas.

Clara Little, the bride for today's appointment, had a reserved personality, like Clarissa. The relationship between the two women blossomed with each visit as the number of Clara's public engagements increased. She hugged Clarissa in lieu of a handshake. That's the type of person Clara Little was.

"Relax. I can see you quivering. It's just me." Clara's smile brightened. "Let me introduce my bestie slash maid of honor, Amanda Collins, and my surrogate mom, Imogen Collins."

Imogen Collins surprised Clarissa with her gentle Manchester accent. "No need to be worried, dear. We are quite normal folks."

Everyone exchanged welcomes and seated themselves. Taking a deep breath, Clarissa thanked them for their patience. She introduced Sonya to Amanda and Mrs. Collins.

Clarissa admitted to the Collins women, "I have seen your photos in quite a few places on social media with Prince Eddie. As cliché as it sounds, Sonya and I find it so utterly romantic."

Amanda flashed an infectious grin to Clarissa. "We do make a pretty awesomely awesome couple." Clarissa chuckled.

Sonya chatted animatedly with Amanda for a few minutes. Sonya had the gift of knowing exactly what to say to every single person she met, as if she had known them her entire life. Clarissa wished she shared the same quality.

From the counter by the register, Clarissa retrieved her black design folio. All eyes in the room focused on the designer. The conversation quieted down. Clarissa's heart picked up its pace as she slid out her sketches. Her palms grew sweaty.

"From past consultations, I am aware of your preference

for gowns with an empire waist. Depending on if you intend to follow the tradition set by past royal brides, I was uncertain if you required a dress that covered your bare shoulders. If you follow suit, I thought three-quarter lace or cap sleeves would be the most appropriate choice." Clara nodded in understanding.

"All of my inspiration behind these sketches comes from the magic of Kew Gardens. Flowers, no matter how perfect they may appear in the distance, each have their own small differences and individual nuances that make them unique. Rain may cause a flower to lose some of its petals; a bee landing on the flower may take off and alter the direction of a petal. One just has to know where to look." Clarissa had everyone's rapt attention.

"Dress option number one draws inspiration from the Santa Cruz water lily. The flower only lasts for perhaps two days and is a soft cream with a gold center and pale pink undertones. For this dress, I decided on a V-cut neckline with a lace overlay and three-quarter length sleeves. The gold crystal belt highlights the dropped waist and fitted A-line style skirt. This dress would feature an asymmetrical overlay where the panels would be cut in the shape of the lily flower petal. I want to give the dress some movement. I sketched the skirt to have a small train and corset ties in the back."

Clarissa handed the sketch of dress number one to the ladies.

"Dress number two is inspired by your role as Princess Aurora in *The Sleeping Beauty*. Act I, if we are being specific. You may notice the color of the sketch floats between ivory and champagne. I looked for references from your tutu at the Westminster Ballet and attempted to match the pink and gold tones. This color is the closest in my mind's eye. This gown sits just off the shoulder with cap sleeves. The top half of the dress is fitted to your body, playing off the corset of your ballet costume. I would embroider dainty roses into the corset. In contrast to a tutu, the dress is fitted in a mermaid style and shows off your silhouette. I would create butterflies and roses out of tulle or a similar fabric."

Clara and Amanda studied the second option as Clarissa went on to explain her last concept. Clara's eyes danced in excitement.

Clarissa's hand lingered on the third sketch. This one was her favorite of the three and the one she hoped Clara might select. "This gown features an illusion halter-style neckline with a keyhole cut-out in the back to reveal just a hint of skin. This dress is inspired by the wildflowers of England. I have sketched a few different abstract floral applique patterns into the top of the dress to represent the wildflowers you may encounter in many of the meadows around the UK in spring. The dress is fitted to your body and flares outward at the hips. It is the closest dress to your favored empire waist. This dress features a detachable skirt to add volume to the dress and to appease the more conservative members of the royal family. It provides both a ball gown and a more fitted contemporary look."

The last sketch made its way around to the three ladies in the room. Everyone was silent as they exchanged sketches and compared them side by side, reexamining the details. Clarissa fidgeted with her hands as she waited for a reaction.

Sonya stood off to the side, chatting softly with one of the security guards, yet shot her a wink. *Five pounds tells me she has his mobile number or a date before this afternoon is over.*

Clara's eyes darted to-and-fro. Finally she flashed a bright grin, and her cheeks glowed a rosy red. Clarissa bit the inside of her cheek.

Amanda let out a long whistle. "No wonder Clara is taken with you. You are *very* talented, Clarissa. I'm impressed. Each one of these screams you, C. You could pick any one of these and look ammmmmmmmmmazing. You definitely know Clara's style better than she knows her own style. Can you help *me* out next? I normally go vintage, but I looooooooove all of these designs."

Clarissa accepted the compliment. "Thank you. I'd like to think I have a thorough understanding of my clients."

Mrs. Collins cleared her throat. "Amanda Tabitha, that is not how we behave. You may ask if Clarissa is even available to design a dress for you. She has her hands full enough with Clara. Designing a royal wedding dress is a difficult enough task to undertake."

Amanda deflated. Having the ability to design for Prince Edmund's girlfriend would be another amazing opportunity. Clarissa was uncertain if she should volunteer.

Clara hugged the sketches to her chest, overwhelmed with emotions. "These are stunning! I am not sharing her, A. I found her first."

Her eyes roamed over the sketches and back to Clarissa. "I love that you went for the ivory and champagne color! It's so unusual. David would want something traditional, but I'm not a traditional bride. I want to stand out in my own way; a subtle hint of color is the perfect bit of unexpectedness. I love all three. I knew I could count on you to find the perfect designs for me. You didn't manage to make one, though. You've created three spectacular options!"

I never expected to garner this much of a positive reaction. Being able to bring out the inner glow and radiance of a client was why she chose to design—to bring out inner beauty.

Clara's eyes glazed over. "I actually think I want *two* dresses. One for the ceremony and one for the reception. I wish I could try these on now. It's so difficult to pick only two. I do not think I can justify three, however."

Which two does she prefer? I never considered she might want a reception dress too!

Trying on a sample might narrow the decision down. Clarissa inclined her head toward the back storage area. "I have two gowns from my next collection that are of similar silhouettes to the halter and A-line dresses. Let's see how they fit you. Just please bear in mind, they are not wedding dresses."

Clara nearly bounded out of her seat, poised to try on the dresses the moment it was suggested. "Please! I'm a visual person. Comes with the territory of being a ballerina and watching and studying choreography all day."

Clarissa and Clara exchanged laughs. Then Clarissa slipped out of the room and sagged against the wall as she closed the door. The jittery excitement nearly caused her to burst.

Two dresses? Wow. Which ones will she decide upon? The water lily dress? The Aurora dress? Or the wildflower dress?

She walked quickly into the workroom where two silky evening gowns sat inside non-descript garment bags waiting to be placed on display. Although the silk fabric was much lighter than the real wedding dress fabric would be, they would serve as an adequate stand-in for the real thing. Amanda squealed with joy as the dresses were carried out.

She opened her large purse and pulled out a bottle of champagne, five glasses, and a container of chocolates and strawberries. "I came prepared. Let's get this party started. You only get to shop for your wedding dress once, C."

Clarissa quizzically stared at Amanda's tote. How had she fit all those in there? *I'm not usually so easily impressed.*

Imogen Collins shook her head at her daughter and placed her hand on her head. "Really, Amanda? Champagne and strawberries? I shouldn't say I'm surprised. I raised you, after all."

Amanda shrugged. "I did call ahead to ask permission first. I'm not that bad. Sonya cleared it with Clarissa. And it's from the king's private reserve, meaning it probably cost more than my monthly salary."

Clarissa and Sonya nodded in confirmation. "That she did."

Amanda Collins handed champagne flutes to her and to Sonya. Clarissa's cheeks flushed. "You're including us?"

Amanda popped the bottle open and began pouring the champagne. "Why wouldn't we include you two? You guys are doing all the hard work here. C just has to stand at the end of an aisle and say 'I do.'"

Sonya mouthed *drink up* to Clarissa from her spot near the protection officer. *I shouldn't indulge myself. I had enough last night, but would it be rude if I said no? Best drink up. Maybe just not a full glass. I need to be able to have a clear head through the end of this appointment.*

Clarissa had no time to change her mind as Amanda exclaimed, "To the future Duchess of Leeds. Cheers!" They toasted to Clara and clinked their glasses together.

At this moment, Clarissa's body warmed. She belonged; Clara had transitioned from a client into a true friend. She had a budding suspicion Amanda might soon settle in as a member of the family too. After the anxiety her own family caused her, Clarissa, for the first time in a long while, experienced internal peace and inner freedom.

After modeling the two sample gowns, Clara and Clarissa settled on a hybrid design combining dresses one and two for the ceremony dress. Clarissa's sketch appeared similar to the one in her dream she had not quite been able to capture until just this moment.

One of Clara's largest concerns centered on the length of the train of the skirt. Despite being nimble on her feet and a

Prima Ballerina, Clara confessed to being terrified she might trip over it. They agreed upon a one-and-a-half-meter train. They had to give the photographers something to photograph from the back.

Near the end of Clara's appointment, Princess Charlotte, Clara's future mother-in-law, phoned in. "Hello, dear. I hope your consultation is going well."

Clara placed her phone on speaker. "Princess Charlotte! Clarissa has put together some amazing sketches. We're discussing what symbols might best represent my new home. I know it's important to you."

Mrs. Collins added, "Clarissa has suggested having a four-flower motif, for the four countries that make up the United Kingdom, incorporated into the lacework of the dress."

Princess Charlotte replied, "Brilliant. What about the remainder of the Commonwealth? We can't have them left out. Perhaps you can have two to three flowers from each Commonwealth country embroidered on the veil."

Clarissa's eyes bulged. *How am I going to do that?*

That could easily equate to a few hundred flowers. A project like that would take months. All of Clarissa's embroidery was performed by hand. Clarissa wracked her brain for other ideas.

Clara spoke in a hushed voice. "I was hoping to use the veil my late mother used."

Mrs. Collins and Amanda hugged Clara. During one of their many appointments, Clara had mentioned to Clarissa the loss of her parents eight years past. Small nuggets of information they shared with one another helped establish a strong bond.

What about the bridesmaid dresses? Could those be used to represent the Commonwealth instead? They needed to look cohesive and individual all at the same time. *Eureka!*

Clarissa asserted herself into the conversation. "Would you

be open to having each one of your bridesmaids wear dresses representing a different flower from around the Commonwealth? Each dress could potentially have a varied overskirt."

"That is the best idea ever!" Amanda jumped up and high-fived Clarissa.

Princess Charlotte said, "Excellent. I can see my input is not required. Select what feels right to you, Clara. Enjoy the rest of your fitting. I look forward to hearing about the finalized designs."

Clara thanked the Princess Royal and disconnected the call. "Whew. We got off easy on that one! I'm sure it's because, with Clarissa, I'm in experienced hands." Clara grinned.

Clarissa relaxed. *Thank goodness. One problem solved. Wait a moment. Did she just confirm I'm the designer?*

"I have the commission then?" Clarissa whispered.

Clara laughed. "You had the job before we even walked in! I looooooooooove your work. You are a British designer and know how to dress petite women. I am so excited!" Clara smiled. "Let's use sketch three for the reception dress. If you want to make changes to it as it develops, it is completely your call. Just make David silly-grin. You can be as daring or as safe as you want with me. I fully trust your vision."

Ripples of excitement went through Clarissa's body. In a rare show of emotion with a client, she jumped up and down. Sonya sprinted over and hugged her boss slash friend.

This was everything they had dreamed about. As soon as the meeting ended, they were going to celebrate! But first, she needed one more key piece of information.

Clarissa carefully finished making notes in her folio. "I just need to ask, what is the time frame we are working under? I can have a sample completed of the first dress in three months. The finished product normally takes about six months."

Clara's smile faltered. She played with her hands. "So here is the situation. The wedding is in four months, April 29th to be exact. David and Princess Charlotte have been getting on my case for weeks to begin looking at dresses. It has been so busy. I'm a terrible bride in that I don't care as much about the dress as I should. I've really dropped the ball on this one. I have known for months I want you as my designer."

Clara gripped the arm of the sofa. "I understand it is putting a lot of strain on you and the staff, but is it possible to have everything done by then?"

Clarissa understood procrastination. Clara's sketches, after all, had only *just* been completed. Yet, two wedding dresses, a maid of honor dress, and three bridesmaid dresses with a four-month turnaround would take Clarissa up until the very last moment to complete. Sonya might have to assist in this endeavor. She hated sewing, yet in a pinch, her skills stood on par with Clarissa's.

On the other hand, they might be able to utilize some of the newer seamstresses. Could they be trusted on such an important project? All of them were highly talented. She would have to delay the release of her upcoming collection. Did the two shops have enough inventory to last four months?

Clarissa could entrust Sonya to find a solution if they sold through their stock. Clarissa owed much of her newly found success to Clara. She *had* to do this. Her client base was growing but was not overly large yet. Sixteen weeks.

With a determined glint in her eyes, Clarissa proclaimed, "No matter what, I *will* make this work."

Clara let out a relieved breath. "Just so we're on the same page, I want you to know that I truly do not want your business to suffer. If you agree, I want to hire you exclusively for your time until the wedding. If it means buying every single dress off your rack or buying out your clients, David and Princess Charlotte would have no qualms doing it. Would those terms work for you?"

Clarissa resolutely agreed. "I would love to devote myself

just to your wedding dresses. Sonya is a talented business-woman. She has been running my shops for a while now without me. Therefore, if she agrees, I am fully on board. Though, please do not purchase *all* of my dresses. I understand you love my work, but that is taking it to the extreme."

Clara thoughtfully replied. "That's true."

Sonya gave Clarissa a thumbs-up.

One problem was solved. She wouldn't be able to sleep for weeks, but would she ever get an opportunity like this again?

Mama and Baba are going to kill me when I tell them I'm not coming home for the Lunar New Year. This is what dreams are made of, though. This is what I am working for. This is the point of no return.

As Clarissa mused over the prospect of her schedule, Sonya brought up their logistical challenges: the lack of a security system and an adequate workspace.

"While the majority of our equipment is in this location, the Bond Street shop is larger. Unless Clarissa has another idea, realistically speaking, I'm not certain of how she will be able to work on such a top-secret project in tight quarters *and* keep it under wraps."

Amanda proposed, "I had an idea for that too! So I am basically the admin lady for the Leeds-man. We have a *ton* of office space at Kensington Palace. The Waleeds Trust only uses maybe ten percent of its allocated area. You could set up your operational base there. I kind of ran this idea by him the other day, without him knowing what he was agreeing to, of course. He and Princy usually don't mind letting me run the show. Besides, anything C wants, she gets. And with Princess Charlotte on our side, they really don't have a say in the matter."

Amanda Collins means business. I like her a lot.

Amanda continued, "So to confuse any would-be spies, we could have you show up here or to Bond Street and then have a driver sneak you out to KP. Anything you need, we will order for you, or you can bring it with you. My boyfriend's security team is highly efficient at moving." Amanda's eyes sparkled in mirth. "Only you and whomever you handpick would have access to the workrooms at Kensington Palace, plus me, Clara, Mom, and Princess Charlotte."

Clarissa didn't know what to say. "You really have thought of everything."

"So, officially, is it a yes?" Clara clapped her hands together, her eyes looking longingly to Clarissa.

"That's a yes!" Clarissa exclaimed. They hugged tightly. Clarissa winced as her tender left wrist ached for the first time that morning, still bruised but not overly swollen. She made a mental note to ice it when she had a spare moment.

Clarissa had never been prouder and more terrified in her life. Designing a royal wedding dress could define her career. There was so much at stake. Only adrenaline kept her going. No matter what, she would relish each and every movement of the process.

Chapter Eight

PATRICK

Patrick pulled at his tie as he sat in the back seat of a London taxi. He checked over the lenses of his backup glasses for any specks of dirt before replacing them on his face. His hands shook.

The impressive seven-hundred-and-seventy-five room home of King Reginald came into view as the car entered the grounds of Buckingham Palace's visitor's entrance. David, stood waiting to greet him.

"Paddy! About time you accepted an invitation to see me! How are you, mate?" David clapped him on the back, then eyed his friend over. "Wow! I almost didn't recognize you. What a difference."

Patrick self-consciously looked down. "Good to see you too, Leeds. The black eye?" He frowned.

David shook his head in disbelief. "No, no. The fitted suit! You've really transformed yourself."

"I truly hadn't realized I had changed that much until last night. No matter what, I can still best you in the saddle anytime, anyplace." Patrick, with a determined look in his eye, stared at David who laughed. Patrick added, "You just wait until I get my hands on a foil. Have you kept your fencing skills up to par?"

David walked in step toward King Reginald's study. His tone sobered. "You're much happier than last time we spoke. You're healthy and you have a light in your eyes I haven't seen since your father was still around. I'm glad to have you back, mate."

Patrick returned the salutations. He carefully regarded his longtime friend. David, for the first time in recent memory, had a smile that reached his eyes. They glimmered in delight from behind his glasses. He walked and carried himself with a certain spring in his step.

"Is this the same David who I couldn't pry away from his laptop or mobile?"

David placed his hands in his pockets. "You can thank my fiancée and my persistent new assistant for that. Uncle Reg awaits us."

Should I be afraid of what Leeds has up his sleeves? If he asks me to learn to make shoes from him, it's a flat no. Honestly, how did the man find shoemaking so fascinating? *I understand the satisfaction of being able to make an object from scratch, but I could never fathom spending all day and night obsessing over it.*

Patrick nearly laughed at the situation. Never had he pictured his thirty-two-year-old bachelor mate getting married, much less to an American ballerina. David always had a faraway glint in his eyes when he spoke of his fiancée. This was what Patrick wanted for himself. Once more, the universe brought forth the prime example of what love *could* look like.

Meeting Clarissa brought questions to the forefront of his mind. Happening upon Clarissa had evoked feelings Patrick was certain Mary had caused him to bury and destroy.

With Mary *finally* out of his mind, Patrick embraced the notion of opening himself up again to love, should the right woman come along. Maybe there was still hope. Last night certainly left him with an impression.

Patrick joked, "This must be serious business indeed for the king to be involved in the prospective project."

They followed the well-trod pathway through the state-rooms, portrait gallery, and past the offices of the Princess Royal up to the stairway leading to the king's private study. David knocked twice on the wooden door outside the room.

"Enter," a commanding voice bellowed. Per protocol, David and Patrick bowed.

King Reginald lazily waved them off as he stood from behind his favorite desk and gestured for his guests to help themselves to the array of refreshments fresh from the kitchens.

The king poured himself a cup of coffee. "Lord Renbrook. It's good to see you."

Patrick acknowledged the greeting. "Likewise, sir. Mother sends her regards."

Patrick's attention was taken by the soft whimpering of Francine, the royal family's English springer spaniel, better known as Franny. A young litter of puppies chased after their mother's tail.

Patrick knelt down to have Franny investigate his scent and scratched her behind the ears. "I see congratulations are in order for you." Franny licked Patrick's hand and rolled over onto her belly. He chuckled. "Same old girl. I haven't brought you any treats today."

The king whistled. Franny jumped up and moved with surprising agility as she took up her begging post at the king's feet. She rolled over for a treat and a belly rub. "It's rude to beg for treats from our guests. You know better than that, my girl."

Patrick sat on one of the red velvet, wingback chairs across from the king and David. He helped himself to some tea as Franny returned to her motherly duties.

Eyeing Patrick's keen interest, the king asked, "We've accounted for three of the litter of pups, but there are still two more available for adoption. Edmund and Amanda have selected the smallest for themselves. My Alice will more than likely want one, and David and Clara have agreed to take one. Can I interest you or your mother in a puppy? If I recall, Lady Renbrook last kept a bull terrier and cocker spaniel?"

Patrick attempted to be as diplomatic as possible. "Excellent memory, sir. We still have the cocker; she's getting on in years. I'll ring Mother and pass along your generous offer. As for myself, puppies take quite a bit of training up. I'm not certain if I'm ready to commit to one just yet."

The king recounted, "Lucy used to adopt every single creature she encountered. She and Agnus almost convinced me to have a menagerie constructed at Balmoral. I always suspected your mother would have made an excellent vet had she not met and married your father."

Patrick never knew mother was so invested in animals, but upon reflection, it made so much sense. She'd always championed many animal welfare charities. Even now, she took great care of the horses and other animals on the home farm. A smile crept up on his face at the fond memory of his mother and animals.

David offered Patrick a biscuit to accompany the cup of tea in his hands. He declined. "Thank you. Just tea for me." David raised an eyebrow and chose not to comment.

Patrick almost regretted declining one of the nice, strong cups of Buckingham Palace coffee. He missed the rich taste of chocolates and nuts in the dark roast. He'd been doing so well sticking to tea. He had a cup of coffee at Rainridge. Would another cup do him in?

I knew it was going to be hard to limit myself once I had the first dose of deliciousness. Must. Resist. The. Urge. Can't have myself addicted to coffee again like David.

It had been difficult to snap the habit a year ago after completely altering his lifestyle. He walked a slippery slope when it came to caffeinated beverages.

The king moved to the red sofa closest to Franny, sat, and crossed his legs. "Good to have you back in London, son. David tells me you were rather eager to leave the countryside," the king joked, engaging Patrick in conversation.

"Yes, sir. Country life suits me well; however, I've been sequestering myself away from everyone for far too long. The repairs on Rainridge have consumed all my efforts, but I no longer need to be in residence *all* the time. Truthfully, I used it as a convenient excuse to hide away." Patrick paused, not ready to reveal his newfound revelations to David or the king yet.

He cleared his throat. "Mother and I have an events business venture. She is performing a splendid job and only asks me to make myself available on the weekends during the wedding season. Going forward, I plan to spend more time in London and weekends at Rainridge."

The king nodded. "Indeed. Had I the ability, I myself would never stray from Balmoral or Sandringham. Many of the older homes have been forced to find ways to fund their upkeep with tourism. Clever to capitalize on the events business. I'd imagine Gloucestershire is a favorite destination for weddings these days." His eyes turned to David. "If David decides against Windsor as a wedding venue, Rainridge might be a prudent alternative option."

David shuddered. "You can be the one to speak with Mother. Clara and I have only just convinced her Windsor is the ideal location for us."

Everyone in the room laughed. "Perhaps the reception then?" the king put forth.

"As much as we would love to host you at Rainridge, the

manor isn't large enough to accommodate the sheer number of guests you likely have on your list."

David snorted and mumbled under his breath.

The king took a moment to study Patrick. "Changing topics, I venture you are rather curious as to why I've asked David to arrange today's meeting." Patrick had the distinct impression he was about to receive an offer he hadn't counted on.

"Over the last year, I've been investigating ways for the monarchy to engage more with the British public. After a recent chat with Alice, I've resolved to create a new museum on the grounds of Buckingham Palace. You are the candidate I have selected to oversee the entire project. Over the years, you have continually impressed me with the breadth of your knowledge and appreciation of history. Many years ago, I distinctly remember you working up the courage to ask permission to utilize the family archives to write your under-graduate thesis." Patrick's cheeks grew warm at the memory.

"You argued passionately with me about the merits and the importance of having plenty of primary source material to draw conclusions from. You made such an impression upon me that I asked you that summer to organize a special exhibit in tandem with the summer opening of the Buckingham Palace staterooms. You have since continued to serve as an advisor to the Royal Trust each subsequent summer on my behalf. Moreover, few people of my acquaintance hold a first-class degree from Oxford. As far as I am concerned, there is not another candidate better suited to the job." The king looked expectantly at Patrick.

Patrick's mouth felt dry. He blinked several times. *Me? He truly wants me?*

Patrick had always dreamed of an opportunity like this. A museum under his control? It was much too good to be true. He'd truly enjoyed working on the yearly exhibits, but had never considered diversifying his portfolio with museum work.

He stuttered. "Thank you, sir. I am rightly honored by your offer. If I may ask a few clarifying questions?"

David looked out the window. Patrick wondered to what extent he had been aware of the project.

"Certainly. Ask away." The king drank his own coffee.

Patrick asked, "What type of museum are you looking to create? How much space do you intend to dedicate to its creation? Would it house permanent collections? Temporary exhibitions?"

The king slowly blinked. "The offerings would be entirely at your discretion, as with the summer projects. I *would* prefer to see whatever you decide upon somehow or another involve areas around the Commonwealth. Space-wise, the venue will be housed in the back gardens where one of the dilapidated Victorian conservatories has been cleared away. Its entire design is at your discretion."

A carte blanche. This was a dangerous proposal.

The timing could not be more ideal now that Patrick had more time than ever on his hands. The events business was his mother's. This was just the change he needed. A project perfectly suited to his interests. Patrick didn't have a single con to argue against the king's offer.

The king stood and went to his desk to pull out a small-scale map of the museum's proposed location. "David advocated strongly for you as the museum's director when we initially discussed the idea. Admittedly, I already had you in mind. The Waleeds Trust shall serve as a joint-operating partner with the crown in the initial inception."

David couldn't hide his sheepish expression any longer. "You always spoke of a desire to create a modern-day Great Exhibition of your own, like my ancestor Prince Albert. Was that not the topic of your undergraduate thesis? Uncle Reg was immediately enthusiastic. It has been difficult to keep this under wraps. Alice, on a recent ride, encountered the dilapidated conservatory's space. She pressured Uncle Reg to put it to use in some form or another. You can thank her."

"I'll do it," Patrick agreed. What would a modern Great Exhibition entail? Science? Natural History? What would excite people? They could incorporate Uncle Reg's love of the military into it. Patrick could reach out to his old school friends, Pascal, Andrew, and Brandon, and inquire about working with him.

The king stood and shook hands with him. "That's a lad. Excellent to hear. Regrettably, I am unable to stay and chat. Do keep me informed of your progress." The king reluctantly slipped away to his afternoon engagements.

Elated, Patrick couldn't wipe the smile from his face as he departed with David. *I couldn't be happier right now.*

He wanted to begin researching possible ideas straightaway. Were his father alive, Patrick would share all his thoughts and ideas with him. Mother would be excited. He wished he had another person to share the good news with.

David's countenance lit up. "I knew your answer before you did, Paddy. Welcome to the team. Officially, you'll be working on behalf of the Waleeds Trust, yet unofficially, you answer only to Uncle Reg," David informed him as they walked.

Patrick's eyes shined. "Thank you, David. You truly have no idea how much I appreciate everything you two have just offered me. This is a brand-new beginning for me."

"I am ecstatic to hear you are approaching this as a new chapter in your life," David replied. "Our new assistant, Amanda Collins, is off this afternoon to shop with my Clarbear. When they return, I'll finally be able to introduce you two!"

Patrick smiled. "I'm looking forward to meeting both of

them. I've heard they are as thick as thieves. The rumor is she knows her way around the kitchen. I may have to see if we can exchange recipes."

David said, "Amanda is dating Eddie, believe it or not. He's certainly matured over the past few months. I would pay large sums of money to have you and Amanda hash it out in the kitchen. Speaking of which, are you *ever* going to share the story of how you earned that black eye with me? Uncle Reg may have been too polite to inquire about it, but I am not."

It's taken him until now to ask for details? That's a new record.

"Shaving accident?" Patrick lamely offered.

Did he want to tell David how he *really* had come by the black eye? Could he endure David's teasing over him being distracted by his mobile, slipping on a puddle, and essentially walking into a doorknob? If he mentioned Clarissa, David might want details. In some respects, David could be a large gossip, like his mother.

David deadpanned. "Nice try. There's a lot more to the story about last night than you're letting on, isn't there?" They walked outside the building down to David's driver waiting to take them to Kensington Palace.

"That is for me to know and you to find out. If you buy this ol' bloke lunch, I'd be happy to share my tale of woe with you... It was a dark and stormy night..." Patrick acted out.

David held his hands up. "Lunch it is."

Patrick left, hoping he'd see Clarissa when he arrived home. How was Clarissa this morning? How had her meeting gone? There was a lot he didn't know about Clarissa, even after speaking with her into the early hours of the morning. What did she do for a living in fashion?

Come to think of it, I don't even know her surname.

Chapter Nine

CLARISSA

Clarissa and Sonya exited the black cab dropping them off near the intersection of Harrow Place and Middlesex Street in Shoreditch—an area of London that had become trendy in recent years with numerous restaurant and entertainment options.

Today, however, they were here for an entirely different reason—the fabulous fabric shops. Some of the best fabric shops were in the dodgy areas of London, yet being able to source rolls of fabric from a warehouse and walk out with said fabric on the same day made the trip worthwhile.

Clarissa normally ordered samples of fabric, but with their timetable, she couldn't risk how long they might take to arrive. She had never before been offered an unlimited budget to purchase anything she wanted. She left it up to Sonya to ensure she did not become overly distracted. In the world of fashion, the designer typically constructed a sample garment from muslin or a similar material.

Yet, oftentimes, working with the *real* fabric brought out new challenges. Their intended choices of silk, organza, and satin were notoriously unforgiving. One wrong stitch or cut could spell disaster. She had sixteen weeks to complete the two wedding dresses. In reality, that meant fourteen weeks.

The question of the color and overall logistics of the dresses for the remainder of the bridal party lingered in the back of Clarissa's mind. Following Sonya's recommendation, three handpicked seamstresses from the two shops would collaborate on the dresses for the maid of honor and three bridesmaids.

As much as Clarissa wanted to manage all the tasks herself, she did not want to compromise the quality of the dresses. She *had* to learn to delegate and have faith in her team. As her business grew, so did the growing pains that came with trusting others to see her vision. She let out a deep breath.

Clarissa slipped out of her musings as Sonya said, "Thanks for bringing me along. Shopping for fabrics was one of my favorite things about our design course at uni. This is my contribution to the royal wedding. Sewing, patterning, and all the other bits and bobs, I leave to you and our team. I mean, I am available should you need an extra set of hands, but there *is* a reason I switched over to the fashion business course and away from designing."

They both laughed. "You truly made some ghastly creations. I remember you napping in one of the workrooms right near the end of term as I struggled to fit my dress form with our modern take on women's workwear. That had to rank among the most stressful end of term projects," Clarissa reminisced.

Sonya agreed. "I only managed to barely scrape by because of you. I was a sod of a partner for that module. I went out much too often. The workrooms were always quiet, but the lights, much too bright." She and Clarissa examined a few of the shops on the street corner, debating on where to begin.

Clarissa said, "When you transferred courses, I was amazed at how quickly you ranked among the top of the class. You truly are the ideal business partner. Without you, I doubt I would have been able to come this far. Truthfully, both of our names should be on the shop's branding. Considering my learning disabilities, I had serious doubts over my future just a few months ago."

Sonya stopped in her tracks. "Never doubt yourself, Clarissa. You have earned every single client and accolade that has come your way. I have never seen another person work so hard to overcome so much. I am so proud to be a part of the journey you are on, but let me make one fact clear. There is no way my name should be listed with yours. I am the silent partner for a reason. I *like* being in the background and just here to help. I am not as driven as you."

Clarissa hugged Sonya tightly. "I could never ask for a better friend." She wiped a small tear from the corner of her eye. Goosebumps appeared on her arm. An eternal warmth of happiness spread through her body. "I know you don't require a title, but you are officially the Worldwide Chief Operations Officer of Clarissa Lee Atelier. You are exclusively in charge of the shops as if I don't exist. Promise not to do anything too crazy."

Sonya crossed her heart and held her hand up. "I promise."

Clarissa pointed to the small alleyway one street away from Harrow Place. They crossed the street and soaked in the scent of freshly baked fish and chips from a neighboring restaurant. Sonya glanced at the restaurant, but a determined Clarissa pressed on. Sonya received the message and jogged to catch up with Clarissa.

Clarissa switched tones. "In all seriousness, do you think the Bond Street shop is secretive enough for our bridesmaid team to work out of? I'm not as concerned about the designs of their dresses being leaked as Clara's dress. Can we trust Stephanie, Amy, and Elaine?"

Slightly out of breath, Sonya said, "You worry far too

much. They will be brilliant. Since we have brought the girls on, they have performed masterful work. Their references were impeccable. As part of the onboarding process, I had them all sign confidentiality agreements. Let your COO handle the details. I hate to see the amount of anxiety you are already causing yourself." Sonya had a point.

She continued. "I'm happy there is a *man* in your life, even if he's just the new neighbor. This is the first time you've mentioned anyone in a long time. I hope he proves to be a welcome distraction. I have seen you struggle through taking on too much responsibility too many times to count, Clarissa-rella. It is good to know I can knock on your next-door neighbor's door and potentially have an ally in my goal to keep you from overworking yourself to the point of collapse."

"Yes, my fairy Sonya." Clarissa eagerly rubbed her hands together. The very thought of Patrick sent tremors through her body. The soft feel of his Savile Row suit against her skin was a feeling she had not forgotten.

Would Patrick become a person she could turn to when she needed a friend to chat with outside of her bubble? After their long conversation, she knew just how passionate he was about gardening and his newly acquired interest in aquaculture. They'd spoken for hours, and Clarissa barely scratched the surface of the gem underneath. She had no idea what he even did for a living.

Despite the shops with vivid window displays drawing in a lot of people, the two stopped in front of a bland, nondescript warehouse. A worn, wooden sign labeled the warehouse as Wentworth Textiles. The door was propped open with several antique pieces of luggage.

Clarissa could hardly contain her enthusiasm. "Shall we?"

The moment they walked through the entrance, the magic began. Clarissa often thought of Wentworth Textiles as a treasure trove, not unlike Aladdin's cave, where she needed to unearth a diamond in the rough.

From floor to ceiling, roll upon roll of fabric stuck out at odd and various angles. Clarissa welcomed the slightly musty odor. Stripes, polka dots, neons, neutrals, tartans, carpets, and many other fabric options provided an almost overbearing feast for the eyes.

Clarissa's eyes darted to-and-fro. She muttered under her breath. "Washed silk? No, start with satin. Charmeuse? Crepe? What type?"

Clarissa had her reference sketches in her handbag, yet preferred to let the fabric tell the story and speak to her. The dresses lived in her head. She just needed to make them come to life. She willed her fingers not to touch everything in sight.

Sonya dutifully took charge of Clarissa's belongings and, like a bloodhound on a mission, let her search for the needle in the haystack. "Okay, boss, you lead and I will follow. If I see something, I'll holler at you. I have the notebook ready to go for any stock numbers you see."

They circled the first three floors of the factory twice. Finally, on the basement level, Clarissa stopped in front of a roll of pearl-colored, off-white silk. "What do you think?" she asked Sonya.

Carefully she exposed the edge of the fabric from the middle of the stack. She wiggled her fingers and closed her eyes. It felt glossy and light. Would this be the bridal fabric? She couldn't tell just yet. The muse struck on its own accord.

Sonya moved in closer to the silk and held it in her hands. "Good start. Excellent thread count. It's soft and the perfect layering base for organza. I'd look for ivory and a blush, too, in case Aurora doesn't approve of the pearl." Aurora was the nickname Sonya and Clarissa had agreed to use in public for Clara.

"Two bolts or three?" Clarissa, who struggled with math, let Sonya perform the mental calculations.

"Refresh my memory. How long is the potential train?" Sonya questioned.

"One and a half meters, plus some extra for any mistakes I make." Clarissa resumed searching the surrounding stacks.

"Two rolls should be plenty. It is doubled over." Sonya nodded and wrote down the fabric number and location to keep on their list for the shop assistants to gather up for them.

They spent another hour compiling a selection of blues, greens, pinks, oranges, and purple satins for the prospective bridesmaid dresses. Clarissa reviewed the lace selection but hoped to be able to find a lace maker who could fabricate her bespoke design by hand. Everything else they needed could be ordered or they already had in her design studio.

"I think you have enough for an adequate start. Have you even sketched out any of the bridesmaid dresses yet?" Sonya wearily eyed the mountain of colors and fabrics that would be delivered to Clarissa's Kensington Palace workstation via the Bond Street store later that day.

Clarissa rubbed the back of her neck. "I have Miss Disney's dress and some rough, working ideas. However, Aurora promised me a quick chat tomorrow to learn more about the other ladies. I need a better understanding of what suits their personalities and tastes before I finalize any designs per Aurora's special request." Miss. Disney was the codename for Amanda Collins.

Sonya sighed. "I remember… the fabric tells the story. Call me once you're ready to have the girls start on the dresses. With any luck, they can at least pattern the Disney mock-up dress today. Who do you want specifically working on it?"

Clarissa hesitated. "You?"

Sonya laughed. "Nice try. I recommend Amy."

Clarissa nodded. "I trust you."

This was part of the process of learning to grow and mature. The first *real* test of trusting the team behind the Clarissa Lee label, while terrifying, was also incredibly exciting.

~

Later that evening. Clarissa opted to ring her parents from the privacy of her flat instead of her atelier studio. In the background, Clarissa's mother yelled to her father in Mandarin.

As long as they had been in the United Kingdom, her parents still spoke a mixture of the Chinese dialects of Mandarin, Cantonese, and, of course, English at home.

Clarissa's mother shouted over the phone as Clarissa cringed. "What do you mean you aren't coming home for Lunar New Year? Clarissa Wing Lee, you missed Christmas with us two weeks ago! There are *no* exceptions to this kind of behavior. These are the only times we are together as a family. You *will* be coming home to Birmingham if I have to drive all the way down to London to pick you up myself. Ay-ya! Wei, come talk some sense into your stubborn daughter."

Mr. Lee came onto the line. She heard him take the phone out of her mum's hands. "Hello, Baba," she greeted her father.

Mr. Lee cut straight to the point. "What's this about you not coming home? Clarissa, we only expect you here two days a year, Christmas and Lunar New Year. Only two days. You know how important this is to us. What's stopping you this time?"

Clarissa pleaded, "Baba please. I tried to explain to Mum that I can't come home this year for Chinese New Year. I can't give you all the details, but it wouldn't be unless it was exceedingly important. I have a V.I.P. client I've been working with who is going to—" Clarissa's father cut her off.

"No. Family always comes first. We should never have indulged in your desire to become a fashion designer. At your age, you should have a home, husband, and children. Do you understand how disappointing it is to have to tell your relatives that you *still* aren't married? You can't even make the basic Chinese dishes!" Clarissa gulped as her father ranted.

I can't even get a proper word in.

Every single time they spoke, the conversation always followed the same pattern. When are you coming to visit? Do you have a boyfriend? When are you quitting the fashion business? Have you spoken to Mark Leung? Are you attending your brother's next tennis match?

Her family was one reason she had sought to settle in London, away from her childhood home.

"Baba. This is a once-in-a-lifetime opportunity." Clarissa knew she was on the losing end of the conversation. All parties grew frustrated. "How about we compromise? I will come home for Lunar New Year, but in return, I can only stay for the day."

Her mind turned briefly away from the countless times she had heard this lecture to Patrick. Clarissa sought to break free of the vicious cycle and desperately wanted to appease her parents.

To sweeten the deal, without considering the consequences, she panicked and added, "I'll even bring somebody special with me for you to meet." The words appeared to have the desired effect on Mr. Lee.

"Very well. I will speak to your mama. We are extremely disappointed in you. We see you so little as it is. It's almost as if we don't have a daughter," Clarissa's father disconnected the call.

When did everything turn so ugly? Six years, and her parents still had yet to understand a relationship with her ex-boyfriend, Mark Leung, was out of the question. For all her success, Clarissa would exchange it in a heartbeat if she could have her parents, for once in her life, on her side.

Emotionally drained, the pressure and disappointment bored down on her chest. Her mobile rang just as she was about to stand up from the sofa. Checking the caller ID, she saw it was her younger brother, Henry.

"Hello, Henry? What's the situation?" Clarissa's only saving grace was her younger brother. Henry, who still lived at home, was the apple of their parents' eye. Despite being able to afford a home of his own, Henry saw no point in moving out when he was often out of the country as a professional tennis player.

"Mama and Baba are having a fight, but they seem to have calmed down. Not coming home for the annual New Year's party?" Henry asked.

Clarissa's voice lowered. "I wasn't going to, but I'll be there just for the day," she quietly said. "I can't tell you why, but it's important."

She could picture Henry shrugging. "I bet it is. I wanted to ask, how about we have lunch in London in a week or so. I'm down there to meet with my sponsors before I leave for the ATP Tour stops in Rome and Padua. You can show me your swanky new shop. I read about it online. Sounds like you're doing really well for yourself. I'm so proud." He always understood her passion and determination.

"Thanks, Henry. You always know what to say to make me feel better. Lunch on Wednesday?" Clarissa inquired.

Henry attempted to lighten her mood. "Wednesday is brilliant. One of these days, Mama and Baba will understand you have long moved past Mark Leung. You still have me on your side, and you are always welcome to join me out of the country on tour. I support you no matter what. I love you, older sister."

Henry yelled to their parents in the background when they kept asking who he was speaking with.

"You had better go. I don't want you to get in any trouble. I love you too." Clarissa disconnected the call.

In the Lee family world, success was measured by two things: a university degree and a relationship with the right Chinese person. Henry could do no wrong. At age seven, he was proclaimed a tennis prodigy.

The sports media had coined Henry as the best chance for a British man to win Wimbledon when he was only twenty years old. He held the number twenty world ranking among male tennis players and was the number two British player. Clarissa could not have been more proud of Henry, yet the two of them walked very different paths.

Henry had sailed through his university degree program, earning first-class honors while playing professional tennis. His beautiful girlfriend, Lily Chung, would graduate from the University of Edinburgh in the spring, likely with a first-class degree.

In contrast to Henry, Clarissa, in the eyes of her parents, failed on both accounts. Her fashion school degree didn't equate to that of a traditional university degree.

Then there was Mark Leung, her emotionally abusive ex-boyfriend. His name still invoked painful memories for Clarissa. Her stomach clenched. She would *never* be dependent on anyone again.

Every day she reminded herself she *was* a success and had literally built her own business from the ground up. Would she ever be free from Mark's shadow? She cried softly to herself, curling up into a ball on the couch. She truly felt alone.

Chapter Ten

PATRICK

Patrick knocked for the second time in as many minutes on Clarissa's front door. He shifted from foot to foot in eager anticipation. Was she home?

I shouldn't have gotten my hopes up. Everything today was going so well. Bugger off.

He eyed the bouquet of flowers purchased from the corner shop on a whim. The flowers had strangely reminded him of Clarissa the moment he set eyes on them.

Looks like you're coming back to the flat with me. His shoulders hunched in disappointment.

Patrick stopped as he heard sniffling and the telltale unlatching of the deadbolt on Clarissa's door. It opened a crack; Patrick could just make out Clarissa's face under the dim lighting.

"Are those for me?" she asked quietly.

Patrick moved closer as the door opened wider. He stared at the ground and hastily threw the flowers in front of him, like a shield, afraid to look her in the eyes. He gathered his courage. His hands were unsteady. *Do it now, man.*

Patrick's voice rose up an octave higher than normal as he asked, "Wouldyouliketohavedinnerwithme?"

Clarissa sniffled. "I'm sorry, can you please repeat that? I didn't comprehend what you said. I've worked myself up into a state, and my ears are a wee bit stuffed up."

Patrick cleared his throat. His gaze shifted from the floor to her face. Why was she crying and alone? Dinner plans forgotten, he examined her closely. He noted her tear tracks and swollen cheeks. Her glow from yesterday was overridden by a dull complexion.

"Are you alright?" His concern pushed out the previous nervous energy.

Clarissa nodded unconvincingly and reached for the flowers. "I've been better. Just a rough phone call home to my parents. We have the same, perpetual conversation each time." She closed her eyes and inhaled the scent of the roses. "These are lovely. They complement the flowers from Kew Gardens. I'm poor company right now, but why don't you come inside. I have a vase for these somewhere."

Clarissa puttered over to the kitchen and clicked the lights onto their lowest setting. Patrick blinked a few times, entered, and closed the door behind him.

The doorknob was loose again. *I'll examine that before I leave.* What a difference twenty-four hours made.

He followed her to the kitchen. "I originally intended to ask if you would like to have dinner with me again. However, I don't think that would be appropriate at present. The flowers are my way of thanking you. My meeting went exceptionally smooth today."

Patrick winced at the way his words came out. *It comes across as if I'm rubbing in my good fortune. It's a turd move when she's in low spirits.*

Patrick was uncertain. Should he leave her alone? Did she prefer privacy?

I would want to be alone. But that's beside the point. I hardly know the woman well enough to know her mind and her mannerisms.

He slowly backed out toward the entryway. "I'm just going to fix my handiwork from yesterday, then see myself out. I don't want to disturb you."

"No! Don't leave! I mean, I'd love to have dinner with you," Clarissa exclaimed. Flustered, she dropped the unwrapped flowers into the sink with the tap running over them. Patrick stopped in his tracks.

"How did you find these in winter? A little color and the scent of flowers go a long way in lifting my spirits." The bouquet included roses, rosemary, viburnum, a few magnolias, and winter heather. Clarissa turned off the tap.

Patrick watched her arrange the flowers to her liking into a vase and place them on the center of the kitchen island next to the wildflowers. "I have to admit, I picked them up from the corner shop. Normally I prefer fresh cutting from the family greenhouse. We keep multiple blooms in season year-round. Mother loves fresh flowers."

He debated offering to discuss the source of her discomfort. "Speaking of family, would you like to talk about what happened earlier?"

His chest tightened. Was it too early in their friendship to inquire about her personal life?

Clarissa violently shook her head in refusal. "No. They've ruined my evening as it is. I arrived home in high spirits until I spoke to my mama and baba. I need an escape. Dinner sounds like just the ticket. Would it be an imposition on my part? This *is* the second night in a row."

Patrick sagged internally in relief and sat at Clarissa's kitchen island. "As I explained last night, cooking for me is one of the more enjoyable experiences I've discovered. It's relaxing to be able to prepare ingredients and even better to have brilliant company to share my culinary skills with. I prepped all my ingredients in the event you were available tonight," Patrick admitted.

In the long term, cooking had become an outlet that he could utilize to manage his grief and depression.

Clarissa smiled.

She's beautiful when her eyes light up. Even when she's been crying, they're warm, mocha colored, and so inviting. She's so natural. She wears her emotions on her sleeve.

Playing with the top of the flowers, Clarissa said, "I do have one question for you that I've been pondering since last evening."

Patrick held his breath, hoping he could answer it. He gripped the counter. His knuckles turned white. What was on her mind?

"What's your surname?" The tension fled his shoulders.

"Blimey. Is that all? I thought you were going to say you had changed your mind." He leaned back onto the stool and almost lost his balance but recovered in time. He attempted to cover the blunder by casually leaning on the kitchen island. Clarissa hid a giggle. "My surname is Nelson. May I ask the same? What is your surname?"

"Lee." Clarissa's long hair fell in front of her face. Patrick caught a whiff of gardenias. Patrick couldn't help but stare at the long, glossy locks. Her hair was so dark, it almost appeared violet.

In the meantime, Clarissa searched for her phone and a jacket. "I'm not typically so disorganized." She found both items on her sofa. She slipped on her shoes by the entryway and gathered her keys from the hook on the wall. "I've been thinking about you throughout the day today. It's refreshing to have a person to talk to outside of my small work sphere."

Funny, I've been thinking about you all day too.

There were so many questions he wanted to ask her. He

desired to know how her day went until the low point. He wished to find out what telly shows she enjoyed. Was she originally from London? Each complex layer of Clarissa he discovered made him eager to know more.

Patrick waited for her by the door. "The feeling is mutual. My few friends always want to dash out and about. As we have collectively aged, their priorities have shifted to spending time with their children and families. I'm the lone wolf these days. In recent times, I have become a recluse. It is something I am working to rectify. You are just the remedy I seek."

Clarissa signaled she was ready to depart, and her cheeks flushed once more. "I am honored. Decent conversation can be so difficult to come by. I only wish my parents would understand life is not just about dating and marriage."

Patrick chose not to comment. When she was ready, he hoped she'd trust him enough to confide in him. The mention of dating brought up memories of his past with Mary. Their entire relationship had been based around her. She never even thought to ask about Patrick's troubles. He knew now just how unhealthy that was and how it led to his depression. Patrick shivered.

Clarissa was so unassuming and relaxed. Even after a rough night, she was willing to indulge a stranger like him. *She is a soothing balm.*

Chapter Eleven

CLARISSA

Four weeks passed. Clarissa and Patrick developed a daily ritual where they met after breakfast at eight-thirty each morning and walked the short distance together to the Holland Park tube station. They chatted about the weather, books, funny things that they saw on the tube, and whatever else popped into their minds.

Their ten-minute chats each morning always put Clarissa in a positive mood. Patrick often asked for advice about his newly installed aquarium. She lived vicariously through him.

Patrick was her link to the outside world as the design process consumed her entire being. Clarissa closed herself off from the world and ate, lived, and breathed Clara's wedding dresses.

When she arrived at the Kensington Palace complex each morning, she always greeted the security agents before burying herself in her work. Many days passed when she might not speak to another living person for hours on end. As much as she wished for Sonya to check up on her, Sonya's time was otherwise engaged.

At Clarissa's urging, Sonya had designed and launched a

small jewelry line to complement the gowns sold at the two retail locations. Twice, the collections sold through in a matter of days. Sonya, in her own free time, played with new ideas and concepts.

Clarissa could not have been more thrilled to see her long-time friend enthralled by her work. The jewelry line could eventually become its own entity. On top of that, business was growing and required so much of Sonya's energy. Opening a third shop was in the works.

Progress came in stages. The shape of the first mockup dress never quite satisfied Clarissa. Before working with the actual dress fabric, the prototype had to be just so.

Today, with the wedding just twelve weeks away, she finally began fabricating the ceremony dress's pattern. Working with silk and satin was more arduous than working with muslin.

Cautiously, Clarissa triple-checked her patterns and measurements for each layer of the dress. She searched for any minute defects. After steaming out any wrinkles, she laid out the fabric and pinned the pattern to the material. Painstakingly, Clarissa cut and assembled the lining. She repeated the process with the outer layers for the base of the dress.

Time often escaped from Clarissa. She frequently departed Kensington Palace around ten or eleven in the evening. On a night when she was especially fatigued, a brown paper bag sat on her flat's doorway.

She stared at her name printed in small, neat, uniform block letters. "Who's left this for me?"

Suspicious, she examined the contents of the bag. Upon opening the top flap, steam escaped from the carefully packed container. Fresh basil greeted her nose. Digging deeper, she discovered tomato soup and a grilled cheese sandwich. Her perfect comfort food. There was no note.

Without stopping to remove her jacket or shoes, Clarissa

devoured the delicious meal the moment she sat down at her kitchen island.

This is so creamy and good.

The bread was perfectly toasted. She took another bite. The bread crunched; brie cheese melted in her mouth. Clarissa knew of only one person who could make such a perfectly prepared meal—Patrick Nelson.

How does he have time to worry about me? Surely he is just as busy.

Every weeknight following, the pattern repeated itself. Tuesday brought a mushroom veggie burger, Wednesday fettuccine alfredo, Thursday Chinese-style fried rice and spring rolls, and last night, a stuffed bell pepper. Though she had yet to officially confirm that her guardian angel was her neighbor, every sign pointed to him.

By the end of the week, Clarissa truly owed Patrick her deepest gratitude. Without the extra assistance, she would've suffered through night after night of frozen dinners—if she had the foresight to do her own grocery shopping or order takeaway. How long could he go without giving himself away?

Clarissa wondered how she could possibly ever return the favor to him. Her heart fluttered whenever she was near Patrick. Could there be more to their friendship?

Another week slipped away. Eleven weeks remained until Clara Little's big day. Clarissa checked her watch and leaned against her flat's front door. On this Wednesday morning, Patrick was five minutes late.

That's certainly a first. She yawned and wiped away some of the sleepy sand from her eyes. *Ah bugger, I just smeared my makeup.*

Patrick had two more minutes before she needed to leave to catch the train over to Bond Street.

The thought of seeing her neighbor sent a jolt of adrenaline through her tired body. She stood up straighter and checked her hands. No telltale black spots of smeared makeup. *That's a good thing. Wouldn't want Patrick seeing that.*

Patrick was becoming much more than *just* a neighbor. He was her confidant, as she liked to think of him. Would he be interested in exchanging mobile numbers?

Maybe she'd be more willing to pull herself away from the dress once in a while if she had Patrick to text throughout the day. Although, it would be strange for a woman to text message him if he had a girlfriend.

Clarissa had never asked if he was single or in a relationship. What did he do during the evenings? By day, Patrick consulted on a museum project of sorts. He was always vague when asked what type of project. Clarissa chuckled to herself.

When he went to assist his mother on the weekends, it was her job to look in on his aquarium fish. *He puts me to shame. I stay as far away from my parents as possible.*

She had promised her parents that she'd bring a *special someone* to Birmingham for the Lunar New Year. Could she ask Patrick?

If I were in the market for a boyfriend, I'd want someone with all the same attributes as him. But she wasn't in the market for a boyfriend, and he might be dating someone.

Worst case, Clarissa could ask Henry if he had any friends who might be willing to accompany her. Thankfully, Clarissa still had a bit of time to find a solution to her problem.

Labored breathing and heavy footsteps bounding out the door next to hers brought the missing neighbor. "Sorry to keep you waiting. I had a last-minute conversation with my mum. I'll be gone an extra day this weekend. The plumbing is acting up in one of the older parts of the house and—"

Patrick stopped. "I have no need to bore you with the details. You're yawning on me already." They began their daily sojourn.

Patrick pushed the button for the lift as it popped open. They entered. She rested her body against the wall.

She closed her eyes as the elevator descended. "You never bore me. I enjoy hearing about your mum. The fatigue is beginning to wear on me," she admitted. "I have the first fitting with my client next week." The day was moving glacially. Clarissa pondered on what she might be able to drink that was stronger than a matcha latte to get through to midday.

Clarissa was too stubborn to admit she had overexerted herself the last few days. She intended to begin working on the pattern of Clara's second dress today.

I just have to keep pushing through, no matter what. Need to have something substantial for her to review besides the lining of her ceremony dress.

Clarissa bit her lip in contemplation. Would they wish to see all the bridesmaid dresses in addition?

I need to check in with Sonya and see how the ladies are coming along with their end of the work.

Patrick tapped her on the shoulder. Clarissa felt giddy as his warm hand made contact with her. Was he speaking to her too? She lazily opened her eyes and looked over to Patrick through her lashes.

"Earth to Clarissa. Are you sure you're going to be able to survive the day? If you're already this fatigued, I would wager against you." A hint of concern broke through his usually cheerful disposition.

They reached the ground floor. Clarissa yawned again and brushed off Patrick's worry. "I'm an adult. I'll manage. I'll even endeavor to be home before midnight tonight." She laughed, but Patrick didn't join in.

His arm blocked the pair of them from exiting. "When was the last time you had a solid night's rest?"

Clarissa grimaced. Must she answer the question truthfully? Could she downplay her answer? "Rest? What is this nonsense you speak of?"

Patrick scowled. "Clarissa, please. The truth."

She gazed up into his icy blue eyes and saw his serious concern. Clarissa was well aware Patrick's eyes reflected his feelings.

Gray and icy indicates he's unsettled. He will not let me pass without a real answer.

"Three weeks ago?" she questioned.

Patrick pinched the bridge of his nose. He gently grasped Clarissa by the arm and guided the two of them out from the lift and to the side of the building's lobby.

Clarissa's mind was foggy. Her eyes lingered on where he touched her; her stomach fluttered. She didn't fully process Patrick stepping away to make a call and returning to her side.

"You are not going into work today and neither am I." Patrick crossed his arms. His tone was unyielding. "You are staying in. I'm going to prepare a nice proper breakfast for you, then you are sleeping. After that, and only after you have a lie-in, can you leave my sight."

Clarissa blanched. She resisted the impulse to panic. Visions of Mark and his condescending commands flashed through her mind. Clarissa knew deep down that Patrick was only truly concerned for her well-being.

He is by no means Mark. Deep breath. It failed to alleviate the anxiety of her tight schedule. *An off day? I can't afford to not have an unproductive day.*

"I'm sorry, but that's not possible." Clarissa felt herself growing heated.

Patrick challenged her. "Oh ho, it is possible, and I'm

enforcing it. There is not a single person you could possibly be working for that could mind you taking *one* day off."

"I bet there is." Clarissa's mouth was moving faster than her brain.

Patrick stood tall and called the lift back to the ground floor. "Who?"

"The future Duchess of Leeds!" She gasped and clamped her hands over her mouth as her eyes darted around the lobby in horror. "Oh no! I didn't mean to say that aloud. You can't tell anyone! I've signed about a million confidentiality agreements."

Patrick broke out into resounding laughter. "In that case, this works out so much better!"

Chapter Twelve

PATRICK

Clarissa's face turned red in anger. She clenched her fists. She lifted her hand as if to strike Patrick. "You are acting like a sodding ignoramus. I am so tempted to slap you right now. I've just broken the confidence of my friend and VIP client, and all you can do is laugh at my misfortune?" Her hands shook.

Patrick scanned the lobby and held up his hands. Three people passed them, walking with purpose to their morning appointments. He waited until they were alone again.

"Wait. I promise there is a perfectly reasonable explanation for my behavior. I *will* explain. I can see that I've deeply upset you. I'm sorry. I understand how important your work is to you."

Placing his mobile in his pocket, Patrick took a deep breath. "I'm only thinking about your well-being. I want you to stay healthy and not exhaust yourself to the point you can no longer function. I have let it happen to myself before, and it is not something I'd wish upon anyone. My own father passed away under similar circumstances."

Patrick's shoulders hunched. "I retract my earlier statement. You are your own woman and an adult. However, I insist that you promise me that you *will* be home by six this evening. I will have dinner ready and waiting for you. *If you are* able to take a mental health day, please seriously consider it. I am good friends with the Duke of Leeds. He would never want anyone under his employ, and by extension his future wife's employ, to become ill over their wedding. In fact, if he were here now, he might even insist you take the entire week off."

Clarissa remained silent. At present, with the dark purple bags under her eyes and pale skin, she could pass for a living zombie.

Her eyes closed, resignation written across her face. "I may have overreacted. I was frightened by the way you insisted I take time off. In the past, there was a person who left emotional scars on me in the way they controlled certain situations."

There is more to her circumstances than meets the eye.

His heart dropped at the thought of him frightening her. Guilt arose to the forefront of his chest.

I never, ever want her to be scared of me. I want to protect her. How could anyone hurt her?

Patrick mulled over the new information, yet focused on Clarissa's immediate needs—sustenance and sleep.

Clarissa's eyes opened. Her body released the tension it held moments before. "I am going to have to admit defeat. As much as I *have* to work on hand embroidery today, I simply cannot afford to make any mistakes from my own folly. Therefore, I give in. I will be taking the morning off."

Patrick asked, "Have you had a chance to eat breakfast yet? I make an excellent omelet."

Clarissa's stomach growled. Her cheeks flushed pink. "I

suppose you have your answer. I *can* fend for myself though. Go to work. I can't have you late on my accord."

Patrick shook his head. "I have a fair bit of flexibility in what I was going to research today. Working from home sounds like an excellent idea. Shall we go to my flat?"

They stepped into the lift and rode back up to their floor. Patrick guided them to his front door. Clarissa glided over to his couch, sat down, and pulled her knees up to her chest to rest her head. Patrick slipped off his jacket.

"Please try to stay awake long enough to eat, then you can sleep. Stay here if you wish. As you can see, I *finally* have my desk over in the far corner of the room set up."

Clarissa fought the urge to doze and nodded to Patrick. He left her for a moment to gather the white fleece blanket from his bed.

This will have to do.

Returning to the common area, he offered her the blanket. She accepted it and burrowed into it. She poked her head out of the top of the blanket. Clarissa was so tiny.

With a sudden jolt, Clarissa said, "I need to call my driver and tell him I won't be coming in today. As part of the decoy, I always take the tube to Bond Street and then have a driver to take me from there to Kensington Palace."

Patrick inquired, "Is the driver Michael? I can send him a text straightaway. He is typically the one on call at this time of day."

Clarissa opened her mouth and closed it. She stared at Patrick. "You weren't lying earlier, were you?"

He chose not to answer. He sent the message and helped himself to his well-worn apron. He then proceeded to pull out several containers of fresh fruit and eggs from the refrigerator. "Omelet and a side of fresh fruit alright with you?"

Clarissa agreed. Quietly, she added, "Do you have any

fresh orange juice too? The produce you have always tastes as if it has come straight from the country."

Patrick chuckled. "Absolutely. I purchase all of my groceries from the farmer's market if I am able to." He turned on the heat under the frying pan and began slicing and dicing away as he spoke. He was in his element.

Clarissa said, "Funny, I am more awake now than I was in the lobby. If you wouldn't mind, I think I might like to hear of how you know the Duke of Leeds. I'm rather curious."

Patrick surrendered himself to his memories. "It's not that fantastical of a story. David Leeds and I grew up together. Mum is a distant cousin of Princess Charlotte. My parents have always been close to her, especially after David's parents divorced. We attended the same boarding school, Eton, where we were housemates, and we read history together at Oxford. I was an antisocial child and an introvert. I preferred books and horses to human companionship. David had a similar personality. He was one of my only friends."

Clarissa considered what he was telling her. *She'll connect the dots in a few moments that I have a title. I just hope she doesn't overreact. Will it change the nature of our relationship? Will she be upset I haven't told her until now?*

He needed to trust her. His instincts told him it was the right time to reveal the other side of his life to her. Already today, Clarissa had shared a deep piece of herself with him. It was time he did the same. Nevertheless, he perspired with nervousness.

Patrick focused on the eggs and added cheese, onions, tomatoes, peppers, and olives. He slowly continued. "David has an innate ability to calm those around him. I went through an especially dark period in my life when my father suffered a sudden heart attack and died. David and my father's friend, Lord Greyston, proved to be instrumental when I assumed the title of the twelfth Earl of Renbrook. Have you heard of the Nelsons of Rainridge?"

Patrick's heart picked up a few beats in anticipation of Clarissa's reaction. "Okay. So you—" Clarissa's already pale countenance turned even whiter. She stuttered. "You… you… you're an earl?" Clarissa placed her hands over her mouth. "Why didn't you tell me earlier? Do you not trust me?"

Hurt rolled off her hushed voice, breaking Patrick. He enjoyed being *just* Patrick. He stole a glance at Clarissa. His self-confidence steadily grew.

Patrick's voice wavered. "I'm sorry. I truly did not want to alter the nature of our friendship. You have no idea how much I enjoy and look forward to spending time with you. I've ruminated over it the last few weeks. From my past experiences, my having a silly title has always been my downfall. There are times I wish I wasn't an earl. People have so many expectations and treat me in a way they perceive an earl should be treated. Most associate it with endless piles of money and society. In reality, it is nothing of the sort."

"The Nelsons are not overly wealthy. In fact, the family house just about costs more to maintain than it's worth. We can thank my ancestors for gambling away most of the family fortune. There are so many times I have come close to dropping its use altogether. But I keep circling back to my parents and how disappointed they would be in the loss of the family's legacy. We can't choose the family we are born into. I just wish—" Patrick wretched his hand back from the frying pan.

Pain flashed through him. He was coherent enough to turn off the stove. Clarissa was off the couch and immediately by his side. "Don't burn yourself on my account. If I may…" She gently guided Patrick over to the sink and ran the cold tap.

Patrick hissed as the cold water met his burning skin. "The omelet will be ruined."

"Don't agonize over the omelet," Clarissa scolded him. She moved the pan off to an unused burner.

Patrick retracted his hand out from underneath the cold water. The small portion of his hand that had touched the scorching pan was crimson red, but otherwise fine.

Her touch feels so good to my skin. That's exactly the cooling touch I need. Where she runs cold, I run warm.

"Keep it wrapped in this cloth," Clarissa directed him. "I have an aloe vera plant in my flat." She searched her pockets for her key.

Afraid she wouldn't return, Patrick said, "Stay. I'll be right as rain in a few minutes." He studied the red hand, then the overcooked omelet. "Let me make you another."

Clarissa gazed into his eyes. They locked onto one another. Patrick sensed nervous and conflicting emotions radiating off her person as if he was attuned to only her.

"I'm still peeved," she clarified, "but expect the remainder of your narrative." Patrick nodded to her.

Clarissa hastened to her flat. *She looks as I did when mother told me about her secret marriage. She's hurting as I did.*

A few moments later, Clarissa returned with a cross-section of her aloe plant. Wordlessly, she rubbed the oozing liquid over Patrick's burn. The sappy liquid from the plant was a balm to his aching hand. She wrapped his hand in a moist towel. They both wordlessly sat down on his sofa.

Patrick whispered, "I'm sorry for not trusting you. I am guarded with this part of my life." His eyes watched the fish swimming along in his aquarium, calming him.

Clarissa ran her fingers up the length of his arm. "It's difficult to carry secrets. If you are not ready to share more about your personal life with me, I understand. I needed a few minutes to process what you told me earlier."

Patrick's head looked down, then turned to Clarissa. He swallowed hard and his throat tightened. His hands briefly shook. "No. I should have shared this with you earlier. I was born a viscount. Women have attempted to romantically attach themselves to me for the wrong reasons. David and his cousin Eddie have experienced the same as me. In fact, David and I had made a pact at one point to swear off love entirely. We both agreed we'd be better off."

Clarissa continued to rub small circles on his arm. "My last serious relationship ruined me. Her name was Mary. We shared many interests, yet I was only a pawn of hers in the grand scheme of her plans. In the end, being myself was not enough for her. It broke me to no end. I locked my heart away to keep it safe from being so badly broken again."

Clarissa gasped. Her body recoiled from Patrick, then she pulled him into a fierce hug.

She's mentioned before that she's not looking for a relationship. I understand she's consumed by her career right now. Would she ever be open to something further developing in the future? Why is it that the one woman I'm even remotely interested in is probably off the shelf? What if she outright says she wants to terminate our daily meetings? I haven't even had to know her that long to understand she's special. Patrick wrestled with his innermost thoughts.

Clarissa pulled away. "Thank you for trusting me. I can relate to what you've experienced better than you may think. I'm not mentally prepared enough to travel down memory lane yet, as you have, but when I am ready, I will let you know." She grasped her head and rubbed her temples. "I have the fiercest of tension headaches coming on."

Patrick slowly cupped Clarissa's cheeks. "Eat, sleep, and you and I can chat further once you are fully rested. There is something else I would like to share with you," Patrick whispered softly.

I want to kiss those sweet rosy cheeks, take her into my arms, and hold her tight, never letting her go.

"I'm so tired." Clarissa yawned again and leaned into Patrick. "You've become a good friend. Will you stay with me until I fall asleep?"

Patrick's eyes nearly bulged out of his head. "Yes. If that's what you'd like, I'd be happy to." He didn't dare speak aloud what else was on his mind. It wasn't the right moment.

She made her way to the discarded omelet, ate a few pieces, and prepared for a nap.

<h1 style="text-align: center;">Chapter Thirteen</h1>

CLARISSA

larissa slept longer than she had intended. Naps always caused grogginess. She hated the notion of sleeping away the day; she lost valuable production time. Her eyes opened to relative darkness.

I need blackout curtains like this. What time was it? Did he have a clock nearby? *Where's my phone?*

Clarissa begrudgingly wiggled out of the warm bundle of blankets and sat up against the headboard. She rubbed her eyes.

She was certain she had fallen asleep on the sofa. Was she in his bedroom? She glanced around. The king-size bed, soft silky sheets, dresser, and bedside table revealed the answer to her. She was definitely in his bedroom.

The room contained no personal effects, just furniture. Had it been any other person, save Sonya, her brother Henry, or Patrick, Clarissa would have been overly concerned, but Patrick had earned her trust.

Clarissa sighed. *Patrick was right. I am much more refreshed and alert. My head isn't pounding nearly as much as earlier.*

She stretched and headed outside the bedroom toward the common area. The scent of fresh chocolate croissants lingered in the air and triggered a vague memory. She struggled to recount just what said memory was. Her stomach growled, momentarily distracting her. *I'm glad Patrick wasn't around to hear that.*

Patrick's voice came from the sofa. "Somebody's ready for an early dinner, then?"

He uncrossed his legs, stood, and placed his laptop on the coffee table. Clarissa couldn't help but notice how handsome he appeared with hair disheveled, afternoon scruff, and in glasses.

Clarissa yawned. "What time is it? Have I slept one hundred years?"

Patrick chucked. "It's half-past three."

Clarissa froze. "I've slept for"—she did the mental calculation—"six hours?"

Patrick removed his glasses and placed them alongside his computer. "You desperately required it. The fact of the matter is, you will probably sleep quite well again tonight."

Clarissa made her way to the kitchen island and helped herself to the lukewarm cup of tea awaiting her. "You really didn't have to go to all the trouble to prepare a tea service."

She helped herself to a warm croissant sitting atop a cooling rack. Chocolate made everything better.

She bit into the soft, perfectly shaped, and crispy concoction. The chocolate chips melted into her mouth. Patrick's food always tasted first-rate and smelled divine. The scent returned.

Clarissa recalled the appearance of meals by her mystery chef to whom she was forever indebted. Had it been two or three weeks? In all that time, Patrick had never once uttered a word on the subject.

Patrick started, "I'm afraid the tea is chilled. I needed a

pick-me-up while working through some of these dull invoices and project proposal notes.”

Clarissa sipped her tea. She desired to know why he went to so much trouble for a girl like her. “Patrick?”

He half-heartedly paid attention. “Hmm?” he asked. He sampled his own cuppa. “No, this won’t do. I need to reheat the water.”

Clarissa asked, “Why do you secretly leave a takeaway bag on my doorstep every weeknight? Why have you not said anything? I know it is you.”

Patrick answered too quickly. “I have no idea what dinners you are inquiring about.”

“I never mentioned dinner.”

He sank onto the stool next to her. She examined him in an entirely new light. Taken aback by the longing in Patrick’s eyes, she wondered what the depth of his feelings toward her might be. Everything to this point had been a waking dream. Did he return the same feelings she had harbored for him?

Every bit of her body was yearning to know. “Answer me this… when I was sleeping, I dreamed about you and was afraid you wouldn’t be present when I awoke. I’m confused, but my mind and my heart are telling me that I’m falling for you. I’m breaking every single one of my rules. I have been so hesitant to become involved with anyone. It’s been *six* long years.”

Clarissa stared at the ground, afraid to look up at Patrick. “I’m scared of where this could lead. Am I being too forward?”

Clarissa popped up from the stool and busied herself filling Patrick’s stainless-steel kettle with water before warming it on the stove. Afraid of his answer, she braced herself for a negative response.

“Clarissa,” Patrick breathed out. “I cook for you because I

care about you. But there is, indeed, a deeper meaning. An exceptional woman like you would never have thought twice about a bloke like me. I *never* dared to dream that you might even be open to the possibility of a relationship, but I like you a lot. I gathered every fiber of my being to muster the courage to ask you to dinner the second night we met. I was terrified that if I asked you for anything more, I might jeopardize our friendship. I want to date you and show you the depth of my affections that have grown exponentially since meeting you."

Clarissa's eyes grew wet with tears. She regarded Patrick. "I've only ever had one relationship. Until now, I've been absolutely petrified of opening myself up to anyone. You have changed me for the better. I want to erase the painful past and fill it with love. I want to be around a man who can be a strong friend—a Watson to my Sherlock. You've shown me that love just might be possible. It is an emotion I have never truly known or experienced."

Clarissa could no longer hold her emotions in check. The floodgates released a fresh wave of tears as she flew into the outstretched arms of Patrick. She wrapped her arms around his solid torso tightly, afraid to let go. Her head buried itself in his chest.

"Patrick," she whispered.

Patrick stood. He brought his arms around Clarissa and planted a gentle, chaste kiss on the top of her head. "My family calls me Paddy. I want us to take this slow if need be. Whatever this is, it is brand-new to both of us. We need time to acquaint ourselves with one another on a deeper level. Whatever happens, we do this together. I will treat you as the amazing treasure you are."

Clarissa's breathing slowed. "You've already been doing that. Taking care of me through food is the sweetest gesture. I've been working so much that I haven't stopped, even for a moment to look after myself." Clarissa felt safe and warm within his embrace.

~

With Clarissa, Patrick shared several of his heavy burdens. They connected on a more intimate level. Patrick sat on the sofa with Clarissa resting her head on his shoulder, digesting their dinners.

Patrick spoke softly and played with Clarissa's hair. "I spoke of Mary earlier this morning to you. If we are going to make this relationship work, it is important to me that I don't harbor any more secrets from you. There are very few people aware that for two years, it has been an up and down battle for me with depression and anxiety. I struggled significantly with my mental health after my father's death and even more so after the Mary breakup. It will never go completely away. Mental health is rarely spoken of out loud. Aristocrats have made it a habit of hiding all their problems from the world. Having mental struggles is considered a weakness."

Clarissa sat up straight. "I will take you for all that you are, Paddy, so long as you accept me and all my own faults. In the same light that the outside world sees aristocrats, my family holds similar expectations. They have never understood my learning disabilities. I have dyslexia. I invert letters and numbers. It went undiagnosed for years growing up. In school, I was always the disappointing Lee daughter who barely scraped through GCSEs. I didn't possess the athletic prowess of my tennis-playing brother. Any talents were not considered useful."

Clarissa's face flushed. "You broached being utterly crushed and broken earlier today." Clarissa's fists clenched. "Mark Leung, my ex-boyfriend, emotionally scarred me. It has taken me years to overcome the damage. Even now, I have a difficult time around men. I do not stand up for myself as I should. He caused so much tension between my family and me. My parents and I are still not on full speaking terms."

Patrick clasped Clarissa's hands. He tenderly planted a small kiss on them as her fists opened up. "We are two people who have been shattered and put back together. I will always support you through the good, the bad, and whatever is to come."

Clarissa's anger melted away. "How did I get so fortunate?"

Patrick chuckled. "I'm the lucky bloke."

Clarissa confessed, "I can't give you an answer as to how this is going to work, but I want us to have a full and fair chance at happiness. I am going to be frustrated and tired and working long days until the royal wedding is over. Can you put up with that? Our dates will be sporadic to say the least."

"You are worth the wait," Patrick reassured Clarissa. "Eleven more weeks will pass by in the blink of an eye."

"Thank you." Clarissa stopped just short of kissing him. She wasn't yet ready for a romantic kiss. Agreeing to date Patrick was a huge hurdle for her to conquer.

I never knew a connection with someone like this could exist. Patrick is the person I want around when there's trouble. Should I explain to him the full extent of Mark's abuse? No, today was a lot for me. I'm not ready.

Later that evening as she settled into her own bed, Clarissa reminisced about the day. She was eternally grateful to Patrick for enforcing a day off. The grin had yet to leave her face. She lay down just when her mobile rang.

Until now, she had unplugged herself from the outside world. It had never dawned on her to check her mobile for any missed called or messages.

"Sonya! I didn't expect you to reach out to me tonight. What's on your mind?" It wasn't like her friend at all to call past nine.

"Clarissa!" Sonya's voice bordered on panic. "I've been trying to reach you for the last hour and a half! We have an enormous problem."

Chapter Fourteen

CLARISSA

With trepidation, Clarissa sat up. "You're scaring me. Sonya, what happened?"

Sonya sobbed over the phone. "We *just* had a break-in occur at the Bond Street boutique. The burglars stole almost all the ready-to-wear pieces, and much worse…"

Sonya paused to catch her breath. "They've run off with the three bridesmaid dresses the team was working on. As the business owner, the police need to speak to you in order to formally file their report. I am also still admittedly rattled." Sonya was not easily shaken.

All of the blood drained from Clarissa's face. Three bridesmaid dresses and nearly the entire ready-to-wear selection? Clarissa immediately chided herself for being more worried about the dresses than her staff.

Dresses can be replaced; people cannot.

On edge, Clarissa was finding it hard to not pace the length of the room. Knots formed in the pit of her stomach. She shivered. "Is everyone alright? Was the boutique closing?"

It was nearly ten in the evening. The shop should have closed at eight. She couldn't sit still any longer.

Clarissa heard a few voices in the background. "Everyone is in one piece. The sales floor ladies had already been dismissed for the evening. I was holding a quick meeting with the bridesmaid fabrication team before they departed when we heard the commotion taking place on the sales floor and in the main workroom. Three men broke the front windows of the shop with cricket bats and snatched everything in sight. The backroom happened to be unlocked."

Clarissa's mind was already considering a variety of options. "I'll be there as soon as I can. I don't care what it costs, but please ensure that Elaine, Amy, and Stephanie leave in a cabbie. I don't want them alone. I'm sure they are quite unsettled. We'll brainstorm what the next step is going to be. I need to think." She pictured the damage to the shop.

"I'm so sorry, Clarissa. I know how important this is to you," Sonya cried. Clarissa had a difficult time consoling her. "I am an absolute failure. I know how much is riding on this."

Clarissa placed the phone on speaker, quickly dressed, and slipped her shoes on. "You are *not* a failure! There isn't much anyone could have done. I want to emphasize this is *not* anyone's fault. Rather, it is the result of several poor decisions. The bridesmaid dresses should have been constructed with the bridal gowns at Kensington Palace. Either way, just stay safe. Let the police know I will be there in about twenty-five minutes."

Should she take the tube or a taxi? Bond Street wasn't too far away. *I'll bring Patrick. I need a person with a clear head on their shoulders.*

"I will take care of the girls. See you in a bit, Clarissa."

Clarissa agreed and disconnected the call.

She all but sprinted out the door to Patrick's flat. She dithered once she got to his door.

I hope I am not presuming too much by asking him to come along. He can serve as our liaison to the royals should I have to contact them. I did not even think about that angle earlier. What a way to begin our first official evening as a couple. Patrick is going to question just what he is signing up for.

She knocked a few times in rapid succession. "Patrick? Patrick? Are you free?"

Pounding footsteps had him running up to the door in joggers, no shirt, wet hair, and oversized glasses, different than his reading glasses.

It was one of the first times she could remember him being dressed so casually. If this were any other time, Clarissa would've enjoyed the view. Patrick was really quite pale under all his clothing.

"Clarissa?" His eyes lasered onto her tear tracks. "What's wrong?"

Despite catching up on some rest, the combined shock and exhaustion were finally beginning to settle in. She found herself shaking. Patrick drew her into his arms and steadied her.

"I'm so sorry to interrupt the remainder of your evening. I need a favor, if you're willing. My Bond Street atelier was broken into. I am obligated to survey the damage and make a formal statement to the police. Would you consider coming along for support? I am a pile of nerves and am well aware that as soon as I arrive at the shop, I will not be able to fully focus. I wish to have a person who can remain rational by my side. My boutique manager and close friend, Sonya, is disconcerted. It may take the two of us to calm her down."

Patrick ran his hands over her arms. "You are freezing. Where is your coat? Never mind. Take mine." He glimpsed down at his lack of attire. "Let me just put a shirt and shoes on. I'll be ready in two minutes. We'll take my car over."

He keeps a car? Why is he always taking the train places? I suppose London traffic is horrid. I wouldn't want to bother with it.

Clarissa wrapped herself up in Patrick's black woolen overcoat; its rough texture rubbed against her skin. It smelled of citrus and spice, scents she didn't typically associate with Patrick. It vaguely reminded her of Kew Gardens. Hints of fresh lavender soothed her.

He came out of his bedroom in a hideously baggy and tattered Trinity College jumper over his joggers and trainers. "Let's go." Patrick secured the front door and led them down to the complex's car park. "I am *always* available. I'm especially glad you came to get me. It is moments exactly like these that I am here for you."

They rode the lift down to the basement level. He clicked the key fob, unlocking his car. A bright red Jaguar F-type flashed its lights twice.

He has a red car? Not what I pictured. It's so ostentatious.

"The red was not my first choice. The previous owner of this vehicle, the Prince of Wales, bought a fleet of fast cars a few years ago. King Reginald was furious when he discovered his son's intentions to race with his friends across the continent. He ordered Eddie to immediately sell them off. I bought one of the last three cars. All of them were red," Patrick recounted. "I have a soft spot for cars, horses, gardening, and cooking. You know all my hidden weaknesses now."

That sounds like something I read in the tattler. Though, as I recall, it was a story about funding the numerous speeding tickets Prince Edmund and his friends earned.

Clarissa appreciated Patrick's soft chatter as he drove them through the streets of London to Bond Street. She found her mind otherwise preoccupied with figuring out how to replace the bridesmaid dresses. Patrick parked the car one block from her shop. As they walked in silence, Patrick stayed close.

"This is the second of your shops? The other one is on Portobello Road, is it not?" Patrick asked.

Clarissa's reply died on her lips. The flashing lights from

the police cars stopped Clarissa in her tracks. She let out an audible gasp as her hands flew to her mouth. For a moment, all the air fled her body.

Her heart dropped at seeing one of the two display windows smashed to bits. On the sidewalk in front of the shop, two broken and stripped mannequins lay carelessly abandoned on the ground.

Patrick's hand on her shoulder reminded her of his presence. "Go take care of the shop and your manager. I am here if you need me."

Taking a deep breath, Clarissa uttered a soft, "Thank you." She squared her shoulders and marched into the scene of the crime. Passing under the front doors with broken hinges, she immediately sighted Sonya.

Sonya's bloodshot eyes informed Clarissa of just how hard Sonya had taken the burglary. Clarissa launched herself at her friend and hugged her tightly. "Sonya. This is so much worse than you implied. There is glass everywhere! I am so happy you are safe."

Clarissa released Sonya and checked her over. *I am so thankful I took today off. Everything happens for a reason. I have serious doubts as to whether I would have been able to handle this as exhausted as I was.* Clarissa's adrenaline kicked in.

Sonya said, "I am so sorry. I am utterly devastated right now. The last thing I want is to add to your stress levels and to have to recreate all of the lost dresses."

Clarissa and Sonya had not worked this hard to have the break-in stop them this close to the finishing line. They *would* succeed, no matter what.

"Hey, now. You are always the one who keeps me in check. It is my turn to inform you that we *will* get through this. We will find a way to pivot and move onward and upward. This is the lowest of the low points we can go." Clarissa was pleased with how confident and reassuring she sounded despite the numerous doubts in her head.

Sonya sniffled. "You're right, Clarissa. Where is my head right now?"

Once Clarissa settled Sonya, she set out to find the chief inspector and answer any questions he had in order to file his report. Out of the corner of her eye, she observed Patrick introducing himself to Sonya.

Together, the two of them procured the cleaning supplies from the storage closet and set to work in righting the shop. Her heart swelled. Sonya's coloring returned as she chatted with Patrick.

Once free from Detective Wade, Clarissa paused to truly assess the damage. The emptiness of the shop disturbed her. She slipped into the supply room. Hangers and garment bags littered the floor.

As one saving grace, the more elaborate and expensive gowns were heavy and could not so easily be seized. She counted fifteen remaining. Additionally, Sonya's jewelry line was stored away in the safe room.

Returning to the sales floor, Clarissa tiredly sat upon the now upright furniture. Patrick and Sonya finished clearing the front display window of glass and debris and joined her.

"I have taken a quick inventory of what we have on hand. I thought perhaps we might shift anything that is serviceable over to the Portobello Road atelier," Clarissa suggested.

Sonya nodded in agreement. "That was my line of thinking too. We can have this shop boarded up and closed until the glass is repaired. Until we produce more inventory, it only makes sense to have one shop open. We may need to hire some temporary seamstresses in the meantime."

Clarissa responded, "I agree, but I also think we need to sleep on it and see what other brainstorms we have in the morning. I am planning to come in and see if I can fabricate maybe two or three dresses that are similar to add to the existing collection."

Sonya and Patrick eyed one another. "No," they said in unison. They all laughed.

Sonya said, "Leave the sewing to me. I can get my hands dirty just this once, plus we do have three new seamstresses that I hired due to start next week. I will call them in and have them begin a week ahead of plan. You focus on your wedding gown. You have enough to concern yourself with."

Patrick added, "I've been considering how I might be of use to you and thought that I'd go out and pick up some plywood to cover your broken windows before I take you ladies home this evening."

Clarissa's eyes widened. She hadn't thought of repairing the window and door tonight. "Are you certain? Are you able to board this up so quickly? I doubt many shops would be open now."

Patrick's eyes sparkled in mirth. "I may know a few key people who owe me favors."

Clarissa hoped Patrick would share the full details of just *who* could procure wood for them on such late notice later. Patrick rolled the sleeves on his jumper up. "Leave everything to me. I'll have you squared away in about half an hour."

"Thank you for everything, Paddy. In the meantime, Sonya and I will make a list of physical inventory that needs to be taken over to our other shop."

Patrick pulled out his mobile and set to work. Clarissa and Sonya entered the back room. Slowly they picked up the items off the ground. Sonya was almost back to herself. "I definitely approve of Patrick. He is *such* a gentleman. Just the type of man I would have picked for you from a dating website. Do you have any girl talk you might like to share with me while we're alone?"

Sonya was absolutely on the road to recovery, already

pumping Clarissa for details. It had been a while since they'd spoken in the flesh.

Let's see how her own dating life is going.

Having Sonya to speak with eased her mind. Patrick, true to his word, had the window and door boarded up in record time.

His secret—three of the British Army's finest carpenters. Though Patrick provided some of the labor himself. If there were ever two people Clarissa was happy to have in her life, it was Patrick and Sonya.

Sonya enjoyed her car ride over to Kensington Palace immensely and couldn't stop her excited chatter. "Is *this* how you've been jaunting to and fro? Can you hire a car service for the shops?"

Clarissa was relieved Sonya revealed none of the stress of the last week.

The car service is a luxury I don't even need.

"While I agree it's certainly handy to have a car service available, I am perfectly capable of walking from Portobello Road to Kensington Palace. It's not *that* far. Just as I am happy to take the tube from Bond Street. We're here to work, after all, not pop out to the High Street and back."

"I know it is not realistic," Sonya admitted, "but it won't keep me from continually asking about it."

The truth of the matter was that Clarissa *had* seriously been considering Sonya's request to have a car and driver available for them. There were a number of times they needed to dart from one location to another. With a car service, they could carry more supplies and also potentially offer it out to certain clients.

Clarissa offered a compromise to Sonya. "You may get

your wish. If you are dead set on a car service, I'll have you prepare the numbers for me to see if it might fit into our budget."

Sonya blanched. "That's a lot of numbers to go through. I still haven't balanced the books for Bond Street, then there's the upcoming Shepherd's Bush location—"

"Best get to work on it straightaway then," Clarissa joked.

The Bond Street boutique remained out of commission until the stock was replenished. The police had no leads on the case. Despite having security cameras, the burglars were indistinguishable in their black masks.

The police, however, believed the robbery had not been random. None of the other higher-end shops on Bond Street had been targeted.

The car pulled up to the guard booth demarking the visitor's entrance to the ivy-covered, red-bricked royal residence. As the car was waved through the crunchy gravel pathway, Sonya stared in awe at their surroundings.

She might have even taken out her camera if Clarissa hadn't reminded her they had a strict no-photos policy. Sonya groaned under her breath. She was there for the express purpose of assisting Clarissa with Clara Little's first wedding dress fitting.

Clarissa thanked their driver as they stepped out. Thick trees provided cover over the footpath and doubled as protection from the prying eyes of the public. The building had been one of the childhood homes of Queen Victoria. It was a fact Clarissa never forgot as she patiently waited for Sonya to follow her inside.

Clarissa pointed out to Sonya, "Do you notice the black and white checkered floors? I've been told they are all original."

Sonya nodded as her eyes glossed over every portrait, statue bust, and royal insignia they strode past.

Clarissa continued her running commentary. "We are working in one of the oldest sections of the palace, closest to where Prince Edmund and Prince David conduct their business. I cannot wait for you to see all of the state-of-the-art equipment I've been able to source," Clarissa gushed.

Sonya rolled her eyes and gazed down the hallway. "Unlikely, but I am excited that you are excited. Machines just do not excite me the same way jewelry and fabric do."

Clarissa snorted and refocused. Nodding to the wooden door numbered 234, she entered the secret code into the keypad. The lock turned green and granted them access. Clarissa pushed the door's handle. "Here we are."

Sonya gushed over the work accommodations and view from the room. "Not too shabby, Clarissa. I'm jealous. I might never leave this place!"

Two bay windows allowed in plenty of natural light. The wooden floors echoed as they passed three empty workstations and shelves of supplies Clarissa had painstakingly organized by color, size, and shape.

Situated in the center of the room was a dress form clad in a show-stopping light champagne-colored bodice with a delicate lace overlay. The V-cut neckline and cap sleeves worked in tandem with an empire waist cut where the organza overskirt would attach. The dress diverged from the sketch and appeared different depending on the angle one viewed it from.

The overskirt, at present, was carefully spread out across two worktables. Dozens of tiny hand-embroidered flower appliques sat in small containers waiting to be attached to the overskirt. Each flower was accented in a light wash of pink, gold, or orange.

Sonya ran her hands over the delicate lace and organza overskirt. "Oh, Clarissa. This is stunning. The gold, pink, and orange accents at the very end of the dress invoke the sunset. This fabric is simply magical. I am in awe at your work."

Clarissa almost cringed at anyone, Sonya included, touching her dress. "Upon seeing this dress, I know *exactly* who it is intended for."

She handed Sonya gloves to wear. *Nobody* was going to touch the dress without them! She didn't want any dirt near the light fabric. The flowers on the overskirt had taken her hours and hours of work. She hoped Clara appreciated her effort.

"This dress is my *baby*. Clara is coming in at ten for a first fitting. There isn't a single other person I trust to assist me." Clarissa swept over to her working desk and handed over three revised bridesmaid dress sketches. "These are the replacements I have in mind for the lost bridesmaid dresses."

The original patterns and drawings were accounted for, so Clarissa altered the designs in the event the dresses were leaked to the public. Could her trio of seamstresses create the new dresses in just ten weeks?

Sonya examined the sketches. "These are just as brilliant as the original ones. The girls have the rest of the week off. Have you thought about how to address their safety concerns?"

Sonya passed the sketches back to Clarissa. For now, they would remain stowed away within the safety of Kensington Palace property.

Clarissa guided Sonya back to Clara's dress. "I spoke to Patrick and to Amanda Collins. They both agreed it would behoove me to have them work on-site so that A) I'm not overwhelmed if I need assistance, and B) everything is in a secure location. It was foolish of me to have the dresses worked on in the shop."

Fear had put them in the position they were in now. In order to succeed, Clarissa needed to spread her wings and entrust others with her vision. Every major designer made the jump at some point to trust their team. It was her turn.

Sonya touched Clarissa's shoulder. "No it wasn't. As you

have reminded me innumerable times, it could have happened to anyone. Our luck was just awful. I have been giving the situation more thought. The police may have no leads, but I have to wonder if you were targeted because of your connection to Clara. Did the thieves think you might have her wedding dress on the property? It is worth a *lot* of money to the right media outlet."

Clarissa frowned. *Could it have been because of Clara? The press office never confirmed me as the wedding dress designer.*

She did not have the time to speculate. She needed to prepare for the fitting. How could she get Sonya back on track? An idea struck Clarissa.

"Only time will tell. In more pressing matters, how was your date with the protection officer on the Leeds team? What's his name? Liam?"

Sonya crossed her arms. "If you mean *Charlie*, he was sweet. Very proper and tight-lipped, but he has potential. We have another date lined up, but I don't want to jinx it. Maybe we should focus on today."

Clarissa held her hands up. "As you wish." They shared a laugh. All of the stress from being awarded the rights to design for Clara had built up to this moment. Would Clara say yes to this dress?

"I've been meaning to ask you—" Sonya turned on the steamer to work out the dress's wrinkles. "What are you doing for Chinese New Year at the end of this week? Are you staying in town? While my parents have no notion as to what Chinese New Year is, you are more than welcome to trail along with me when I visit them in Cardiff this weekend."

The Chinese New Year coincided with the lunar calendar. It was celebrated by many different Asian cultures. Usually it occurred in late January to early February. This year, it happened to fall on Friday the 13th of February.

To Clarissa's parents, it was the *most* important holiday of the year. Many members of her family would be in attendance at some point during the weekend. It was the one day of the year Clarissa dreaded.

Clarissa was sorely tempted to take Sonya up on her offer. Cardiff, the largest city in Wales, had so many beautiful seascapes to enjoy. It was a welcome retreat from London and miles different from her childhood home of Birmingham. Still, she could not bring herself to accept Sonya's offer.

I promised Mama and Baba I would come home. I am committed to following through with it so they will not have any additional excuses to find fault with me.

Clarissa exhaled. "There is no backing out. But I did mention to my parents that I was only going home for one day."

Sonya gave Clarissa the evil eye. "This needs to be fixed. You need a holiday. Won't your parents accept that you are already under a mountain of stress? Working yourself in the way you are is unhealthy. Although, Patrick stepping in puts my mind at ease. I just want to see you take care of yourself, Clarissa. I care about you."

I have only just finished the muslin mock-up of dress number two. But a promise is a promise.

Gratefully, she half-smiled at Sonya. "I appreciate you for it. I will be taking Sunday off for myself, perhaps even a spa day." She groaned. "When I mentioned the possibility of staying in London, when I attempted to worm my way out of dinner, well... have you ever heard of a supernova?"

Sonya tilted her head to the side. "Are you referencing astronomy? If I recall correctly, a supernova is when a particularly large star explodes at the end of its lifecycle."

Clarissa glumly nodded. "That's exactly what happened. Mama and Baba exploded. I expect they might have cooler heads by now. My main concern is that Mark may be around this weekend. The Leung family lives across the street from my parents."

She kept her promise to bring a *special someone* home with her to herself. She was positive her parents would never accept Patrick.

Clarissa came to a standstill. Why *did* she care so much? After all this time, *why* did she crave her parents' approval? Nothing she did ever surmounted their expectations. This was *her* life to lead. If she wanted to date Patrick, then she bloody well would. Should she bother subjecting him to the Lees of Birmingham? Would Patrick even *want* to come with her?

The steamer beeped, ready to be put to use.

With those thoughts in the front of her mind, Clarissa felt newfound freedom. She had a *choice*. She had proven she could be a successful businesswoman on her own, and now she was taking command of her private life.

Pure and utter joy radiated through her body. She was Clarissa Lee of London now, not Clarissa Lee of Birmingham. She was designing the royal wedding dress, after all. She'd made her own dreams come true with hard work.

Chapter Fifteen

PATRICK

Princess Alice, the second child of King Reginald and Queen Agnus, was home on a rare half-term break from her boarding school in Wiltshire. Patrick took this as a sign from the universe.

Though he could not pinpoint exactly why, he inherently knew he needed to speak with her in person. The museum project pushed full steam ahead of schedule. Architecture plans and contractors lined up; his aim now consisted of figuring out *what* exactly the museum should exhibit. How could he make this museum stand out from others in London?

She is the key to unlocking the mystery. Alice inspired the museum, after all, and can provide me with a fresh outlook.

There was only one place Patrick would consider looking for her when she was home—the stables. The two children of the king, by Patrick's standards, loved horses more than people. He related. Horses understood emotions better than any human.

His trusty stallion, Chester, always calmed him. Chester

held a special place in his heart as one of the last gifts from his father before his passing.

Patrick envisioned taking Clarissa out for a canter on horseback across one of the wildflower meadows of Rainridge estate in spring, where only the buzzing of the bees, chirping of the birds, and soft fluttering of a butterfly's wings would be around them. The sun would warm her face and bring out the golden highlights within her dark hair. Her cheeks would glow rosy red.

My head is in the clouds. Focus on what you came here for.

Patrick shook his head to clear his thoughts and as he walked to the entrance of Kensington Palace. Whistling a melody that sounded suspiciously close to *Go Ask Alice*, by Jefferson Airplane, a wizened security guard waved him through the security gate without a second glance.

By now, everyone identified Patrick by sight. Having an office at Kensington Palace was a boon. Patrick spent hours combing through the vast archives of the royal family, searching for inspiration.

Hands in his pockets to protect himself from the chill, Patrick followed the gravel pathway to the stables. The crisp, cold air brought with it a dampness and a potential for snow.

London hadn't been privy to a late white winter in many years. He shivered and quickened his pace into the warmer, sheltered stables. The soothing sound of clinking bridle chains and hay welcomed him.

"Good afternoon, Lord Renbrook. How are you getting on today?" Danny, one of the head grooms, inquired. "Did you intend to ride out?" Danny raised an eyebrow.

"Good to see you, Danny. Actually, I'm just passing through to see if Princess Alice is present." *In hindsight, I could've phoned her.*

"Indeed she is, sir. Their Highnesses just rode out ten minutes past. I can have a spare mount prepared if you'd like to join them. I believe Leeds mentioned it had been a while since he'd had a good gallop through the public gardens. Horseback would be faster than by foot." Danny had already begun pulling out various pieces of horse tack before Patrick had given him an answer.

Patrick grimaced. *I am certainly not dressed for riding.* He glanced at his suit trousers, jumper, and jacket. Why didn't he keep a spare change of clothing here at Kensington Palace?

Actually, I need to replace many of my daily wear items.

Once she was finished with the Leeds wedding, would Clarissa be available to assist? She had once even gone so far as to threaten him with altering everything he owned herself.

"Thank you, Danny. I will accept any available mount. You don't have any spare riding kit pieces available, do you?" Patrick inspected the tack room of the Kensington stables. Could he borrow a pair of riding boots too?

Danny followed Patrick's gaze. He appraised Patrick's feet. "I'll see what gear I can wrangle up for you. Size ten boots?"

"Good eye. Yes, please."

For a third time, Patrick urged his docile mount to pick up her pace. The mare had a distinct personality of her own and ignored his request. As Danny had warned him, this stubborn mare performed everything at her own speed, regardless of who was mounted on her back. As a favorite horse of the royals, this spoiled-rotten horse seemed to understand she could get away with her behavior.

Patrick turned to bribery. "Oh, Daisy, wouldn't you *love* to have some extra apples and carrots after your workout today? I can make that happen if you would kindly cantor for me. This trotting nonsense will make me a laughingstock if either Leeds or Wales catches sight of us. You don't want that to happen to a poor ol' bloke like me, do you?"

Daisy snorted and let out a soft whine. *Is she laughing at me?* Daisy continued her trot, her hooves click-clocking against the crunching gravel. Patrick sighed. *It was worth a shot.*

"Oy! Renbrook, is that you?"

Patrick muttered a silent curse.

"It is! Hurry it along and bring Daisy over here. I want to see you properly." Princess Alice's cheery, musical voice rang out across the field.

Appearance-wise, Alice was the female version of her older brother, Eddie. At fifteen, Alice stood about five foot four. A tomboy, she favored a pixie haircut for her strawberry blonde hair due to its low maintenance.

Is this the same Alice I saw last year?

Gone was the quiet, reserved, gangly princess. She no longer had such long, awkward limbs. This Alice was fully in control of her body.

Without signaling Daisy to change her course of direction, she picked up speed, and trotted over to Alice. Under the refuge of a chestnut tree stood three horses and their riders.

"Alice, it's so good to see you. Welcome home. You're quite the young lady now." Daisy neighed in agreement. The group laughed.

Princess Alice answered back. "Thank you, I think. It is brilliant to see you too, Daisy. When you don't see me for months on end, I grow. Funny how puberty works out. I wager I might even be able to contend with you in a fencing match." She smiled. Her braces were gone.

Eddie joked, "Who gave you Daisy to ride? She's the slowest of the lot in the stables. She is the last mount *I* would have picked. It's common knowledge Alice is the only one Daisy will behave for."

Patrick sat taller in his saddle as he came to join the group. "Nice to see you, too, Eddie. Daisy happens to be an outstanding elder-states mare and the *only* one available to take out this morning." He adjusted his grip on the reins. "How are the Life Guards treating you?"

Eddie tilted his head to the side in contemplation. "The army is hard work but rewarding. I will never grow accustomed to being on tourist duty at Horse Guards Parade, though the foot guards have it worse. I could have sworn Poseidon, Skywalker, and Seymour were all available."

"No. All three required the farrier's services today," David answered for his younger cousin.

"My mistake. The days of the week all blend together." Eddie shrugged.

"More likely, you forgot and are trying to smooth over your error," Alice countered to her brother. "Daisy is the smartest horse around. I only wish I could take her back with me to school. She would make a fair dressage horse." Daisy nickered in agreement. The horse Alice sat upon stamped its feet.

Patrick ignored Eddie and spoke exclusively to Alice. "Look who is finally standing up to her older brother. Je suis impressionné."

"Merci beaucoup, Monsieur Patrick." Alice responded in French to annoy her brother.

"Puis-je participer à la conversation?" David added.

"We speak English here in England, last I checked. You three have an unfair advantage. I never studied French in school. I was coerced into learning Latin and Spanish," Eddie whined.

Everybody laughed. "The classics are supremely useful. They form the roots of all words. Nevertheless, I only asked if I could join in the conversation," David explained. "Were you not the one who told me Spanish was supremely useful on your last visit to California? Even Amanda appeared impressed."

Eddie's cheeks flushed. He stayed silent. The group signaled to their mounts to turn about and return to the stables.

"What brings you to KP today? I thought you were going to take an early weekend away from London and the Boring Royal," David said, poking fun at himself. "At last check, you are away to Rainridge every single weekend."

Patrick responded, "To be frank, I came to see Alice. I thought a chat with her might illuminate an answer to a small problem I am having with the museum project. You two may have the luxury of spending all day with her, but I don't."

Patrick pulled his horse up next to Alice. Daisy matched the speed of her mount. "I have never been so popular! Mum and everyone else has been booking my diary so full of engagements that I scarcely have any time to myself or time with Jenna Evans. *I* have an excuse, unlike Eddie."

David chuckled and signaled for Eddie to follow his lead. "We'll allow you two some much-needed bonding time."

David often fulfilled the role of an older brother rather than that of a cousin. Patrick was well aware of how much Eddie and Alice relied upon his guidance. Unlike her brother, Alice was not subject to the same formal behavior as Eddie by her parents.

Patrick inferred it was because she was female and the second child. Alice did not experience the same pressures as Eddie did as heir to the throne. Alice also steered clear of any trouble.

"Papa told me you are spearheading the modern Great Exhibition. Congratulations to you." Alice's large, doe-like eyes glimmered. "I knew the moment I observed the sorry state of the old conservatory it would be the perfect spot for some sort of project. Papa only needed a few words of encouragement."

Patrick smiled. "I owe you several games of chess as a thank you."

Patrick saw a young woman wise beyond her years. It was one of the many reasons he often found himself drawn to her company. From an early age, Alice had exhibited signs of intelligence. He always strove to treat her as an adult, unlike those around her.

Shy Alice had admitted a few times in the past that she was oftentimes lonely. Boarding school had served her well in bringing her out of her shell. Alice appeared more confident and self-assured. More importantly, she was happy.

Patrick updated Alice on his progress. "I have been speaking to a fair few focus groups, yet nothing has yielded the results I seek. We have so many world-class institutions in London. What brings new blood to the table? Perhaps I am approaching this from the wrong angle with you. What initially drew your own interest to the Great Exhibition of 1851?"

He genuinely was curious. Few fifteen-year-old girls would spend their time convincing their father they should resurrect a decaying old building into a museum.

"When I need inspiration, I try to think about what I want others to learn and take from whatever it is that I'm doing. If that makes any sense. I know that is not what you have just asked me." Alice considered Patrick's question. "I was searching for a bit of light reading in the school library when I came across a book detailing the story behind the Crystal Palace."

The wheels in Patrick's head began to turn. *A bit of light reading, indeed.* The Crystal Palace had been one of the largest structures built in the nineteenth century to house the Great Exhibition.

Alice perked up. "I found it absolutely fascinating to read about the Victorians' ability to build and to create. The Crystal Palace was revolutionary for its time. Victorian engineers needed to figure out the maths and architecture to support all the glass paneling and steel for construction to bring their plans to life. It was the size of St. Paul's! Did you know Kew Gardens still has a few Victorian greenhouses?" Alice danced in her seat in excitement.

Alice is a wealth of knowledge. I've never thought about how the Victorians were required to invent new technology for what was essentially the first world's fair. How curious it must have been to see so many new marvels from around the world. We take so much for granted in these modern times.

A lightbulb clicked on in Patrick's head. There was the answer for the museum—marvels in modern science and technology. He could take the best and brightest ideas of young adults from around the Commonwealth and showcase their hopes, dreams, and inspirations. At the same time, he could feature several exhibits on the original Great Exhibition.

Patrick smiled at the young princess. "I know exactly what I need to do now. You have always loved geometry and constructing your own projects. Do we have a future engineer in our midst?"

Alice blushed. Patrick assumed it could also have been due to the cold weather. "I've been speaking to Eddie's girlfriend, Amanda, a lot. Are you aware she is finishing her maths degree at uni? I love speaking to her about advanced-level maths. She understands me so much better than the boys. Physics has been one of my favorite courses too."

"In other words, yes," Patrick responded for Alice.

She focused her eyes on the path ahead. "Maybe. I'm not one-hundred percent sure yet. I've been thinking about what subjects I'll continue to study for A-levels."

David butted into their conversation. "Do not forget

history." He slowed his horse down to reach Alice and Eddie as they neared their sojourn.

"I didn't even take A-levels. You could join the service," Eddie teased.

"No. I would only be interested in the Cavalry, and they don't take any women into their regiment. Besides, I like school a lot. I want to attend uni. I have been researching the Russell Group schools in addition to Oxford, Cambridge, and some of the Scottish unis. Most programs I'm interested in require..."

Eddie groaned. "Alice. Now is not the time for a lecture before we've been fed." Eddie garnered a spiteful look from his sister.

Alice rolled her eyes. She reverted back to her childlike state, proving she was still a teenager at heart. "*You* are the one that inserted yourself into *my* conversation."

"As the higher ranking royal, I declare no more school conversations until the food is consumed." Eddie turned his horse to race back to the stables ahead of his sister. Patrick looked on in amusement at the banter between siblings.

"Not fair. Come on, Sherlock. Bye, Paddy; I will text you soon. It really has been too long. Excuse my rude older brother. Let's go." Alice raced off after her brother to see who could reach the stables first.

David and Patrick remained behind, watching the two siblings take off. "Some things never change," Patrick said to David.

"It's been like this since Friday night. I hope she'll at least say a proper goodbye to you before you leave. I cannot get over how much my young cousin has grown up. Did Alice give you the answer you were after?" David asked.

Patrick reflected on his conversation with Alice. "I have a few ideas to work off of. I owe her a few rounds of chess, and perhaps *one* round of Trivial Pursuit. I am almost afraid to even *mention* the topic."

The last time Alice and Patrick had teamed up against Eddie and David, the game had become so competitive, the king had had to step in. Neither Patrick nor David was willing to back down.

Patrick and David finally reached the stables where two grooms waited to take their horses. Eddie and Alice stood arguing over who could groom their horse the fastest. Patrick was positive the military riding course would give Eddie a leg up. He would never, however, bet against Alice.

David let out a breath. "Let's avoid *that* game for now. Although my Clara and Amanda could probably be trusted to keep us in check, should we decide to play. Meanwhile, can I tempt you to stay for some refreshments? We're eating in. The ladies are due to meet with Clarissa Lee today," David mused.

Interesting. David does not know Clarissa and I are in a relationship. How long can this last before he finds out?

"Oh no. I am *not* getting involved in any sort of wedding details. I have had enough exposure working with the wedding planner we recently hired on at Rainridge. I'm going to pass on today's invitation. I have some prep work for an important meeting later today. Do you know if Hyde Park's annual Winter Wonderland carnival is still open?"

Patrick instantly regretted mentioning the carnival. *So much for keeping this quiet.*

"So have you *finally* asked your neighbor on a date?" They dismounted and slowly walked over to the side of the stables where they could speak more privately.

Patrick colored at the mention of Clarissa. "Yes. We've spent some time together. I'm planning to surprise her this evening with a romantic dinner. She needs a distraction from her work."

David's demeanor sobered. "So she's one of us: a workaholic mess. She needs someone to keep her from going over the edge, so to speak." David bumped Patrick in the shoulder.

"Not so easily done. She's Clarissa Lee. I thought you of all people would've connected the dots by now." Patrick waited for David to process the information.

David rubbed a hand over his stubble. "Oh. So it's a *tad* more complicated. I would never have ventured a guess that Ms. Lee is your neighbor. I just pay the bills. But now that I'm aware *your* girl is working on Clara's dress, I'm infinitely more intrigued."

"Only a little complicated? Clarissa is a perfectionist and under so much pressure to construct the wedding dress of the century. On top of that, she has the added worry of the recent burglary of her shop and all the emotional baggage I come with," Patrick sarcastically shot back.

"You are being too hard on the two of you, mate. Trust her and trust yourself. If there is anything I have learned from my own relationship, it is that love always finds a way." With those words, David clapped Patrick on the back and left him to his own accord as he walked to check in on his younger cousins.

He needed a walk through Hyde Park. *I have told myself I am completely over Mary and have freed myself from my past, but have I really? Can I be the man Clarissa needs? She has her own demons from the past. Is she truly ready to move on?* They both had many questions they would have to answer.

Chapter Sixteen

CLARISSA

Clara and Amanda eagerly rushed inside Clarissa's workshop. "I'm thrilled to finally see all the progress you are making on my dress." Clara clapped her hands together in delight. "In ten weeks, I'll be marrying one of my best friends and the man of my dreams!"

Clarissa's nerves caused her to nearly faint. She rubbed her hands against her legs only to remember she did not want to soil her white gloves. Instead, she clasped her hands together and fidgeted with her thumbs.

Would Clara like the ceremony dress, after all of the countless hours of work she had put in? Clara always appeared to appreciate Clarissa's innate ability to dress her in the past.

Any edits at this stage in the design process would cause difficulty. Her abdominal muscles clenched in response. Doubt lingered in her mind.

Enough negative energy. You need to play your part. There is nothing more you can do until she sees the dress.

Sonya fervently welcomed Clara and Amanda to the viewing. Clarissa mumbled a greeting to the two women. Sonya stood off to the side, signaling for Clarissa to relax by using her hands to make the shape of a smile. She also pointed to the box of white gloves on the table.

Clarissa caught Sonya's not-so-subtle hint and offered Clara and Amanda two pairs of gloves from the box. "I know this may seem strange, but if you wouldn't mind putting these on, please. I've been attempting to keep your dress and fabric as pristine as possible."

They both agreed without any hesitation.

"That explains the white lab coat you have on. Ohhhhhh-hhh, I can't wait much longer. I'm soooooooooo excited." Amanda jumped up and down.

Clarissa crossed her fingers and removed the screen hiding Clara's dress for the big reveal. She counted to three. This was the moment of truth. Clara and Amanda darted forward. The room was silent.

No reaction? No screams?

Clara spent a few moments studying the dress. "Oh. This is so pretty!"

Pretty good? Pretty bad? Just pretty? Not beautiful? Not gorgeous? The soft tone of Clara's voice made it exceedingly difficult to decipher her innermost thoughts.

Amanda ran her hands over the skirt and longingly looked over the embroidery motifs with the bride-to-be. "I like it! It's off to a great start!"

Clarissa exchanged a nervous glance with Sonya. Whenever a woman mentioned the turn of the phrase, great start, it typically indicated the client wanted to make changes.

Clara studied the V-shaped neckline and motifs in the lacework. "I love the way this dress is coming along! It is exactly what I have envisioned. I was wondering if it might be too late to add in a few requests. I've been speaking a lot with the queen, and it's been brought to my attention that as a royal bride, I should really stick with a pure white dress. I absolutely love the gold-white you have now, but would it be too much trouble to change the color?" Clara asked.

Clarissa's eyes widened. Changing fabric or colors would mean beginning the dress again from scratch. The overskirt alone and all the hand detailing she had put into the flower applique had taken days.

I could salvage a few pieces of it.

Her heart was ready to burst. She fought to maintain her professionalism. She shot a keep quiet look over to Sonya whose eyes widened in horror. In the fashion world, the client always had the last word.

"I like this color, C," Amanda said. "It's different. You loved it in the initial consultation. You haven't cared before what others have done and have always wanted to stand out. I remember your exact words were that you are not a traditional bride. Maybe we just change the bottom here and get rid of the orange and pinks," Amanda suggested. "If it comes to it, leave the queen to me. I may have been scared of her when we first met, but I have learned that she respects a strong opinion."

Clarissa hoped waves of tension were not radiating off her body as she offered a sample of the other two possible satin fabrics for Clara to inspect. Nervous energy caused her hands to shake. Neither Clara nor Amanda seemed to notice. Clara held the two fabric swatches up to the champagne dress.

Clara continually stared at the dress. "You're right, A. I want to make my own mark."

Amanda firmly stated, "These other fabrics are too white. No. This is the perfect color for you. Don't let Princess Charlotte or the queen get into your head. They aren't getting married. You are. Their opinions won't matter at the end of the day. Do what makes you happy. Clarissa here knows your taste in fashion to a tee. Trust her vision."

That meant a lot to Clarissa. She shook herself out of her

stupor. *I need to take charge of this fitting. I'm the designer. My opinion counts too. I'm the one putting my name on this dress. Clara did say I could do what I wanted and this is my vision!*

What had happened to her self-confidence and discovery from earlier? What was she afraid of? They didn't know the dress as she did. Every part of the design contained a symbol. Clarissa clapped her hands together to capture their attention.

"I was terrified to say so earlier; however, I'm afraid your dress would simply not be ready in time should you decide to make any significant changes. Under normal circumstances, I'd be more than willing to do whatever you ask of me. The truth of the matter is, I need to finalize your ceremony dress so we can turn our focus to the reception dress. We only have ten weeks."

Clara's and Amanda's eyes opened wide.

Brilliant. They understand the time constraint of working on two dresses.

Clarissa continued. "All of the small flowers you see on the skirt have been hand-embroidered, hand-painted, and hand-sewn over the last two weeks by me. I've sourced the lace for the top part of the dress from Ireland. If you look closer, you can see the lace has the four flower motifs we discussed. It was a bespoke order commission."

Clara and Amanda studied each flower. "Oh. I definitely didn't see that the first time. It's so subtle. Did you truly do all these tiny stitches on the skirt by hand?" Clara asked in amazement.

"Yes." Clarissa hoped this would smooth over any lingering doubts.

Amanda said, "I didn't notice that extra shimmer. When the skirt moves, it gives off a different appearance depending on the angle I view it from. It's a neat effect. Try it on, C, then we can really appreciate the dress in all of its glory."

Sonya chatted with Amanda for a few moments while

Clarissa pulled Clara to the makeshift fitting area. Amanda's dress was also nearly complete. As the maid of honor, Clarissa and Amanda had discussed and settled on a periwinkle blue for all of the bridesmaids. She agreed to model her dress when Clara was done with her fitting.

Clarissa took a deep breath and assisted Clara in stepping into the dress. Slowly, Clarissa buttoned up the back and pinned areas in need of adjustment. The dress fit like a glove.

"Breathe, Clarissa. I can tell how nervous you are. I am too. We are in this together." Clara put a steady hand on Clarissa's shoulder.

Clarissa quietly replied, "I just want everything to be perfect."

Clara answered in a confident voice, "It will be."

Calling to Sonya, Clarissa stepped away and retrieved the overskirt. The two ladies carried it behind Clara's changing screen and guided Clara to step into it. Clarissa repeated the process of pinning the overskirt to the lining layer, checking the alignment and placement in relation to the seams. Clarissa then stepped back to eye her work.

Clara's hands played with the skirt. "This fabric is so light. I thought it would be a lot heavier and scratchy like my ballet tutus. Talk about itchy. Tulle is my best friend and worst enemy. This corset bodice has to rank among the most comfortable ones ever. Can you design my ballet costumes next?"

Clarissa focused on pinning the hem. "Comfort is a high priority. I'm not well-versed in theater costumes. I added a microfiber liner to keep the tulle from irritating your skin and to assist with temperature control. If you like it, I plan to use the same fabric to line the reception dress."

Clarissa let out her breath. "Now, keep in mind, this is only the first fitting. I need your honest opinion on everything. The more descriptive, the better. If you truly would like me to rework the entire dress, tell me. I won't be hurt."

They walked out from behind the screen to the full-length mirror and pedestal. Clarissa and Sonya carried the length of the skirt in order to keep it from touching the ground. Then, Sonya pulled the curtains down over the bay windows.

Clarissa assisted Clara up to the pedestal and turned on two hidden ring lights. Clara needed to be able to see herself from all angles in the best possible light.

Amanda's mouth opened. "I need tissues. The ugly waterworks are about to come out of me. My bestie is getting married."

Clarissa was relaxed now that Amanda had approved of her dress.

"No champagne this time?" Sonya asked.

"Not this time." Amanda's voice was low and awe-filled.

Clara, until this point, had yet to see herself in the mirror. Clarissa wanted it to be the perfect reveal. Clara waited with her eyes closed, facing backward. "On the count of three, please turn and take a good look in the mirror."

She already knew her work to be some of the best she had ever produced. But seeing it on Clara made her stop second-guessing herself and her nerves. "Three, two, one!" Clarissa grew teary-eyed.

Clara turned and screeched. Her hands flew to her mouth. "Is this me?" she asked. She didn't smile; she glowed. The pride in her face, and small droplets of water in the corner of her eyes, revealed all Clarissa needed to know.

Seeing her creation on her star client was what dreams were made of. *I made this. I am creating magic. This is why I became a designer.*

Clarissa experienced pure bliss. Her body light, Clarissa smiled and soaked in the moment.

Clarissa glimpsed many emotions passing through Clara's

face. "I didn't think I'd get to experience the 'bridal moment.' I'm so weepy right now, but I don't want to soil the dress."

"Cry into the gloves. Or better yet, here." Clarissa handed her a box of tissues.

Amanda carefully made her way over to Clara and offered her a careful hug without touching the dress. "Cllllllllllllllllllllll-lllara. You're a fairy princess. If your parents were around, they would have been so proud of you. To see the amazing woman you are. I'm already ugly crying. Better now than on the real day."

Clarissa didn't want to interrupt their moment and moved to stand next to Sonya. Sonya hugged her tightly and whispered into Clarissa's ear, "Well done."

When Clarissa had opened her first shop with Sonya, they had no idea as to what they were doing. The ups and downs, trials and errors had provided such a steep learning curve. Now, here they stood, together, soaking in the experience.

The adrenaline that had kept her going all morning until this point was finally beginning to flee. She should sleep well tonight. Tired, but content.

Clara continued to stare at the dress. Sonya discreetly moved behind the bride-to-be and straightened the skirt for the full effect.

"Forget every single thing I said about the dress. It's perfect as is. You really have to have it on to see how it fits and flows." Clara turned to look at the back of her dress.

"I loooooooooooooooooooove the play of color. Forget what I said too. It's sassy and playful and so well-hidden. You can't even see the undertone in colors until she moves." Amanda picked up the overskirt. "How did you do this?"

"I painted some flecks of gold into the fabric. It will glow in the dark too."

"You are a goddess of fabric and dress design."

Clarissa blushed with Clara's continuous compliments.

Sonya jumped in. "Well, then, I think it's time to ask, Clara. Are you saying yes to your dress?" Sonya was a huge fan of the reality show *Say Yes to the Dress.*

Amanda and Clara looked at one another. "YES!" they shouted.

Clarissa clapped and hugged everyone around her. Clarissa wished she could share her moment of triumph with Patrick. Clarissa pictured Patrick in morning dress attire, standing next to her, beaming in excitement at her. She needed to finish this appointment before she could call him. Tonight she wanted to celebrate.

The energy in the room calmed down. Clara didn't want to remove the dress but understood it still wasn't finished.

"I just have a few questions about some minor adjustments to finish off this piece. As for the reception dress, we are on track to have the first fitting in two or three weeks." Turning to Amanda, Clarissa asked, "Are you ready for your fitting?"

Amanda squealed in excitement and followed Sonya to the same area where Clara had experienced her bridal moment. Amanda's dress featured a modern take on the sweetheart neckline combined with a fit-and-flare skirt and open back with sheer paneling.

The sheer paneling contained the same pattern as Clara's lace—a four-flower motif. Due to the nature of the open-back design, Clarissa was adamant about performing the fitting for Amanda herself before passing it off to her team for alterations.

Amanda's fun personality shone through as she sang the song "Glamorous" out loud from behind the curtain. Clarissa heard Sonya laughing out loud. Clara shrugged to Clarissa.

"Don't I look just fab?" Amanda grinned ear-to-ear and model-walked around the fitting room. Her good mood brought smiles to everyone's faces. The periwinkle blue contrasted with her bright red hair in just the right way.

Sonya added, "I have the perfect gold bracelet to match this."

Sonya darted over to her purse and rummaged through her box of accessories until she found just what she was looking for. Clara snapped photos of Amanda making over-the-top poses while Clarissa confirmed the fit of the dress.

Sonya returned with an Egyptian-inspired gold snake wrap bracelet. "The blue eyes of the snake match the dress. I was playing around with some new jewelry designs last week and this is the end result." Sonya placed the bracelet on Amanda's wrist.

Amanda eyed the jewelry with keen interest. "You made this?" she asked in disbelief. "You two have to be among the most talented crafty people ever. I swear, this is ammmmmmm-mmmazing. So dainty and delicate, yet it makes a statement!"

Clarissa smiled. "Sonya has been making jewelry for a long time. It's only in the past year she has finally agreed to market her pieces in our shops."

Sonya blushed. "It isn't that special. I just create what I like and hope others will enjoy it too."

Clara reviewed the bracelet. "I have to agree with Amanda. It's quite beautiful. I may have to commission a few pieces from you to match the bracelet David bought me when we first met. I would love to be able to have some everyday pieces that I can wear at rehearsal and on engagements."

Amanda said, "Why don't I go change." Amanda nodded to Sonya. "Speaking of jewelry… Clara… this might help you solve the problem with Princess Charlotte."

Clara rubbed her temples. Clarissa and Sonya exchanged curious glances before Sonya followed Amanda back to the changing corner. "I'm debuting *Raymonda* in two weeks and have been supremely short on time. I know this might be a lot to ask, but Clarissa, would you consider working with David's mother in creating a shortlist of jewelry from the royal vault for me to wear on the big day? It would be such a welcome relief to me to have that taken care of. I would much prefer to wear a contemporary piece of jewelry like the beautiful snake cuff, but this is one family tradition I don't want to break."

Clara wanted Clarissa to pick a shortlist of jewelry to wear from the royal family's jewelry collection? She really trusted her with a task as important as this? This was a task best suited to Sonya, who appreciated, and was much more knowledge-able about, accessories.

Saying that Sonya loved jewelry was an understatement. Sonya's jewelry collection included several *very* expensive Van Cleef &Arpels, and Cartier pieces. She splurged on the shiny things. Could she ask to involve Sonya on the adventure? It *was* a once-in-a-lifetime opportunity.

Sonya returned with a wide-eyed expression of longing on her face. Clearly she overheard the exchange. Sonya *had* to be included. "I would be honored to assist you on the condition Sonya comes with me. She has an exceptional eye for acces-sories and details."

Amanda sniggered. "Sonya is your Amanda! You are a two-for-one deal just like C and me. I love it! Of course C will say yes."

Matter-of-factly, Clara nodded. "It's settled then. Amanda will set you up with the office of the Princess Royal. Thank you so much. I won't forget this."

Sonya sent a high-five to Clarissa to the utter amusement of Amanda who turned just in time to see the not-so-subtle gesture.

Chapter Seventeen

PATRICK

Patrick hugged his arms closer to his body as tiny flecks of snow began to slowly materialize and drift down from the sky.

Hadn't he predicted snow earlier? Had it been this cold when he was riding? Why had he not taken his gloves and scarf with him this morning or had the sense to, at the very least, check the weather app on his phone?

He was on the verge of turning around and waiting out the snow with the royal trio. His stubborn pride kept him moving forward as he walked through Hyde Park in search of the original site of the Crystal Palace.

His mobile vibrated in his pocket. He pulled it out and swiped to answer it without checking who the caller was. "Hello?" he said as his teeth chattered.

The familiar voice of his mother sounded in surprise. "Paddy? I did not expect you to answer your mobile. I thought I might take a chance and ring you just in case."

He gritted his teeth and sought to find a tree or another structure as shelter from the wind. It was difficult to hear. "Mother? I'm sorry, the reception is a bit muddled."

His excursion through Hyde Park would have to wait. He needed to find a place to warm up. His fingers and toes were numb. He exited the park and continued walking toward the street.

"Alistair and I are in town taking high tea at the lovely St. George. I wanted to invite you if you were available."

His mother, as much as he loved her, always issued invitations without much warning.

Afternoon tea sounded marvelous, the perfect escape from the cold. He *did* enjoy the pastries at the St. George. Their culinary staff prepared Michelin star-quality cuisine. "I'll be happy to join you. Are you there now? I can be there in one half-hour."

His mother sounded pleased. "Excellent. I'll have Alistair let the maître d' know to direct you to us when you arrive. We're in the Westminster room."

They said their goodbyes as Patrick got into a taxi. He welcomed the warmth and rubbed his hands together. Why was his mother in London? She hardly ever left Gloucestershire these days.

Patrick thanked his driver and dashed up the steps into the iconic lobby of the hotel. He shivered, his extremities still noticeably frozen. Turning right, he walked over to the green and gold gilded tea rooms, noting the glass and steel paneled roof for the first time.

Yet another example of Victorian architecture. The museum could use a tearoom like this. It might prove to be a popular location as any visitor could rightly claim they took tea at Buckingham Palace. The menu could involve teas from around the world and tie into an exhibit on the science of tea.

A host, clad in the hotel's livery, greeted him. "Hello, sir. How may I be of service to you today?"

Patrick observed the host noting his lack of a tie and suit jacket.

Bugger off. I'm not appropriately attired. I'll have to ask the concierge to find me something suitable.

He fidgeted under the stare, "Um yes. I'm here to join my mother and Lord Greyston for tea."

The host reviewed the list of guests. "We don't have a Lord Greyston listed. Would you like me to try another name, sir?"

Patrick was bewildered. What other name would it be under? His mother? "Can you please try Lady Renbrook or perhaps Lady Greyston?"

His host checked once more. "Afraid not, sir." A couple standing behind him cleared their throats and glared at Patrick for holding up the line. He ignored them.

"I'm sorry, but there appears to be some misunderstanding. The woman in the white blouse over there is my mother. She was supposed to advise the maître d' that her son would be joining her party." Patrick's tone remained flat, yet internally he was frustrated.

The host stepped back and had one of the passing waiters go in search of the maître d'. Patrick resisted the urge to insert his title into the situation.

Certainly I could benefit from name-dropping at a time like this, but what purpose would it serve? He let out a deep breath. *Who is Mother and Lord Greyston dining with? She didn't mention any guests when she rang me.*

The host skeptically eyed Patrick over. "If you could, please step to the side while our server checks with the maître d'."

Patrick nodded, not in the mood to play games. "Certainly. In the meantime, perhaps I can have the assistance of the hotel concierge to procure a jacket?"

"Oh course." The couple behind Patrick whispered and pointed at him in hushed tones. Patrick thought he might have heard them say, "The standards of who is able to dine here have certainly diminished." It lightened his mood.

Both the hotel concierge and maître d' appeared as if out of thin air. "Lord Renbrook! We apologize for the inconvenience. I was not made aware you had arrived. If you would please follow me."

To his amusement, the couple standing behind him stopped talking and paled. He was shown to his mother's table less than five minutes after his arrival, suit jacket and tie in hand. He never understood how the St. George's staff could be so efficient.

I never gave my jacket size to the concierge. They are excellent at their job.

As Patrick approached the table, he stiffened. With his mother and Lord Greyston sat his ex-girlfriend, Lady Mary Longwood nee Manners, and her husband, Lord Maxwell Longwood, the Marquess of Carnock.

Chapter Eighteen

PATRICK

Patrick sucked in his breath as he approached the table. He was not by any means mentally prepared for this. His mother, unaware of the tension between the three younger members of the party, stood to greet her son.

He kissed her on the cheek. Patrick had never revealed the extent to which Mary had hurt him. Working through the death of his late father had been difficult on his mother. Patrick had sought to shield his mother from his own miseries, though looking back, his mother was always much stronger than he gave her credit for.

Lady Lucy resumed her seat. "About time, Paddy. It's been over forty-five minutes! Either way, you are just in time for the sweet pastries. They've just taken away the scone course."

Patrick cleared his throat and sat in the only available seat between Mary and Lord Greyston. "I'm sorry for being late. There was some confusion with the reservation." Patrick greeted the rest of the party. "Lord Greyston, good to see you as always. Mary. Carnock."

Max deeply drank his tea. "Renbrook," he managed to say gruffly.

I've long moved on Max. Haven't you?

Mary remained silent, not meeting Patrick's eyes. He had forgotten how silky her tawny locks were. Max possessively wrapped his arm around Mary.

Lord Greyston wiped his face with his napkin. "Renbrook. About time I've seen you, lad. How are you? How's London?"

Cheerful as always.

Patrick never crossed paths with Lord Greyston much these days. He tended to his own estate and was often away for extended periods promoting the Manners family winery.

Did he treat Greyston as a stepfather now that he technically belonged to the family? Lord Greyston had always been kind to him.

Just be yourself.

"Congratulations are in order to you and Mother. We never had the chance to properly celebrate your matrimony. Perhaps we can plan a small to-do one these days." His mother looked to her new husband with adoration. "London has kept me on my toes. I have a new project I'm consulting on with David Leeds."

Max scowled "You and Leeds? Typical. He always had you eating out of his hands."

So Max is jealous. Interesting. Why? He won the girl.

Lord Greyston raised an eyebrow. "Maxwell. Jealousy doesn't become you. It would be nice, however, if *you* would find a *proper* way to occupy your time instead of sulking around the estate. You were released from your job more than seven weeks ago. One would hope you would have found a new employer by now."

Lord Greyston preferred a tough-love approach to his relationships to everyone except Lady Lucy. Patrick suspected Lord Greyston had never approved of Maxwell, yet he kept his opinions and concerns quiet. His manners were impeccable.

Patrick's mother jumped in. "Maybe Paddy could assist. He was just appointed director of a brand-new museum. Reggie always speaks positively about the displays you put together on his behalf during the opening of the staterooms. He sounded exceptionally pleased with the early stages of the project when he rang to congratulate Alistair and me."

"You are working with the king?"

Mary's eyes roamed over Patrick as if truly seeing him for the first time. He blanched at the unwanted attention. Power hungry Mary could not fool him again.

Max muttered, "Some people have all the luck."

The servers brought out trays with sweet pastries. Patrick served himself tea. Mary's hand brushed his as she reached for the pot at the same time as he. Mary quickly moved her hand out of the way. Patrick stared at where her hand had been.

"Sorry," she apologized.

Patrick helped himself to a fruit pastry. "Well, if you change your mind, Carnock, I'm sure I could find something for you to do."

Patrick took the high road. If Max asked for a position, he would offer him one.

Will family gatherings always be this strained between us?

Lord Greyston enthusiastically piled several desserts onto his plate. "Good to hear." He focused on his daughter. "Mary, you and Maxwell, I believe, invited us here to tell us some news." He looked on expectantly. "Am I to be a grandfather?"

Patrick deflated. *Why does it feel as if I have been punched in the stomach? She never wanted children before.*

Lady Lucy placed a hand on Mary's arm. Mary recoiled in horror at what her father had said. "Excuse me? Father? Where did you get a horrid notion such as that? Why would I *ever* want children with my soon-to-be ex-husband?" Lord Greyston's countenance fell, as did Patrick's mother's.

Mary threw her napkin on the table. "Max and I are going

through a separation. We just came from our counseling session. But reconciliation is *never* going to happen. *He's* been seeing another woman for quite a while. I'm tired of all the lies and betrayal." She was close to tears. "He only attended tea this afternoon to keep up appearances. I didn't intend to tell you until our separation was finalized."

Patrick's eyes bulged. Mary was going through a divorce?

Max slammed his fist onto the table. "That is not exactly a fair assessment of the situation. *You* decided to seek the company of that American millionaire from Texas. In fact, Mary is moving to America. *I* have been asking her to start a family since we married. All you care about is money and appearances. I thought you loved *me.* You were utterly miserable with Renbrook, but I see you as you truly are."

Lord Greyston's face flushed bright tomato red. His voice turned deadly quiet. "We shall have *THIS* discussion in the privacy of our own walls." Patrick had never seen him so angry.

Max and Mary abruptly stopped speaking.

Patrick had no idea what to say. He needed to leave as quickly as possible. "Mother, it was wonderful to see you, but I have another engagement this afternoon, if you wouldn't mind seeing me out. Greyston, we shall set a date for your celebratory dinner soon."

Patrick's mother shot out of her seat like a cannon.

Mary's eyes were wet with tears but her expression resentful. "You've changed. You look quite fit. I should have stayed with you. Then I might have had *some* sort of interesting company to mingle with."

Patrick stopped in his tracks. He clenched his fists. "Mary, I should have done this a long time ago. Once upon a time, I loved you. I gave you my heart, and what did you do? You shattered it. You told me you had *never* loved me to begin with. I've worked hard to overcome all of the emotional baggage *you* wrought. I swore off ever having another relation-ship. I never wanted to be so low and hurt again. I see I was the lucky one. I've always strived to be cordial to you and Carnock. After today, I have had no need to ever see you again. Good day to you both."

Unused to rejection, Mary stammered, "But you were overweight and unattractive. You were so serious and lifeless, working all the time. Even the law cases I worked through were more intriguing. I needed to be engaged and occupied. Maxwell at least has a decent body and more money than you. You cannot place all the blame on me."

Patrick couldn't believe what he was hearing. "My father had just died. I was *grieving*. I had so many lessons to learn and was overwhelmed. Your own father understood that and took me under his wing. As for your other remarks, physical attrac-tion comes and goes. What's left is a personality, which you certainly lack. I have no words left for you. Goodbye, Mary."

Lord Greyston's face was stormy. "Mary, you are my daughter, and I love you. That will never change. It pains me to say this, but Renbrook, you're too good for the likes of her. Where did I go wrong as a father?"

Patrick guided his mother by the arm and led her out of the Westminster room. Patrick was sorely tempted to look behind him but resisted the urge.

Once outside, Lady Lucy gripped her son in her arms and fiercely hugged him. She whispered into his jacket, "Why did you never say anything to me, Paddy? Have you truly felt that way for so long? I would have been there to support you, no matter what. You are *my* son. I can be a fierce lioness if anyone were to ever hurt you."

Patrick needed his mother's embrace. She had always been there when he needed her. "I was so afraid of seeing you take on more grief. You had just lost Father. I couldn't burden you with my woes. I see now I was wrong."

Lady Lucy sighed. "Since your younger years, you have always sought to protect me. Sometimes, Paddy, you must trust those around you. People are more resilient than you think and are made of sterner stuff." Lady Lucy straightened Patrick's tie. "Just promise me one thing. Don't give up on love. The right woman is out there for you, my son." Lady Lucy released him.

Patrick laughed. The absurdity of the afternoon hit him full force. "Actually, Mother, I'm seeing someone *quite* special. She's the one I have been waiting for."

Lady Lucy asked, "Is she anything like Mary?"

Was Clarissa anything like Mary? The truth of the matter was yes, she was, but only the good parts. She was driven, determined, stubborn, broken at one time, but also proud, and a person who wanted to be her own woman.

He kissed her on the cheek. "Partly yes. She's special. She's—"

Lady Lucy placed her pointer finger on his lips. "Your body language tells me everything I need to know. Bring her 'round soon. And eat more. I dare say you are too thin. I need to save Alistair from the mess inside. His heart will be broken over Mary and Max. I am preparing for war. Wish me luck."

Patrick watched his mother square her shoulder and march right back into the Westminster room. His mother was a force of nature, like Clarissa. He thought himself fortunate to have two excellent women in his life.

He returned the tie and jacket to the concierge. Walking out of the St. George, Patrick was relieved. Mary was officially out of his life. Tonight he would celebrate with Clarissa. She just didn't know it. How could he make the evening special for her?

Chapter Nineteen

CLARISSA

Clarissa left Kensington Palace around six in the evening, later than intended. She shot a text message off to Patrick on her car ride home, hoping he wouldn't be too annoyed at her. She truly had tried to leave before five. Time had slipped away from her, per usual.

Clarissa: The car is departing the palace complex now.

Patrick: Excellent. I'll pop dinner into the oven.

Clarissa: I told you I was going to order sushi takeaway today! It's my turn to provide dinner. You don't have to go to such lengths to take care of me. Are you still alright with staying in and watching *Strictly Come Dancing?*

Patrick: Of course. I know it's your Tuesday evening guilty pleasure. Just send me a text when you reach the lobby. See you in a few.

The car dropped her off outside her building. She gathered her belongings and stepped inside. She checked her phone as soon as she entered the building. Rubbing her hands together, she pulled off her gloves and alerted Patrick to her arrival.

Clarissa shivered in delight. What did Patrick have planned for tonight? He had been secretive when they spoke at lunch.

He hadn't replied to her earlier messages checking on how their days were coming along. She soon received her answer. As soon as the lift doors opened, Clarissa was greeted by a tuxedo-clad Patrick holding a single blood orange rose.

She had butterflies in her stomach and quivered at the sight of Patrick in an *actual* fitted garment.

"My lady. I've been eagerly awaiting your arrival. We have a reservation for you at Chez Nelson." Patrick presented her the rose and offered his arm to her. He escorted her over to his flat's door.

Clarissa's cheeks were already rosy from being outside. "Patrick, this is unbelievable."

She rested her head against his arm as they walked. He smelled of garlic and butter. Was this what they were having for dinner?

This is much better than sushi. I wanted to celebrate tonight, but how did Patrick know?

Patrick's flat was already unlocked and encapsulated in total darkness. Soft jazz music played in the background. The door clicked shut behind them.

Clarissa's eyes readjusted to the dim lighting of the sitting room. She made out two candles and a table set in the spot normally claimed by the couch, which was pushed to the far wall.

She dropped her tote in surprise. "Dinner by candlelight? Just preparing dinner for me is more than enough, not to mention overly romantic. I've been supremely spoiled by you in so many ways."

She wanted him to know nothing was ever expected of him. Just having him in her life was enough for her.

Patrick sensually kissed her hand. "I better warm this up. As I tell you every single day, I know you don't expect anything from me. I *want* to do this for you. It's my way of showing you how much I care for you. I know how hard you've been working."

Clarissa trembled as his hand rested on hers. All she could think about was showing Patrick her appreciation.

As Clarissa was escorted over to the table, she made up her mind. *Tonight I tell him I'm ready to jump head-first into this relationship. If we take things any slower, I will simply go crazy.*

Patrick had two place settings and two glasses of rose wine. Clarissa's heart beat rapidly. She stopped him short as he pulled her chair out.

Her breathing slowed, and she wrapped her hands around his. "Patrick," she whispered. "This is the sweetest surprise I've ever been given."

Time slowed. Clarissa pushed up to her toes and boldly pulled Patrick closer to her body. She licked her lips. They were cracked from being out in the cold. However, her focus was on the tall, brown-haired, blue-eyed giant in front of her.

She ran her hand over the black silk lapels of his tuxedo and wrapped her arms around his neck. "You're finally wearing clothing that fits. The look suits you and is the sexiest garment I have ever laid eyes on."

Clarissa planted her lips on Patrick's mouth. His stubble rubbed harshly against her face as he greedily responded to her passionate kiss. Clarissa's eyes half fluttered open.

Patrick's husky voice whispered into her ear, "You can thank my tailor, Andy, though he doesn't work nearly as efficiently as you." Patrick claimed her mouth a second time. "Two can play this game, Miss Lee."

Her knees grew weak as she melted into him. Nothing else mattered in the world except the two of them.

Clarissa felt lightheaded in delight as he released her. Her spine tingled. She was no longer the shy neighbor afraid of who Patrick might be. She was in love. All of the signs and feelings she had so desperately tried to ignore were suddenly made clear.

I was so afraid of falling in love. I want to be with him.

Clarissa only half-paid attention to Patrick's words. "Huh?" she jumped.

Patrick quietly repeated, "I said we should probably eat before either one of us gets too carried away again. I fully expect the same type of entertainment after dessert."

Clarissa, embarrassed by her blunder, grew hot to the tips of her ears. Would he notice in the dim lighting? She dumbly nodded and allowed Patrick to guide her into her pulled-out chair.

Patrick kissed the top of her head. "You are so adorable when you blush. What are you embarrassed over?"

The last thing she wanted to share with him was her newly discovered feelings. She wasn't ready to yet voice them out loud. "Um... it's a state secret?"

Patrick flashed his pearly white teeth. "I'll let your answer slide, but we shall revisit this after dinner, which is more than likely cold by now. Let's see then." Patrick pulled off the stainless-steel covers from the place settings.

Clarissa stared longingly at the eggplant Parmesan and thickly sliced garlic bread in front of her. Her eyes grew moist. "You've recreated our first meal together."

Patrick sat across from Clarissa. His eyes shimmered under the candlelight. "You remembered."

Clarissa affectionately met his gaze. "How could I forget? 'Twas the beginning of a beautiful friendship."

Patrick looked down. His face held an unreadable expression. He murmured, "Friendship indeed."

Clarissa pushed her plate forward with apprehension. What was wrong with friendship? "Patrick?" she inquired.

Patrick put down the cutlery he was holding. "I had an afternoon encounter with my ex-girlfriend today."

Clarissa's stomach churned. She lost all interest in her meal. "Oh."

Just when I thought he might return my sentiments, he is going to tell me he's reconnecting with his ex.

Patrick immediately realized his mistake. He jumped up. "No, no. Nothing of that sort. Ah, bloody hell." He reached for his wine glass and took a long swig. "Let me try this again." He placed the glass down. "What I wanted to say is that I am not interested in just friendship with you. As we spend more and more time together, I realize there are so many things I want to share with you. You're the *only* one I want to be with. Today was the first time I have truly been tested, and I had no feelings for my ex. Only pity. I told her I never wanted to see her again. I am free."

Clarissa's lips quaked. He *did* return her affections. "Patrick. I've learned a lot about myself over the last month and a half. I know exactly what my feelings are for you. I wasn't sure if you might return them." She brushed her fingers along his forearm. "I'm falling for you hard and fast, and it scares me. I wanted to wait to take things slowly, but I've changed my mind. Whatever happens will happen."

Her senses dulled. Patrick gently kissed her. Her thumb brushed his lower lip. They gazed into one another's eyes and finally understood that they both wanted the same thing. Clarissa was suddenly keenly aware of how close Patrick was to her. Her self-control was hanging on by a bare thread. "If you want to eat dinner, we had better do it now."

Patrick laughed, "I see I'm not the only one who is easily distracted."

Patrick reheated their dinners. Clarissa and Patrick enjoyed their first date into the early hours of the morning. After the candles had long burned out, Patrick and Clarissa sat on his sofa, now facing the window, staring at the falling snow. A small fire glowed in the background as they sat entangled in one another's arms, falling fast asleep.

Chapter Twenty

CLARISSA

Clarissa had procrastinated, and now she was paying the price. She bit her lip and placed her head down on one of the few empty spaces on her worktable. In the background, sewing machines hummed rhythmically.

The bridesmaid dress team chattered in hushed tones. What if Patrick said no? Could she face the Lee family alone? If she couldn't bring him, it was her own fault. Clarissa pulled at her hair.

Sonya exclaimed, "You had four days to ask him! I can't believe you're being so chicken about it."

Clarissa couldn't sit any longer and paced the room. "I know. Go ahead and berate me. I kept coming up with one excuse after another." Sonya snorted.

Clarissa stared at the phone to her right. Could staring at it long enough melt a hole in it? Sonya grabbed ahold of Clarissa's phone.

Clarissa spluttered. "What are you doing?" She reached for the phone but wasn't quick enough. Sonya wickedly held it out of her petite friend's reach. Clarissa chased Sonya around the room.

Sonya said, "If I give this back to you, will you *please* call Patrick before lunch? The longer you put it off, the more difficult the task becomes."

Clarissa successfully wrestled the mobile from Sonya's grip. "Fine. I will do it now. Will that satisfy you?"

Sonya replied, "Yes."

Secretly, Clarissa was elated to have Sonya urging her to place the dreaded phone call.

Her fingers fumbled as she unlocked her mobile and scrolled through her contacts. Beads of perspiration formed on her hands.

Patrick's voice filled the room. "You're calling early. Miss me already?" Clarissa was at a loss for words. Patrick's voice grew tight. "Clarissa? Are you there? Is everything alright?"

Sonya, a safe distance away from any projectiles Clarissa may have hurled her way, answered for her. "Hi, Patrick. It's Sonya. We are safe, and yes, Clarissa is still here. She has a question for you."

Clarissa panicked. Her jumper itched. Her throat constricted. "Pat... Pat... Paddy. I... erm..."

Patrick's voice calmed. "Clarissa? You can ask me whatever you would like."

Before her courage fled, she clumsily asked, "Would you be my date to my parents' home on Saturday for the Lunar New Year?"

Papers shuffled in the background. "I have to consult my work diary. One moment."

Sonya shrugged, offering no sympathy. Clarissa sank to the floor, not caring if she was sitting on the ground. "It's no problem if you aren't available. I understand it's extremely short notice on my part. I know you have to travel up to Rain-ridge most weekends."

Patrick's voice barked out in laughter. What did he find so amusing? "Clarissa. I am sorry. I could not resist toying with you. For you, my schedule is always open. I do need to be in Rainridge on Sunday, but my Saturday is yours."

Clarissa facepalmed. *Why was I so worried to begin with?*

Patrick's voice never wavered. "You can fill me in on what I'm agreeing to tonight. I'll be over at Buckingham Palace until about half-past four." He had explained recently that he was overseeing the groundbreaking of the new World of Curiosities Museum.

"Alright, thank you, Patrick. See you tonight." Clarissa ended the call.

Sonya said, "There now. That wasn't too difficult, was it?"

Clarissa deadpanned, "Oho, the worst bits have yet to begin." She shivered at the memories of the last six years of family gatherings. If Patrick wasn't scared away after this, he was a keeper.

For the last six years, Clarissa evaded any unnecessary trips home. Gatherings with her family always began with a barrage of questions into her personal life. From there, her parents compared her to her brother and how her cousins could learn from Clarissa's failures in school. To add insult to injury, her ex-boyfriend, Mark Leung, resided nearby. Mark turned on his charm for her family, and everyone always fell for it.

Though she and Mark had long since gone their separate ways, her parents always attempted to rekindle their relationship. In their eyes, Mark appeared to be perfect husband material. He was Chinese, from a family her parents knew well, and a dentist. Clarissa had endeavored several times to explain Mark's true controlling nature, yet they never believed her.

She had long given up attempting to correct their vision of Mark. Her parents had funded a large part of his dental school bills, calling it a future investment. Clarissa never understood how her parents could afford it. Their restaurant was successful, but not *that* successful.

Chapter Twenty-One

PATRICK

Rain plunked down sporadically against the windshield of Patrick's red jaguar as it moved down the M-40 from London toward Birmingham. Clarissa stared out the window at the darkened clouds that reflected her mood. Patrick's right hand remained on the wheel with his eyes glued to the road.

Every once in a while he gazed over at her. Clarissa's had yet to move an hour into their drive. He took hold of Clarissa's hand several times to reassure her the day would pan out just fine. She remained quiet.

Patrick turned the heater on. Clarissa fidgeted. He couldn't stand the silence any longer. "Clarissa. Please. Tell me what is on your mind. I have absolutely no idea why you are so nervous and sullen. It's only your family. They love you. I've seen the photos on your flat's wall. Can you tell me a bit about them? We never did get around to discussing them."

Clarissa had attempted every trick in the book to avoid speaking about her family. The only information Patrick had to go on were small snippets of information he gleaned from Clarissa.

He was aware the Lee family owned a successful restaurant near the Birmingham Hippodrome and that her brother was a professional tennis player.

She sighed and turned off the heater. "Thank you, but I'm not cold."

Patrick offered a small smile at his little victory. "At last, she speaks."

What was she hiding? Why was she so reluctant to share any information with him? He had told her about Mary and about his own family.

He understood how much energy it took, and how mentally draining it could be, to relive the past. He wished Clarissa might entrust him with part of her past.

Patrick slowed the car down as he navigated a roundabout near Banbury, the official halfway marker.

Clarissa gripped the edges of her seat, "I'm sorry for not speaking more. I'm just mentally preparing myself for tonight."

Patrick stole a glance at Clarissa. She was pale and pinching her lips. He frowned. This would not do. "Clarissa, I promise I won't turn the car around. Please let me into your thought process. What are you so concerned about? Working through the past can be one way of expelling demons."

Clarissa stalled. "You're right. You have been so helpful to me and a soothing balm, Paddy. It is just so difficult for me. Even *thinking* about the past forces up ugly memories. It traps me in a mental prison from which there is no escape. You understand the effects of anxiety."

Clarissa sighed. "I should have shared this with you a long time ago. It's complicated. Once I start my story, please don't interrupt me. I need to be able to get through the entirety of it. You can ask me anything you would like afterward."

Patrick gripped the steering wheel tighter. "I promise. No interruptions."

Clarissa let out a breath, "Mama and Baba came to the UK from Hong Kong in the early 1980s. They always garnered high expectations for their future children. As immigrants, they worked hard and came from practically nothing. They began learning English, and found a home and a steady paying job. I failed them the moment I was born female. In Chinese culture, boys are prized over girls. They carry on the family name and lineage. On top of that, growing up, I struggled tremendously at school, earning among the lowest marks. I was the smallest child, the one who was from a strange family who didn't even speak English. I had very few friends."

Patrick processed the information. As a male child himself, he had been the celebrated heir to the earldom. Had he been a female child, the title would have been lost to his family and passed down instead to the next closest male relation to his father.

Patrick could only imagine the difficult circumstances Clarissa was required to bear at such a young age. One couldn't control the circumstances of their birth. He did understand loneliness. He had few friends of his own, and although he had David while at boarding school, that was it.

She sniffled. "I worked extra hard each and every step of the way. I would stay up late hours into the night trying to make sense of my books. I asked my teachers for assistance, but the language barrier presented a problem. My marks never reflected my efforts. When I was about ten years old, we learned I suffer from dyslexia. I invert a good amount of my numbers and letters when reading. A sad fate for a girl who struggled enough with learning English. It only added to the pressure already on me. At home, we only spoke Chinese. They insisted I learn their native tongue."

"I don't remember the exact moment, but one night when I was working in the family takeaway, I discovered a fashion magazine left behind by one of our customers. Here was a magazine that didn't contain so many words, it was mainly photographs! I connected to it instantly; it was as if an entirely new world was opening for me. From that point onward, I became absolutely obsessed with creating and sketching my own designs. I had a refuge to escape to when times grew tough. I wanted my creations to appear in that magazine. Through experimentation, I taught myself how to sew, pattern, and create. Before I knew it, I was accepted to the London School of Fashion on a full scholarship."

Patrick smiled. His Clarissa was indeed highly talented. Hearing she had taught herself to sew didn't come as a surprise. The ability to prosper with a learning disability and with learning a completely new language revealed how resourceful and clever she was. His respect for her deepened.

He wanted her to understand how much he admired those qualities in her, yet he had given Clarissa his word not to interrupt her. Instead, Patrick chose to draw small circles on her hand with his thumb as he drove. They reached another roundabout. The rain remained their constant companion.

"I thought Mama and Baba might be proud of my efforts. Just the opposite occurred. My A-levels were dismal." Clarissa shed a few tears. Her tone darkened. "Mark Leung entered my life when his family moved near mine in the sixth form. My parents were always particularly keen to assist those new families emigrating from Hong Kong. Mark and I bonded over the similarity of our backgrounds. At first, I was flattered that a boy would be interested in a shy girl like me. He understood what it was like to have a family with high expectations and to have to learn a brand-new language. I was especially vulnerable. We dated on and off throughout the year. I thought he was handsome and charming."

Clarissa had to take a few deep breaths. "Looking back, all of the signs, however, pointed to an unhealthy relationship. I was always eager for acceptance and did anything he might ask, fearful of being left alone and disappointing my parents. When we dated, they had a pride in me I had always yearned for. A vicious cycle began. Mark was always critical of me. I was constantly reminded of how I was lucky to have him around. He was always angry with me. When I moved to London to begin my studies, it became worse. He would randomly show up at my shared flat and go through my phone, emails, and my belongings. He took to following me to classes at one point. It was only thanks to Sonya I was able to break free."

It is a wonder she is opening herself up to me. The mental toll and the scars that this good-for-nothing Mark must have left behind linger. It says so much about Clarissa's mental fortitude that she was able to push forward. I thought Mary was bad, but this is so much worse. Oh, Clarissa.

Patrick's anger began to build.

Clarissa whispered, "The worst bit is that Mark continues to charm his way into my family's good graces. He is everything they want in a son-in-law, and as a neighbor, he is constantly around. My parents paid for a good majority of his dental school. In the long run, I think this is the *real* reason why he used me. His parents were not financially well off. I don't know if they still take on some of his debt, but my parents hold the belief that our relationship has failed due to me. To this day, they refuse to hear my side of the story. I have long since given up. Not a single person, save my younger brother, ever came to my defense. It's been six years, and I've had a strained relationship with my family ever since. Each year, I am constantly berated for ruining my chance at a 'successful future.'"

Patrick had heard enough. He turned on his signal and pulled over to the side of the road. The hazard lights clicked on, filling the silence. Patrick unbolted his seat belt, opened the car door, and went around to Clarissa's side. He opened the door and pulled her out into the rain.

The droplets began to drench clothing. He pulled her tightly into his arms, not releasing her for a single moment.

In a soft tone, Patrick commented, "I want you to yell out into the fields around us. Let that good-for-nothing twat have it. I'll yell with you. Release your anger, frustrations, and emotions. They won't hold you prisoner any longer." Patrick held her hand and squeezed it.

Together they screamed into the wind until their voices were hoarse. She was emotionally spent. Patrick held Clarissa to his body. Her breathing calmed. She relaxed in his embrace. His feelings were torn between wanting to thrash Mark and needing to be a steady rock of support for Clarissa. Patrick guided them back to the car and assisted her inside.

From the boot of the car, he found a towel and blanket. He passed them to Clarissa. His cologne of cedar and sandalwood lingered in the air. Clarissa dried herself off as best she could and stopped crying. Patrick's feelings deepened for Clarissa.

He was supremely angry at Clarissa's parents. How could they fail their eldest child? Under his skin, his blood boiled. He huffed. He needed to be strong. Clarissa was emotionally fragile after expending so much energy on reliving her past.

He needed to tread lightly. "Clarissa," he began, "Nothing I can say or do will ever make up for what happened. We have both been through some difficult experiences. They have molded and shaped us in different ways. Together, we will be a strong source of love, support, and strength for one another."

Clarissa, emotionally raw, reached out for Patrick. They listened to the soft pitter-patter of the falling rain, holding hands. Clarissa mumbled a quiet, "I'm happy you're here with me now."

The Lee family resided in a four-bedroom, relatively modest, terraced home in the Aston district of Birmingham. Patrick pulled his car in front of the red-brick building. A string of bright lanterns and banners with Chinese calligraphy decorated the front door. A single front window looking into the lounge showed a gaggle of family members chatting amongst themselves.

As he turned the engine off, Patrick reminded Clarissa, "If anything goes amiss, we can leave at a moment's notice. All you need to do is let me know. You look beautiful, by the way."

Clarissa appeared more at ease. Her cheeks flushed. "Thank you. This is a modernized *cheongsam* dress I made myself. It is a take on the traditional Chinese dress. Red and yellow are lucky colors of the New Year."

Having retouched her makeup in the car, Patrick could see no signs of her emotional reaction from earlier.

She's always been beautiful, but the dress really brings out the warmth of her brown eyes.

She played with the strap of her purse. "Okay then. My mama and baba will be the first ones to greet us. You are aware of what my brother looks like from the photos. He will likely be inside. It is a toss-up as to whether or not my auntie and uncle will meet us outside, but be prepared for their onslaught of personal questions. Try to stick with Henry. I fully expect to be curtailed into kitchen duty for my own interrogation."

Patrick kissed Clarissa on the cheek. "I'll keep that in mind. I do have *one* trick up my sleeve." He chuckled to himself. "Do I look presentable? Is my tie straight?" Patrick smiled as Clarissa pulled it a centimeter to the left.

Clarissa puffed her chest out as they got out of the car. She plastered a fake smile onto her face. Patrick clicked on the alarm. They crossed the street. Just as Patrick's hand moved to unlatch the steel entrance gate, the front door opened. The couple Patrick recognized from Clarissa's photos rushed out. Clarissa stiffened.

Her voice was much more reserved than normal. "Mama, Baba, gong xi fa cai. Happy New Year. I'm so happy to see you both. There is someone important to me I would like for you to meet."

Patrick didn't waste any time and jumped right into the greetings. "Xin nin kuai le."

Clarissa's mask slipped into surprise.

Let them find fault with me wishing them a happy Chinese New Year. Yes, Clarissa, thanks to the magic of the internet, I speak a few phrases of Mandarin.

Mr. and Mrs. Lee remained rooted in their spots. "Happy New Year, Clarissa. And who is this young man you've brought with you?" Mr. Lee asked in heavily accented English.

Patrick surmised the Mandarin introduction had served him well. Mr. Lee appeared intrigued and unsure of what to make of him. Mr. Lee had salt and pepper hair and a small frame.

Patrick debated how to answer. *Might as well use one of the other two limited phrases I have.* "Wǒ de míngzì jiào pàtèlǐkè. My name is Patrick," he replied.

He winced at his pronunciation. *Maybe I should have run the phrasing by Clarissa.*

From Clarissa he had learned there were four different Mandarin pitch intonations. Being off-pitch could easily change the meaning of a word.

Mr. Lee nodded to Patrick. A small smile extended the corners of his mouth. *He looks like Clarissa. Same round face and dimples.* Of Clarissa's two parents, Patrick could tell he was the more relaxed of the couple. Mr. Lee offered his hand to Patrick.

Excellent, we are off on the right foot. Mrs. Lee stood stout with jet-black hair swept back in a tight bun. Her eyes roamed Patrick up and down as if to say, *But he's not Chinese!* Patrick met her gaze with kindness.

Regardless of their past history with Clarissa, he was meeting them for the first time. He would give them the benefit of the doubt until he had the opportunity to get to know them better.

Clarissa approached her mother and kissed her on the cheek. "Mama, I'm happy to see you. I've missed you."

Mrs. Lee returned the sentiment. She hugged her daughter tightly. Patrick, however, couldn't help but notice some tension in greeting her daughter. He shook hands with her. Mrs. Lee's eyes softened.

Mrs. Lee directed them inside. "Welcome home Clarissa. We are happy to *finally* see you. Can you not spare a few more visits home to your mama and baba? We both miss you. You two are late. You have missed lunch. There are not many dishes left. Come through to the kitchen and fix yourselves a plate. You are both too skinny. Then your baba can show Patrick the home. We must finish the last few courses before the remainder of the family arrives. I need you in the kitchen since Mrs. Leung will not be present."

Clarissa blanched, but kept her composure. "Yes, Mama. Does this mean Mark will not be here this year?"

Mrs. Lee frowned. "Mark has a standing invitation, but he is not here at the present."

Patrick observed Clarissa's relief as they entered the home. Everyone slipped off their shoes and assembled in the hallway to greet the arriving guests. They ate lunch, then Clarissa followed her mother toward the kitchen.

He was tempted to offer his culinary services and join Clarissa, but as she had already warned him, the kitchen was the domain of the women of the Lee family. It was where they gossiped, exchanged family stories, and complained about the men in the family. His assistance, no matter what, would not be accepted.

Mr. Lee offered a pair of indoor slippers to Patrick and welcomed him into the sitting room with the men. Many curious eyes settled upon him as Mr. Lee introduced him to various uncles, cousins, and, finally, Clarissa's brother, Henry.

Henry, tall with the lean muscles of a tennis player, kept his hair cropped short. He grinned at Patrick. "It is nice to finally have a face to put to the name. I'm Henry, Clarissa's younger, handsome brother. You are just in time for a round of Trivial Pursuit. Can I interest you in joining us?" Patrick appreciated Henry's efforts to put him at ease.

Why is it always Trivial Pursuit? This game is the bane of my existence.

Clarissa's identical twin, nine-year-old cousins groaned. "Why can't he join our team? We saw him before you."

Henry laughed. "Patrick is new to Lee family gatherings. I need all the assistance I can get. You two always win."

The cousins replied, "Fine. But the losing team has to do the washing up later tonight."

"Tough crowd." Henry laughed. "What do you say, Patrick; are you in?"

Patrick rubbed his hands together. "Henry, I would not be anywhere else in the world. Sign me up."

Chapter Twenty-Two

CLARISSA

Clarissa washed her hands and donned a red apron to keep her dress clean as she chopped the green string beans and onions.

I am so happy Paddy is playing with the boys. He appeared so relaxed. She sighed. *Leave it to Mama to find the one kitchen task I am suited for.*

Around her, the idle chatter of her female cousins and aunt allowed her to work in blissful peace. The tantalizing smells of fresh meat filled her nostrils. The room was full of steam. Every available cutting board and knife were being used, and the counter space was packed full of ingredients.

Lea, her twelve-year-old cousin, hugged her tightly. "It's so good to see you Clarissa. We missed you on Boxing Day. At least we had Henry's girlfriend for company. I was sad she couldn't be here this time, but it is important she's with her own family too. She was fun to be with but not a replacement for you. Abi and I are in desperate need to catch up with you. Where did you buy your dress from? It's one I would actually wear, and I *never* want to wear traditional clothing."

Abi, Lea's ten-year-old sister added, "It's so chic. You

always have the best clothes." She scrunched her nose. "All I have are secondhand clothes from Lea."

Clarissa twirled. "I'm happy you like it. This is one of my own creations."

Lea didn't seem overly surprised. "I wish I had your talent. I'd love to be able to make my own clothes. Mama never buys me anything."

Abi said, "Will you make me one, pretty please."

Clarissa could relate. She'd been about Lea's age when she discovered she could alter her clothes to fit her own aesthetic.

"If you put your mind to it, you can find a way to sew and design. Talent is only a small part of the design process. Maybe the next time you are in London, you can stop by my shop." Clarissa turned towards Abi. "I will make you any dress your heart desires. All you must do is pick out your favorite colors for me."

Abi's eyes danced in delight. She hopped up and down and hugged Clarissa. "Thank you!"

Lea's eyes sparkled. "I would love to see how you make a dress. Can you teach me?"

Clarissa's mother caught the tail end of their conversation and chided the three girls to keep washing and cutting the vegetables. "No time for chatting. We have eighteen people to feed. The pork, duck, fish, chicken, spring rolls, and chow mein will not prepare themselves."

Her Aunt Wong artfully arranged two piping hot plates of fish and dumplings. Not so subtly, she said, "Clarissa. We saw that man you brought with you. He's quite handsome. Are you engaged? Should we expect a wedding this year? It is your lucky year, the year of the dragon! What zodiac sign is he?"

We made it almost forty minutes into food prep before she asked. That's a new record.

Clarissa wiped her hands on her apron and placed her

veggies on the counter near the stove. Her mother handed her the next set to wash, slice, and dice.

She wandered over to the sink. "Patrick is someone I just started seeing. We've been friends for a few months. However, dating is brand-new to us. We plan to take this slow. Please don't scare him away. I *really* like him a lot. In fact, I am *crazy* about him. I believe Patrick was born in the year of the tiger."

The Chinese zodiac may have been taken seriously by her parents and Auntie Wong, but Clarissa never put much stock into it.

Aunt Wong whistled and nodded in approval. "You two have a good connection. I could tell from the energy when he entered the house with you. The tiger is a good match for a dragon despite what your mum may say."

Aunt Wong raised her eyebrow to Mama. "The tiger is brave, confident, and unpredictable. Together, the two signs are both headstrong. I hope he knows what he is after."

Her mother added, "Dragons are imaginative and ambitious. Maybe too much for their own good, but in time, maybe they will learn to make compromises." Her mother stopped what she was doing. "Are you happy, Clarissa? Truly happy?"

Confused, Clarissa carefully placed her knife and vegetables down. Why was her mother asking her if she was happy? Clarissa hesitated before answering. Taking inventory of her mother, Clarissa observed for the first time the fine lines in her mother's youthful face.

Wisps of gray hair poked out from her bun. Were those dark circles under her mother's eyes? Her mother appeared to have aged overnight.

She answered, "Mama, I am happier than I have been for a long time. Patrick is a good man and a true friend."

Satisfied, Clarissa's mother nodded.

Glancing at the dishes scattered around the kitchen, a

sudden, horrible thought struck her. *Patrick is a vegetarian. Everything here, except the spring rolls, are meat-based! I could make some rice and maybe Mama has some tofu?*

"Mum?" Clarissa bit her lip, "Do we have any meatless dishes?"

Her mother raised an eyebrow at her. "Our first dish, the jai, is. Why?"

Clarissa pulled out a plate from the white cabinet above her head to the left of the sink. "Patrick does not eat meat. He's a vegetarian." Lea and her cousins sniggered. Aunt Wong glared at them. They immediately quieted.

"Ah-ya. Why didn't you tell me sooner? I will not be the hostess who doesn't have enough dishes for her guests."

Her mother dropped what she was doing and began moving around the kitchen faster than Clarissa had ever seen her do. Her heart warmed to see her mum go to so much effort to accommodate her faux pas.

In no time at all, Mrs. Lee procured five vegetarian-friendly dishes. Energy jolted through Clarissa's body. The corners of her eyes moistened.

"Mama," she cried. Clarissa flew into her mother's arms. Auntie Wong ushered out the other occupants of the kitchen to give mother and daughter a few quiet moments together. Clarissa sobbed and pulled her mother closer into her body. "I have missed you."

Mrs. Lee hushed her and rocked her only daughter back and forth. "My baby."

Clarissa carefully pulled back. Her mother wiped a few tears from Clarissa's face. Neither one spoke. Actions spoke louder than words.

For the first time all afternoon, Mrs. Lee smiled. "Come on, then. We have a family to feed." Mrs. Lee's eyes sparkled in pure joy. Clarissa felt lighter than air and shadowed her mother's movements as they prepared to bring out the evening's dishes.

~

Being in the kitchen for a good part of the afternoon kept her busy and her mind occupied. Dinner swiftly arrived. She had not had time to process the roller coaster of emotions from earlier.

She relaxed into her seat next to Patrick, exhausted but content. Clarissa wondered just what Patrick had been up to with the rest of the family. Henry and Patrick exchanged a wink.

The eyes of her twin cousins, Kai and Bo, widened as her mother and aunties brought out dish after dish for the first course. They whispered to one another.

Clarissa's curiosity took hold. "Just what did you boys get up to? The twins are never this quiet. Are they *nervous*?"

Patrick coyly replied, "The young Padawans have learned that Henry and I make a formidable team. We are two Jedi masters of trivia."

Clarissa gasped. "You and Henry defeated the twins at Trivial Pursuit?"

Henry high-fived Patrick. "Indeed we did!"

Mr. Lee cleared his throat. "Next time, Patrick will be on *my* team." Her baba made his way around the table, pouring the drinks.

Everyone was ready to begin serving themselves just as the doorbell rang. Who would be arriving at this hour? Clarissa glanced around the table. All spots were occupied save one.

"Clarissa or Henry, would you mind answering the door?" her mother called out. Henry, in conversation with Patrick, failed to hear their mother's request. Clarissa removed her napkin from off her lap and muttered to Patrick, "I'll be right back."

She padded down the entryway. The door creaked open. Clarissa's chest tightened. "Mark!" she exclaimed.

⁓

Clarissa stared in shock. The hairs on the back of her neck stood up. Mark regained his composure quicker than she. To this point, they had successfully avoided speaking to one another for three years.

"So the hopeless wannabe fashion designer, if you can even be called that, has returned home. I'm shocked you managed to turn up. Last I heard, you were still selling clothing out of your dingy flat." Clarissa had owned her own shop for three years. Mark's petty words rolled off her.

He pushed past her as he entered the house. Mark's voice was quiet and sharp. "I wager you're still all alone. Nobody would want a woman who cannot properly read, do math, or cook. Lucky for you, I am willing to overlook these faults." He pulled her arm toward him.

Clarissa pushed against his chest, trying to escape his grasp, but Mark only tightened his grip. "Let me go. The only reason I'm even speaking to you now is because you are a *guest* in my parents' home. I would never have let you enter if it weren't for them. I told you six years ago, I would *never* be trapped by you again."

Mark ignored her. "Well, woman, you can hang my coat up and get me some house slippers."

Clarissa swallowed hard. She could stand up to Mark. She took a deep breath as she tried to wiggle out of his grip. "No." Clarissa firmly stood her ground.

Mark's eyes glared into her. "What did you say to me?"

A cold, cutting voice answered for Clarissa. "You heard her perfectly clear the first time. You are a grown man. As a guest, you are perfectly capable of doing those tasks for yourself. There is absolutely no reason for you to even speak to Clarissa so rudely."

Patrick's eyes narrowed dangerously to where Mark held Clarissa's arm.

Mark demanded, "Who are you to Clarissa? We have a long history together. She knows to do *exactly* as I ask her. Or else."

Patrick stepped forward. "I know all about you, Mark. If you know what is good for you, you'll release her this instant. You are clearly hurting her. Her arm is purple from your grip. You and I clearly need to have a chat outside."

Mark threw Clarissa with force into Patrick. He stumbled, but caught her before she fell. Clarissa, pale, but otherwise fine, placed one hand on Patrick's chest. His face grew red. Clarissa, strangely, enjoyed seeing Patrick riled up, and no longer feared Mark.

She was a dragon and her tiger was ready to pounce should Mark make one false move. They were a team, prepared to handle Mark together. "It's time I faced my demons."

Clarissa's claws came out. With venom, she used the same scare tactics Mark had used for years on her: a deadly quiet and calm voice. "This is Patrick. He's my *boyfriend* and is among the best things that have ever happened to me. Thanks to Patrick, I know *exactly* what love and a true relationship built upon friendship are supposed to be like." Clarissa crossed her arms. "You sought to manipulate me for many years, and because I was too scared of you, I let you have your way. I've changed. Clearly, you haven't. This is the last conversation we will ever have."

Mark pushed Clarissa's shoulders. "We shall see about

that. The Lees trust *me*. Your boyfriend isn't even Chinese. There is no way the Lees would *ever* approve of a relationship between you two." Patrick stepped in and blocked Clarissa from Mark's reach, using his own body as a shield.

What would keep Mark out of my life for good? Money? That has to be it?

Clarissa decided to take a chance and see if money was what he might be after. "My mama and baba have been utterly blinded by you. You have been living in their good graces for far too long. How much money will it take for you to leave us alone, permanently?"

Patrick remained quiet. Clarissa felt his muscles shaking beneath his shirt. She was utterly impressed with his self-control.

Mark appeared to consider her offer. "Make it a quarter-million pounds, and we have a deal."

A quarter-million pounds? That was a substantial sum of money. *I don't care what it costs. If I need to take out a loan to rid him from my life, I will do it. Although I am certain the business can support that much.*

Clarissa hoped Patrick would stay quiet. "Done. You'll have your money delivered to you by tomorrow. Leave my mama and baba alone."

Clarissa's father emerged from the shadows behind Patrick. To Clarissa's disgust, Mark played the victim. His eyes turned soft, and he hunched his posture.

Breathlessly he said, "Mr. Lee. Thank goodness you are here. I have been trying hard to talk some sense into Clarissa. You will not believe what I caught this man doing to your precious daughter. Look at her arm! Should I call the police?"

With lightning speed, Mr. Lee opened the door. "You can end your charade here, Mark. I have witnessed the entire exchange from the moment Patrick asked you to stop hurting my daughter. For years, you have spread your lies and nearly destroyed my family. My son, Henry, has always spoken out against you. I should have listened. I have been an old fool. Being privy to the way you've treated my daughter has disgusted me. I have never been the best father; however, it's time I rectify the situation. Leave my home."

Mark attempted again. "Perhaps you are mistaken, Mr. Lee, and did not hear what I said correctly."

"I will say this one more time before *I* call the police. Leave my home."

Clarissa saw a glint of fear in Mark's eyes as he scrambled out the door under the glare of Clarissa, her father, and Patrick. Clarissa sagged into Patrick. The full reality of what she had just experienced took hold.

"I'm free," she whispered into Patrick's chest.

Mr. Lee appeared much older. He sniffled and held his head in his hands. Clarissa looked up at her father. She had never observed him crying before.

"Baba. Are you alright?" Clarissa stepped away from Patrick and checked on the well-being of her father.

"I am the one who should be asking you. I have failed you in so many ways. How can I ever be worthy of hearing you call me baba?" Mr. Lee sadly shook his head.

He looks as if he is carrying the weight of the world.

It hurt Clarissa to see her father suffering from so much grief. Despite their treatment of her, her father was her one and only father.

"Baba, come here." For the second time today, she hugged one of her parents. Clarissa could not remember the last time she had been so close to her baba. She soaked in the scent of his aftershave. The rough texture of his skin rubbed against her cheek. How strange it was to be the one to console her father.

"We need to have a long chat after dinner. You, me, and mama," he managed to say as they released hold of one another. He kissed the top of her head.

Patrick cleared his throat. Clarissa had momentarily forgotten he was present. "Some ice for your arm."

Mr. Lee excused himself to check on the remainder of their guests and returned to the dining room. Patrick and Clarissa lingered in the entryway a moment longer. She needed to know. "How did you know Mark was going to be at the door?"

"Call it a sixth sense. I had a tingling sensation in my gut that I needed to follow you. Your father distracted the family with alcohol and followed me. I'm quite certain by now everyone's forgotten we're not even sitting at the table."

Clarissa smirked. "I'm sure you're right. Funny. Mark was born in the year of the snake."

"How fitting," Patrick leaned over and planted a peck on her cheek. "I suppose we should make our appearance at the table now."

Everyone was indeed well into their cups by the time the first course was actually passed around. Patrick enjoyed being able to meet and share a holiday with Clarissa's family. Course after course was served.

Mrs. Lee locked eyes with Patrick and nodded to him. She ensured his plate was never empty for long. For the first time in a long while, the waistband on his pants felt uncomfortably tight. He placed a hand on his stomach. If he needed to go up a size, at least he knew a woman who could work magic with thread.

Clarissa chatted animatedly with her cousins. She sat up taller with her shoulders pulled back with confidence. He was proud of her. She didn't let any of the day's earlier events affect her. Looking at her, an electric pulse radiated through his body. Patrick was still trying to figure her out, but one fact was undeniably true. He loved his small, fierce dragon.

At the opposite end of the table, Mr. Lee played with his water glass between conversations. He longingly stared at his daughter. Henry glanced curiously between his sister and his parents. Mrs. Lee kept busy, taking care of her guests. Patrick hoped their ensuing conversation might go smoothly. Clarissa appeared to be through the toughest portion of the night— her encounter with Mark.

There wasn't a time in recent memory where Clarissa stayed long enough at a family gathering for all the guests to depart. It was nearing eleven in the evening. Neither Patrick nor Henry had the heart to wake up the twins and enjoyed their game of seeing just how fast they could complete the washing up of all the dishes used for the dinner. It served as a stark contrast to the three members of the Lee family currently sitting in Clarissa's childhood bedroom.

A light scent of lavender lingered in the air. Ironically, lavender was supposed to promote healing and calming, two much-needed qualities for the ensuing chat. Both her parents appeared sober. Tension weighted heavily in the air. There was a deafening silence in the room.

Clarissa spoke first, her voice shaking. "Mama, Baba, I am unsure of where I should even begin. Growing up, you both always made me feel so inadequate to Henry. I worked so hard to please you with all of the extra tutoring and classes. But all you two could speak of was Henry and his success in school and on the tennis court. Never once did you tell me, I had done well. I was never an equal." Her parents listened. The longer she spoke, the more defeated her parents became.

"In my eyes, I was an outsider. I was so lonely and desperate to make you proud of me. When I earned a fully-funded place at the London School of Fashion, I thought perhaps then, the status quo might change. Instead of celebrating the achievement, you both grew upset that I had not been accepted to a traditional university." Clarissa had a few tears running down her cheeks. "You know a bit about Mark. He assisted me with the move to London and from there, our relationship festered. I learned of his true nature. It is here, my heart broke.

"Mark hurt me in so many ways, to the extent I never thought I'd be willing to trust a man again. Mark turned you against me. Despite Henry stepping in and explaining the toxicity of Mark, you sided with him over me. I stayed away because I was broken, hurt, and unloved. It took so much courage for me to come home to Birmingham each year, knowing I might see Mark. Despite all of this, I love you both too much to stay away forever. You are the only mama and baba I have.

"I am so tired. I don't think I can go on as I have much longer. I need you two in my life. I've built myself up as Clarissa Lee of London, the successful fashion designer, yet underneath all these layers, I am still Clarissa Lee from Birmingham. A daughter who just wants you to accept and love me." Hearing from Patrick about what it was like losing a parent made Clarissa feel an urgency to mend their relationship. It remained her highest priority to reconcile.

Mr. and Mrs. Lee looked at the floor. Neither one spoke for several moments. Clarissa sniffled. Mrs. Lee cupped her daughter's cheeks, almost afraid to touch her as if she were made of glass.

"I've never been more ashamed in my entire life. Can you

not see *I* have always been proud of you? Your baba and I have always pushed you because we understood you to be capable of greatness. You are so stubborn and strong. As a child, you had the gift to do just about any task you set your mind to. Your baba and I could not keep up with you. You pushed yourself so hard."

Clarissa fiddled with a loose thread on her dress. "Why did you never tell me you were proud? Why did you accept Mark's word over my own? When you berated me for not being able to be the 'kind of girlfriend' I should be and I tried to explain that he was emotionally hurting me, you failed to listen."

Her mother sobbed. "I thought you did not need to hear it. Henry is not like you. He is delicate and always asked your baba and me for help. I have no answer for Mark. He was so charming and sweet, and we did not want you to lose him. We lost our way, deceived by all of his falsehoods. I am not fit to be called your mother."

Clarissa held her parents' hands and looked into their faces. "Yes you are. What is more important, though, is forgiveness. We have already lost so much time, and I am not willing to lose you for another moment. I want us to be a *real* family again. I have missed you so much. I want you to be back in my life. I've failed at letting you understand my feelings. I failed to fight for us. We all make mistakes; it is what makes us human. We need to make every moment count, beginning now."

By the end, none of them had a dry eye.

"My baby." Mrs. Lee sobbed and pulled her daughter into an embrace. Mr. Lee joined them. They stayed intertwined, breathing heavily.

She had hugged her parents individually earlier, but this instance was different. Clarissa could not recall the last time she had been embraced in this way. She soaked in her mother's citrus perfume and her father's spicy clove musk.

The stiff cotton of her mother's jacket brushed her arm. Her father's calloused hands rubbed her arms up and down. Faint memories came to the forefront of her mind of the happier times of her youth. She added this moment to them, closing her eyes to imprint this memory. While their relationship might never be perfect, they were on the path to healing.

Chapter Twenty-Three

PATRICK

On their drive back to London, Clarissa slept peacefully, leaning against the glass of the window. A smile played over her lips. Patrick wondered what she could be dreaming of. She was innocent and youthful in her sleep. So relaxed after the tension of the day.

Clarissa awoke fifteen minutes from their building complex. Patrick yawned, fighting sleep. His eyes weighed heavy, but he needed to see them safely home.

Clarissa turned his radio on softly in the background. "You should've said something to me so I'd stay awake. I feel guilty at having slept most of the way home."

Patrick yawned once more. "S'alright. You needed the rest. It was an emotional visit."

He did have one burning question lingering in the back of his mind. "What was inside the red envelopes everyone exchanged after dinner?"

Clarissa laughed and stretched. "During the Lunar New Year, everyone exchanges red packets with money."

Patrick's eyes widened. He arched in the driver's seat stretching his sore sitting muscles.

"I can imagine that's one of the highlights of the evening for the children. I had wondered why the twins were so extra energetic and running around to collect the packets."

Patrick peeped over at Clarissa. Her eyes danced in the evening lights. "Absolutely. I remember as a child lining up everything and having Henry assist me with summing up just how many pounds we were given. The twins loved you. So did my eldest female cousin, Lea. I think you have an admirer." Clarissa placed her hand on Patrick's shoulder. "I owe you a large debt for being present tonight. You've become so special in my life, Patrick."

Patrick shivered in delight under her touch. "It is I who am lucky to have you in my life. Before now, I was only half a man. You complete me and make me whole."

Clarissa is a part of me now in so many more ways.

Clarissa did not reply. She smiled goofily at him as Patrick glanced over. The content in her eyes and her rubbing his neck expressed her sentiments.

Her touch is so natural.

Patrick turned on his signal indicator and entered the car park of their complex. Pulling the car into his reserved spot, he turned off the ignition and let out a sigh of relief. Patrick yawned and rested his head on the steering wheel for just a moment.

"Come on, sleepyhead. Time to get you into bed." Clarissa opened the car door and led the two of them up to the sixth floor. They walked slowly, hands intertwined, parting only when Clarissa was safely inside her flat.

"Goodnight, Patrick. I love you." Clarissa's lips lightly brushed over Patrick's. Her scent of vanilla and orange lingered with him, and he stared at the flat door closing in front of him.

She loves me. He closed his eyes and happily sighed. *She loves me.* He shuffled into his flat, drunk in love, and sat on his bed still dressed in his suit and shoes, thinking about Clarissa.

"I am an idiot." Patrick realized what Clarissa had just told him. Without a care for the lateness of the hour, Patrick rushed back to Clarissa's door and wildly knocked on it. Clarissa took but a moment to answer.

"I love you too!" Patrick exclaimed and again, they kissed.

Chapter Twenty-Four

CLARISSA

S onya and Clarissa stood before the gates of Buckingham Palace, staring up at the unmistakable gold and green gates adorned with the lion and unicorn of the British monarchy. Buckingham Palace was an impressive sight to behold. In all her years of living in London, Clarissa had never actually seen the palace in person.

In the distance, the sound of the marching band of the foot guards played softly as they returned to Wellington Barracks. Even on a mild late-February day, the area around the Queen Victoria statue was flooded with tourists, though the Changing of the Guard ceremony *had* just commenced.

A light breeze and warmer weather signaled the impending arrival of spring. Flowers around the grounds and across the street at the edge of Green Park awaited the signal from Mother Nature to bloom in full force.

When April arrived, it would be the perfect setting for a royal wedding. Clarissa fantasized about seeing Clara wearing her wedding dress, waving from the balcony of Buckingham Palace to the thousands of well-wishers that would assemble in London for the big event.

No pressure on me at all.

Sonya didn't speak until they headed to the security gate just outside the visitor's entrance. "I'm honored to be included in the meeting today. I know you didn't have to advocate for me to join you. I will not take this experience for granted. I am soaking in each and every moment." Sonya was serious. Clarissa watched her eyes glisten in the afternoon light.

Clarissa stopped and hugged her friend. "I wouldn't have it any other way. Now let's go into our meeting today and find some jewelry for Aurora."

Reflecting on two nights ago, Clarissa's mind buzzed with excitement. Patrick eloquently articulated the three most beautiful words in the English language, *I love you.* Clarissa floated through Sunday in disbelief, speaking to her seahorses as she performed her routine cleaning and tank maintenance.

And still, in the very depths of her mind, Clarissa harbored a few seeds of doubt. Was she too happy and setting herself up for eventual failure? In the future, could Patrick accept a woman with a completely different upbringing than his? In spite of her newfound confidence, shades of the past remained.

Sonya carefully examined Clarissa. "Are you alright? You are just about to walk straight into that lavender bush."

Clarissa brought herself into the present. "I suppose I am just nervous."

Sonya sighed. "If there is anyone who can do this, it is you. Leave your doubts at the door. We have to be on our mental 'A' game for this appointment."

Clarissa did not want to explain that her nerves were over Patrick and not the appointment. "You're right, Sonya. Let's do this." Clarissa nodded to her friend as they entered the interior of the palace.

~

Clarissa held her breath. She observed the pale-yellow wallpaper and antique china in the display cabinets next to the desk of Princess Charlotte's assistant.

In spite of having met Princess Charlotte before, Clarissa was never quite comfortable in her presence. Sonya stood next to her as they waited in the reception area to Princess Charlotte's offices. Her heart beat nervously in her chest.

Sonya, unable to stand still, paced the foyer with uncontainable energy. "Eight weeks left, Clarissa! I am so utterly proud of you for *everything* you have accomplished so far. We are down to the wire now. The bridesmaid dresses are just about complete. The girls have worked so hard. You may have to pinch me! I cannot believe I am truly standing here. What do you think we'll see today? Diamonds? Rubies? Emeralds? Sapphires?"

"I suppose we might see some pearls and diamonds." Clarissa giggled at Sonya's frown.

Sonya said, "Only you would be so nonchalant about one of the world's largest collections of jewelry and tiaras."

The door in front of them opened with a creak.

Abigail, the private secretary to Princess Charlotte, bade them to come forward. "Her Highness is ready for you."

Clarissa and Sonya thanked Abigail, straightened their attire, and glanced at one another in reassurance. Sonya and Clarissa performed their secret handshake. "For good luck," Sonya whispered. Together they passed through the double French-style doors.

The pale-yellow wallpaper from the waiting area continued inside. It brought a cheery air to the interior. Three large windows overlooked the Buckingham Palace gardens. The bright sunlight streamed into the room and highlighted two ballerina portraits painted by impressionist artist Edgar

Degas. Two wooden chairs, an oak antique desk, and three bookshelves filled the room. Clarissa noticed article clippings and several thick binders overflowing with photos lining the desk.

Princess Charlotte, who stood about five foot six, had bright red hair with wisps of gray. Princess Charlotte preferred to style her hair in a low chignon. Approaching her late fifties, she was the oldest of the three late king's children—King Reginald and the rarely seen Prince Francis, the Duke of Albany. Princess Charlotte stood up from behind her desk as Sonya and Clarissa entered the room.

They attempted the dreaded curtsy. Clarissa stated, "Your Royal Highness, it is a pleasure to see you today."

Princess Charlotte tsked at the two. "No need for such formalities ladies. If everyone bowed and curtsied to one another *all* the time, we might never be able to stay on schedule. In time, you might come to find that my siblings and I enjoy informality where possible. Now then, we have a number of issues to discuss. As with the first time we were introduced, just Princess Charlotte will do. Please sit and help yourselves to some refreshments. As my good friend Dr. Evans has taken to reminding me of late, I am *quite* detail oriented."

Was this why Clara and Amanda had asked her and Sonya to meet with Princess Charlotte? Because she was organized? Clarissa wondered just what she might be getting herself into. She sat on one of the two unoccupied chairs.

Sonya followed her lead. Princess Charlotte gathered one of the three-inch-thick binders from her desk and thumbed through several pages. She put on a pair of red reading glasses to examine a page closer.

She spoke to herself. "This is the one."

Opening the rings of the binder, she took the page out and handed it to Clarissa. "As I am not privy to the design of the dress, you are the best person to ask on the subject of flowers. I would like you to glance over my short list of the following one hundred varieties and advise as to which ones you are utilizing in Clara's and the bridesmaids' dresses. I need to ensure we do not have any duplicate flowers represented in any of the bouquets the girls will carry."

Sonya stared wide-eyed at the princess. Clarissa schooled her face into a neutral expression.

She wants to go over one hundred different flowers? So this is why Clara asked me to stand in. If this is just one small example of the level of details Princess Charlotte wishes to discuss, I can only empathize with how fatigued Clara must be. Clarissa's eyes twitched. *Remain calm.*

"Thus far, I have incorporated a shamrock, a thistle, a rose, and a daffodil into the ceremony dress. We have replicated the motif on the reception gown's wrap, though she has yet to see it in person. The plans for the bridesmaid dresses have changed from the original design meeting. Unfortunately, my shop experienced a burglary; the original sketches were stolen. In the revised dresses, each girl will be styled in periwinkle blue and will represent the golden wattle, the lotus, the desert rose, and the bougainvillea flowers."

Princess Charlotte spoke slowly, "I see."

Sonya recovered her wits and added, "Clarissa did quite an extensive amount of research. She studied books on the Victorian language of flowers, has made several trips to Kew Gardens, and even procured live specimens to aid her. Each flower for the bridesmaid dresses comes from a different continent."

Princess Charlotte chuckled. "I can see I'm not the only one who goes the extra step. Well done."

Clarissa's nerves settled. Princess Charlotte continued through a staggering amount of questions. They covered footwear, undergarments, hair accessories, rain contingencies, and even discussed the color of ribbons the horses pulling

David and Clara's wedding carriage should have braided into their manes and tails.

No stone was left unturned. Sonya jumped in to assist Clarissa whenever she could. The afternoon proved tedious, yet rewarding. Clarissa and Sonya were leaving their own mark on the royal wedding. Finally, they reached the topic of jewelry.

The Princess Royal said, "I hope you are not overly weary. The jewel vault is a bit of a trek."

Sonya jumped to her feet, her excitement unbound. "We are ready. Shall we leave straightaway?"

Princess Charlotte's eyes danced in amusement. "As soon as I clear it with security, yes."

Clarissa restrained Sonya from all but sprinting to the doorway. "Patience," Clarissa reminded her.

Sonya's face flushed bright red. "Please accept my apologies. Jewelry is a passion of mine. Just having the ability to see the gems up close and in person has been a lifelong dream of mine."

Clarissa laughed. While she enjoyed suggesting jewelry to her clients, Sonya's expert eye for accessories could not be understated. She truly could find the perfect piece for each and every person. They often joked it could be her superpower.

Princess Charlotte nodded in understanding. On her intercom, she called to Abigail. "Please let the guards know I have two visitors joining me in the jewel room."

Clarissa's excitement grew. She might not know as much as Sonya about jewelry, but she couldn't imagine what they were about to see.

I am living a dream. I am about to search for a tiara for Clara. A real-life tiara! I never could have pictured myself even thinking about this just last year. And to think, I have the chance to share this moment with Sonya. We have come so far from skimping on groceries and doing what we can to scrape by.

~

Many floors below Buckingham Palace sat the otherworldly ice-skating-rink-sized vault. The amount of items sparkling under the lights must have numbered in the thousands.

Artfully arranged in case after case stood enough jewels to last one person several lifetimes. Clarissa's eyes glazed over, taking in the never-ending array of options: diamonds, emeralds, aquamarines, rubies, jades, sapphires, and opals.

Wow! No wonder Sonya was so enthusiastic.

"This is one of the world's most valuable collections of jewels after the Russians." Princess Charlotte opened the closest jewel case and lifted out a crown made up of platinum adorned in diamonds and pearls. "This particular piece alone is worth ten million pounds." Clarissa flinched and took two steps back. Princess Charlotte chuckled.

"All of the jewels are insured, and we have our jeweler on permanent standby for fixes and adjustments. You do not need to handle these as if they were constructed from glass. I can vividly recall my own mother once breaking this tiara getting out of a car for a state banquet. This setting has been repaired several times."

Sonya observed the tiara in awe. Normally never this quiet, Clarissa found it eerie to have Sonya be so reserved. In a hushed voice she asked, "Do we require gloves to handle pieces from your magnificent collection?"

Princess Charlotte replied, "No, no. Just with your bare hands is fine. You may even wish to try them on. It helps to understand how heavy a certain tiara might be. If Clara is to wear one for the duration of the wedding ceremony, we want to find one that will be perfectly suited to her."

Sonya's eyes fluttered. She stammered, "Tr... tra... try them on?"

A ghost of a smile formed on Clarissa's lips. When they

left the meeting later, she was sure Sonya would chat nonstop about their day. Taking a key out from the pocket of her burgundy blazer, Princess Charlotte opened two other jewel cases. "Of course. As I have mentioned, please do not be overly shy with the jewelry. It is intended to be enjoyed. Now where shall we begin?"

Clarissa suggested, "Knowing Clara, as a ballerina, she is used to wearing some type of headpiece. She is not the type of person who would want to wear anything too ostentatious. Perhaps we could start by examining the simpler tiaras in the collection? Something with pearls."

Sonya perked up. With unsteady hands, her fingers lingered over a tiara set in gold and silver. Spikes of diamonds ran across the top. A row of pearls loosely hung in the arches below the spikes.

"This is the Cambridge Lover's Knot tiara. I have seen Queen Agnus wear this in photos a few times." Sonya's cheeks flushed. "It would look so well with the slight off-white coloring of the organza overskirt of Clara's dress."

Sonya gingerly picked up the tiara and turned it over several times in her hand. She tested the weight in her hands and offered it to Clarissa. Her fingers brushed across the pearls as they rocked to-and-fro as the tiara moved.

Princess Charlotte explained, "This is a Gothic revival tiara. As you mentioned, it is one of the queen's favorite pieces. The pearls can be detached and turned into a necklace. An excellent choice."

Clarissa studied the diamonds. "It is heavier than it appears."

Sonya sighed. "I think this tiara might take the attention away from Clara's dress. Are there any pieces that may not have been out on public display for a long time?"

Clarissa agreed and placed the Cambridge Lover's Knot tiara back in its resting place.

Princess Charlotte's eyes sparkled. Clarissa thought it strange the Princess Royal appeared to be giving her and Sonya complete control over the choice of jewels. Was there an underlying reason? She pondered the thought.

Princess Charlotte guided them farther down the jewel vault. The lights within the vault reflected the jewels, almost hypnotizing Clarissa.

The Princess Royal said, "Each tiara has a unique history. Agnus prefers to always wear the same classic Russian-styled pieces like these." Princess Charlotte pointed to two tiaras constructed entirely of diamonds.

"What may interest you is in this case over here. This was my grandmother's debutante tiara." Princess Charlotte paused.

Sonya and Clarissa followed her gaze. Their eyes settled on an art-deco-styled tiara. The band consisted of vines from which small diamonds and amethysts arose to form various-sized roses.

"This was never a royal tiara until my mother married into the royal family. It belonged to her family. We call it the English Rose tiara. If memory serves, it was designed by the Catchpole and Williams silversmiths."

Sonya and Clarissa exchanged glances. "This is it," they both said to one another.

Sonya took up the tiara and tested its weight in her hands. From varying angles, Clarissa noticed different colors of gems shone brightly. From the angle Sonya held the English Rose tiara, she could see pink sapphires worked into the rose.

"It's stunning," Clarissa breathed.

Sonya brushed Clarissa's hair back and placed the tiara on her. Princess Charlotte passed her a small handheld mirror. "This looks quite like the Nelson family tiara."

Clarissa sharply breathed in. "It's beautiful."

Thoughts of Patrick swirled in her mind. Patrick's family

had a tiara like this one? The words of the Princess Royal added weight to the tiara as she gazed at her reflection. For the first time, Clarissa began to understand just how different their backgrounds were—Patrick inhabited the world of nobility and Clarissa the world of working-class immigrants.

This is not about Paddy or me. I'm here for Clara.

She removed the tiara and passed it back to Sonya. "This is the one for Clara. It's her in the form of jewelry. A true English rose."

Princess Charlotte's eyes misted over. "I have waited so long for my David to find the right woman. Clara is everything to him."

On instinct, Clarissa hugged Princess Charlotte. Sonya offered her a tissue from her purse.

"Thank you both." She dried her eyes. "We are still several weeks away from the wedding and already I am emotional. I shall need an industrial pack of tissues over the course of the day at this rate." She smiled brightly at Sonya and Clarissa.

The trio spent another hour reviewing earrings and necklaces. At the end of the three-hour appointment, the entire party was emotionally and physically exhausted, yet excited.

Leave it to Sonya to find the perfect pink sapphire and topaz pieces.

The orange and pink were perfect complements to the reception dress. She hoped Clara was pleased when she saw them all together. They were supposed to find a short list of items for Clara. Instead they found only a single tiara, necklace, and set of earrings.

Sonya and Clarissa declined the use of their normal driver and planned to leave Buckingham Palace for a stop in Piccadilly

Circus. Most Londoners avoided this major tourist area at all costs, yet today marked an exception for Sonya and Clarissa.

"It's been so long since we've treated ourselves to a pistachio gelato! I cannot wait for that magical first bite," Sonya gushed.

Clarissa laughed. "You and pistachio. Everyone knows the Neapolitan is the best of all worlds. The perfect blend of vanilla, chocolate, and strawberries."

Sonya stuck her tongue out in distaste. "Too traditional."

Clarissa's mobile alerted her to a message. They crossed the street into Green Park and strolled along one of the pathways at a leisurely pace.

Rummaging through her purse, Clarissa found her phone and unlocked the screen to reveal several missed calls and one message from Patrick. Clarissa swallowed and hoped it wasn't anything too overtly worrisome. She frowned as she tapped into her voicemail.

"Clarissa, it's Patrick. Please ring me as soon as you receive this message. It's urgent."

She stopped walking and breathed in sharply. Sonya responded. "Everything alright?"

"Do you mind if we stop for a moment? I have a message from Patrick asking me to call him as soon as possible."

Patrick's voice came on the line short two rings after she dialed the number. "Clarissa. Thank goodness. I wanted to reach you as soon as possible." His voice was tense.

On a premonition, Clarissa gripped Sonya's arm. "Patrick. You're scaring me a little. Has something happened?"

Patrick huffed on the other end. "I am so sorry to have to be the bearer of bad tidings, but I have had to ring the police. When I was leaving my flat this morning, I found your door ajar. I knew you would be meeting with Princess Charlotte today and thought it odd that you might be home. When I stopped to check in on you, there were two burglars. They rushed out as soon as they saw me, but there is rubbish every-where. Detective Wade is here and needs you present to make another formal statement."

Clarissa swayed. Sonya guided her over to a park bench. On pins and needles, Clarissa spluttered. "My flat has been ransacked? Two burglars? Are you alright?"

Sonya gasped.

She heard Patrick swallow hard. "I'm fine. I'm just concerned about you and your safety."

She abruptly stood. "Tell the police I will be there straightaway."

Patrick paused, "Just be careful. I worry about you. I love you."

Clarissa whispered back, "I love you too."

She disconnected the call and stared blankly at the phone in her hand, touching it where she had just heard Patrick's voice. There was much information to process. Her emotions swirled in a sea of confusion over the magnitude of the news and her feelings toward Patrick.

Sonya's eyes roamed over Clarissa. She waved her hand in front of her face. "Earth to Clarissa. Let's go. Taxicab. Now. I am coming along, and there is no talking me out of it. My mind is made up."

Clarissa's nerves took hold; her stomach grew heavy with dread. *There is not a chance this second break-in was accidental. What am I going to find when I reach the flat?* Clarissa and Sonya high-tailed it to the street where Sonya waved down a taxi. *I only have a few weeks to finish off Clara's dress. This could not have come at a worse time.*

Clarissa stared out the window at the passing scenery. Sonya broke the ice. "You are welcome to hide away at my flat. It doesn't begin to compare with your posh Holland Park digs now, but you are always welcome. It can be as if we are going back in time to our uni days."

Clarissa tightly smiled. Sonya was always reliable in a pinch and always there for her, yet she didn't want to be scared away from her own home. "Thank you for the offer Sonya. I'm hoping it won't come to that."

Sonya sighed. "You are so stubborn. While it is a quality I find endearing in you, please take this seriously, Clarissa. I do not want you to get hurt or put yourself at risk. What would I do without my business partner and one of my best friends?"

Clarissa hugged herself. "I know. My mind is having trouble processing all that is going on."

Chapter Twenty-Five

PATRICK

The sun wouldn't set for another half-hour. Patrick stood, waiting to receive the taxi conveying Clarissa and Sonya. He sighed with welcome relief at their uneventful arrival.

Clarissa has so much on her plate right now. It's fortunate Sonya happened to be nearby. I would not have wanted her to receive the news by herself. Should she even be traveling alone? Will she agree to stay with me?

The black cab's doors opened; Clarissa slid out, then Sonya. Patrick greeted Clarissa with a peck on the cheek and guided the ladies into the complex building and up to their floor. She brushed her hand over his face. Patrick enjoyed her cooling touch.

"Paddy!" Clarissa admonished. "You have a cut on your cheek and your shirt is torn! What happened?"

Patrick glanced down. *Leave it to Clarissa to notice a rip.*

Patrick winced and abruptly changed the subject. He may have understated his involvement with the burglars. In their haste to escape, Patrick had chased them from Clarissa's flat. He fell as they fled down the building's fire escape.

He gulped. *Will Clarissa be able to handle the mess that was once a spotlessly maintained flat?*

"I can explain in detail later. The chief inspector on the case from your shop is waiting for you. A word of warning… it is quite an ugly sight to behold when you reach our floor, Clarissa. I'm sorry." Patrick ran a hand through his hair.

The lift bell indicated the arrival on their floor. Sonya clapped a hand to her mouth and Clarissa's jaw dropped. Strewn across the hallway, leading up to her flat, lay pieces of broken glass, fragments of sketches, and fabric samples from her workroom. She gripped Patrick's arm.

Detective Wade greeted Clarissa with tired eyes. "Miss Lee. I am sorry we meet again under such dire circumstances. Mr. Nelson informed us of what he could. I am required to take a statement from you and also need you to let us know exactly what is missing from your home. If I could have you follow me. Mr. Nelson and your friend will have to wait here. I am afraid this flat is now a crime scene."

Patrick kept his arm on Clarissa's back for support. Sonya stood on her other side. Both were poised to argue with the detective. Clarissa held her hand up. "I can do this." Clarissa nodded.

"If you could, please follow me."

Chapter Twenty-Six

CLARISSA

Clarissa shuddered. Furniture turned over, vases broken, water on the floor.

At least my little seahorses are alright. I have had them for three years. I don't know what I would do if they were lost.

Clarissa picked up a fallen photo of her parents. She stared at it for several seconds and carefully placed it back on the wall.

Surveying the room, she said, "Other than being out of place, the kitchen and the sitting areas appear to be fine." The bedroom also stood untouched.

The detective made several notes and followed Clarissa to the last room to investigate—her sewing studio. The door stood ajar. Clarissa resisted the urge to vomit.

Her sewing machine was overturned, all of her magazines and books were opened with some containing missing pages, and her meticulously maintained collections of trim items lay in a million pieces coating the floor.

Sadness took hold. "All of my reference binders and notes, and parts of my fabric swatch collection have been taken. They were probably the most valuable items here. They contained all of my work for the upcoming collection and the notes of every clothing item I have ever worked on, save my um... private client notes. Those I keep in my shop. My laptop and tablet are also gone."

The inspector sighed. "We will do our best to track down your valuables, Miss Lee. This case is admittedly tricky. The attack on your shop was well organized and, until earlier today, we had a few leads to operate off. Ironically, I had hoped to ring you with an update. The original bridesmaid dresses and several of your sketches mysteriously popped up for sale in an online auction this afternoon. We have our IT department working to trace who the seller might be. As for the break-in on your flat, I daresay the two cases are related."

"I suspected as much." Clarissa crossed her arms over her chest.

"We believe that an organized crime group has narrowed down the potential list of fashion designers for the impending wedding of His Royal Highness, the Duke of Leeds. Within the last three weeks, we have had no less than three robberies at high-end fashion shops. Each break-in has gotten progressively more aggressive. There is a large amount of money at stake for any information relating to the royal wedding."

Clarissa's heart sank. "There is?"

"Unfortunately, yes." The detective closed his notebook. Grimly, he glanced around. "This is the part of the job I dislike the most. Your home is a crime scene. At present, I have a few of my team dusting for fingerprints and searching for any potential clues or evidence. It may take several hours or more for us to finish our work. I would like my team to take a little extra time if possible."

Clarissa agreed. "Take all the time you need. To be honest, I'm not so certain I feel safe here."

The inspector sighed. "It is highly unlikely the assailants will return, but I agree there is always the possibility. If I were to give you a risk assessment, I would recommend you stay away for a few days. I have high hopes that based on the information from today, we will be able to identify and make a few arrests very soon."

Clarissa hesitated. "Thank you for the update. I'll take everything you said under advisement."

A strange feeling took hold as the detective left to check in with his team. Clarissa lingered in her entrance hallway.

I do not want to impose on Sonya or Patrick. I don't want them to be targets too. As nervous as I am to be alone right now, maybe it's better if I don't involve them. The detective said the attacks were getting worse.

Could I find a hotel room for a week? Clara's dress could not be a more welcome distraction. Maybe I could stay in the Kensington Palace workroom. Her eyes closed. The weight of the world seemingly sat atop her shoulders.

She clenched in anger. *Why did this have to happen now? I have worked so hard to build up the Clarissa Lee brand. Why couldn't they leave me alone? I'm just one person.*

Her anger faded as she reflected on how lucky she had been to be patronized by Clara, without whom she would have not had the means to move into her current flat and meet Patrick. Patrick was one of the best things that had ever happened to her. He had truly shown her what love could feel like and how it was to be taken care of.

Her eyes opened. She needed the support of two of the most important people in her life right now, Sonya and Patrick. They would keep her sane in the time of crisis. Exhaustion began to take hold.

Clarissa didn't trust herself to think clearly. As she exited her flat, she spotted the two standing with their heads together in deep, hushed conversation. Upon seeing Clarissa, they jumped apart.

Not one to waste any time, Sonya slowly asked, "How bad?"

Clarissa put it bluntly. "They hurt me in the worst way possible. My entire sketch collection is gone. It is as if it never existed."

Sonya rushed over to hug Clarissa tightly. Clarissa leaned her head onto Sonya's shoulder. "There is not a stronger or more resilient person I know. You will come through this stronger than ever."

Clarissa willed back her tears out of sheer determination. She wanted to believe Sonya but couldn't bring herself to do so. Despite feeling so low and vulnerable, she put on a brave face. Crying would make it seem as if the burglars had won. She would not let them succeed.

"It's fine." Her words came out flat, not even truly convincing herself. She stepped back from Sonya.

Patrick hovered in the background, anxious to be near Clarissa. He stayed silent. The lines of worry on Patrick's forehead nearly resulted in her tears rushing down. She frowned at the cut near his eye that had begun to swell.

Stay. Strong.

Patrick said, "There is no way you are *fine*, but I won't ask you about it right now. We can speak on it when you're ready."

Clarissa loved Patrick even more for not asking about how she was doing. He hugged her tightly into his chest and kissed the top of her head.

The smooth fabric of his shirt and musky scent assisted in calming her. Enough time passed for her mind to clear somewhat. Though she was not letting go of Patrick, she was ready to hear what they had to say.

Chapter Twenty-Seven

PATRICK

"Sonya and I have spoken and we both agreed you might need a change of scenery."

Patrick hesitated. Would Clarissa be open to their suggestions? He wanted nothing more than to squirrel her away to the safety of Rainridge, but upon learning more of her past with Mark, he understood that Clarissa needed to be the one to make the decision.

Clarissa stared at the ground. "Under normal circumstances, I would disagree with you, but the detective has recommended I spend some time away from the flat. I thought perhaps I might book a hotel."

Patrick sharply breathed in, internally groaning.

Sonya stepped in. "As I mentioned earlier, you are always welcome at my flat, but in this case, I think you might want to hear what Patrick has to say."

"Thank you, Sonya." He paused. "While you spoke to the detective, I rang David to fill him in on the situation. Despite being a royal, David is one of the few people I trust to examine a situation from a completely objective point of view. I suppose it comes from him having been in the army."

Patrick did not add he had privately tossed around a few ideas about how best to address his security concerns for Clarissa. Once more, Patrick had to remind himself this was *Clarissa's* decision. It was a separate conversation he would have with her tomorrow.

"David and Clara have graciously extended an open invitation for you to stay with them as long as you wish or to even put you up in a hotel. They feel responsible for much of the chaos."

Patrick cleared his throat. "I wanted to add my own option for you to consider. Rainridge Manor, while not as grand as Kensington Palace, is situated in the Cotswolds away from the hustle and bustle of London. You are more than welcome to stay there for as long as you would like. The selfish side of me wants you to pick Rainridge because then I have an excuse to show you my ancestral home. Additionally, I am well aware Clara's wedding dress is understandably your top priority. At Rainridge, you could have an entire floor of the manor to work on the dress."

Clarissa looked up from the floor to Patrick. He didn't like the dark circles forming under her eyes or the semblance of defeat in her body language. A glint of determination in her dark brown eyes informed him Clarissa had already made her decision. "I want to go to Rainridge."

Chapter Twenty-Eight

CLARISSA

The trio agreed that they did not feel up to dinner with David and Clara. They ordered takeaway and discussed logistics. Sonya would stay in London to oversee the boutiques, bridesmaid team, and Patrick and Clarissa's prized aquariums.

After procuring a few personal items, Clarissa and Patrick set out for Kensington Palace where she supervised the packing up of Clara's nearly-completed reception gown, Clarissa's sewing machine, and several other containers of supplies. Even with the extra space in David's SUV, the items nearly did not all fit. Clarissa was especially careful to wrap and lay the dress out on the back seat of the vehicle.

Under the cover of darkness, Patrick drove them in the borrowed car to Gloucestershire. Clarissa was mentally exhausted; nonetheless, she eagerly anticipated seeing the place Patrick loved so much. It was a clear evening as they drove out of the city limits along the M40.

Clarissa burrowed into a soft green, plaid, wool blanket that smelled of Patrick. "This blanket has some of the softest wool I have ever touched." The fabric was just heavy enough to keep her toasty.

Patrick chuckled. "Where we are headed is famous for its wool."

Clarissa scrunched her face. "What do you mean?"

Patrick shared, "The wool is local. Before the Industrial Revolution, the Cotswold area of England was famous for its wool from Cotswold sheep. It is how the region earned its name. The wool was once said to be the best in the world. A gold standard, so to speak. Unfortunately, the industry crashed with the rise of machines. Luckily, it eventually recovered. These days, the area is more famed for the many Londoners that keep homes in the Cotswold."

Clarissa perked up. "Fascinating. I never connected the name of the sheep to the area."

Patrick said, "Indeed. My family earned much of its fortune from wool. We still have a farm that includes a handful of sheep, but most of our estate income comes from opening our home to event bookings."

Clarissa blanched. "Event bookings?" Panic flashed through her body. "Oh no. I hope we are not going to be arriving in the midst of a busy weekend. Paddy, you should have mentioned it earlier."

Patrick attempted to calm her with a quiet, soothing voice. "No events until May. I promise. We are in our winter season. Mother and I agreed that winter is the time to perform upkeep and general maintenance on the estate. It is one reason I pop up to Rainridge weekly. I check on how certain projects are coming along."

Clarissa relaxed. "I should not have jumped to conclusions. I'm sorry."

Patrick disagreed. "Please don't apologize. It has been an extraordinarily long day, and you are obviously exhausted. We should be there in about twenty more minutes. Then you can enjoy one of the soft new guest beds."

Clarissa blinked a few times. "A soft bed sounds wonderful right now." She rested her head on the window.

After two hours of driving, it was close to midnight. The Rainridge property was nestled in the heart of the Gloucestershire area of the Cotswold. Though it was pitch black outside, Clarissa could make out the fuzzy outlines of the forestscape and rolling fields. It was a far cry from the urban sprawl of London.

Up in the sky, the stars shone brightly. They changed to the A40 near Oxford which took them past several townships and villages. Clarissa was charmed by the Tudor revivals and many row houses illuminated by the moonlight. She pictured the stone shingles on the homes and thatched roofs of the cottages they passed.

Patrick yawned. "Here is the turn-in for the drive," he offered.

Clarissa, who began to fall asleep throughout the last third of the journey, bolted awake as the car slowed. Patrick maneuvered the car skillfully through the dark. Clarissa held her breath.

Once they made it over the small hill, illuminated before her was one of the most beautiful homes she had ever laid eyes upon. She instantly loved the brick exterior and cottage-style front garden.

Patrick parked the car and turned off the ignition. "I didn't think to bring a lantern with me, but I had our groundskeeper switch the interior lights on. With Mother off at Belshaw Hall, the manor should be empty. Welcome to Rainridge Manor."

Clarissa's eyes bulged. "There have to be about thirty rooms!"

He zipped his jacket up and stepped out of the car. "No,

only twenty rooms. Of those, we only use a handful. Time has not been kind to the building. It has taken a massive effort to upkeep the exterior and slowly update the interior to modern times. Most of the former servants' quarters and second-floor suites are dusty and full of oddities. The attic has a leak I'm still working on patching." He shook his head.

The sounds of insects resonated through the night. Gravel crunched under Patrick's shoes. He made his way over to assist Clarissa from her side of the car.

Clarissa slowly slid out of the vehicle. After sitting for so long, her legs lacked blood flow. "So long as I have a bed, blankets, and electricity, I'll sleep anywhere."

Making his way to the boot of the car, Patrick removed their hand luggage. "If you'd like, I can set you up in the stables." Clarissa's eyes darted toward the three or four outbuildings.

Stables? I didn't anticipate the property being so large!

Clarissa rubbed her hands together to keep warm. She was reluctant to leave the blanket in the car, yet anxious to see the interior of the home. Opening the back door, Clarissa reached for the garment bag with Clara's dress and lifted it carefully to avoid any dirt.

Patrick asked, "Are you alright to leave the remainder of your work items in the car until tomorrow?"

Clarissa agreed. She just wanted to go inside out of the cold. Patrick clicked the security alarm on the car and led Clarissa up the pathway to the three-story home. Near the doorway, he took out a large iron key and inserted it into a lock. Clarissa couldn't fathom using such an antique key.

"I can have you situated in your room as soon as we are inside, unless you are up for an abbreviated tour?"

As the door swung open onto the ground floor, Patrick set Clarissa's hand luggage down as they entered the home.

"I would love to have a tour please."

He motioned toward a large hallway closet where Clarissa could store the dress. Immediately, Patrick noticed the heat had not been turned on.

He muttered under his breath and adjusted the thermostat. "It'll take a while for the central heating system to warm the entire house. I'll build us a fire in the study while we wait."

Clarissa's eyes danced in mirth. "You can build a fire?"

Of course he can. I bet he chops his own firewood too.

Patrick smugly replied, "Comes with being the lord of the manor. In the meantime, I'll start our tour down here. The ground floor is the oldest portion of the house. The Nelsons of Rainridge once used this as the dowager house. A fire in the late 1870s destroyed most of the main home. It was then demolished in 1915. The kitchen, sitting area, library, my office, and one of the three guest suites are on this level. I was going to install you on this floor tonight and on the second floor tomorrow. My rooms and Mother's rooms are on the first floor."

Clarissa soaked in the antique wooden floors and paneling covered in a red-carpet runner. Wooden crossbeams ran across the entryway's roof. Portraits of Patrick's ancestors lined the walls. The kitchen appeared modern with new appliances.

Poking her head into the study, Clarissa enjoyed the masculine feel of the room. Floor-to-ceiling bookcases lined walls. Clarissa could easily picture Patrick sitting in front of a fire, in a wingback chair, enjoying one of the hundreds of books.

Patrick laughed at Clarissa's expression. "This room was always my father's pride and joy. As you may have guessed, we harbor a large collection of rare and antique books. All of them are cataloged and organized according to the author. My father was meticulous about how the books were arranged."

Patrick set to work on the fire. "I remember so many times in my youth coming into this room to practice my Latin.

Father and I often read through Cicero and debated upon the writings of Tacitus and Suetonius, Roman historians. I found my love of history in this room."

Patrick stared into the fire as it grew larger, providing much-needed warmth.

Clarissa sat on the couch opposite the fireplace, lost in thought. Patrick rarely spoke of his father.

"He sounds like quite an intelligent gentleman. I'm sorry I don't know much about the Romans other than they built an empire."

Patrick stood and wandered over to the second bookshelf on the left. He blew a thin layer of dust off the shelf. His fingers caressed the spines of the book, stopping at a particularly large volume.

"This is a first-edition copy of the *Decline and Fall of the Roman Empire.*" Clarissa watched as Patrick joyfully brought the book over to the couch. He beamed with pride, eyes dancing. "It is among the best histories of the Romans. I would love to share this book with you."

Clarissa's heart sank. It was evident Patrick loved his books and reading; however, she was unable to share the same passion.

The gesture is so sweet, but the book is wasted on me. How do I gently remind him I can't read well?

Her brain just wasn't wired for proper reading; it was comparable to reading a book upside down.

Clarissa placed a hand on Patrick's. "I am so honored you want to share such an important book with me." Clarissa's cheeks flushed red. "I will need your help though..."

Patrick breathed in sharply, the spell broken. "Your dyslexia!" he spluttered. "Clarissa, I wasn't thinking. I'm a dunce for even putting you in such an awkward position."

Clarissa winced. "The gesture is so thoughtful. Your heart

is in the right place. Maybe we can read a small section of the book together each night."

Patrick abruptly stood. "Absolutely," he replied and placed the book back on the shelf. "I am just going to step out and check on the heat. I'll be back in a moment."

Clarissa watched Patrick retreat, his cheeks pink with embarrassment.

I shouldn't have said anything. Why did I have to bring it up? Clarissa frowned. *Even if I could read well, it isn't as if I can match Patrick's intellect.*

His parents had sent him to boarding school and set him up with a top-tier education. She had barely passed school and had *only* attended a fashion university. Patrick attended Oxford and was in the process of establishing a museum.

I don't bring much to the table. What does Patrick see in me? Am I even worth all the trouble?

Her head ached. The full extent of the day finally took a toll upon her body.

I need sleep.

Chapter Twenty-Nine

PATRICK

Patrick angrily clenched his fists. *How could I have overlooked such an important part of Clarissa? She has shared with me before how self-conscious she is about her dyslexia and how much she had to come to terms with it growing up.* He leaned against a wall outside the kitchen.

Seeing her light up when they first set eyes on Rainridge made him glow with pride. He had been certain she would love the estate as much as he. Clarissa loved stories and histories. Instead, he had spoiled her first impression of Rainridge with his faux pas.

Patrick ran a hand through his hair. *She's had a difficult day. All I have done is add to the list of difficulties. I'm so angry at myself and those blasted burglars.*

Patrick counted to thirty. He held his breath and waited for some of the pent-up anger to flee his body, one of his many coping mechanisms. *It will do me no good now to be angry. I am human, and as mad as I am at myself, I have to realize I am going to make mistakes from time to time. I'll apologize again to Clarissa and find a way to make it up to her.*

Patrick checked on the thermostat and returned to the

library. Before entering, he pushed all anger at himself aside. He took several deep breaths. Entering the room, Patrick found Clarissa asleep on the couch.

He hated to wake her, but sleeping on the coach would not do. Patrick remembered just how sore his back was the last time he had fallen asleep reading late into the evening.

He lightly touched her shoulder. "Clarissa, are you ready for bed? I can carry you, but it might be better if you see where your suite is."

Clarissa's eyes fluttered open. "Sounds marvelous. You lead the way, please." She stood and stretched.

Patrick added, "I wanted to apologize again for my behavior." He stayed quiet, leading her down the corridor opposite the kitchen. Clarissa shuffled behind him.

As they reached their intended destination, Clarissa rose up onto her toes and pecked Patrick on the cheek. "Don't concern yourself over it, Paddy. I need to sleep though. I'll see you in the morning."

He bid her goodnight. Clarissa slowly closed the door. Patrick lingered in the hallway and remained staring at the door. He crossed the hall and ascended the flight of stairs to his own suite.

I hope she sleeps well tonight.

Try as he might, sleep evaded him. Patrick lay awake for hours, contemplating having Clarissa under the Rainridge roof and just how much she had changed him in a few short months. Clarissa brought out a light in him that had long been extinguished. His life was finally coming together with Clarissa as the missing piece of the puzzle.

He loved her so much. She made him laugh and experience feelings he had long repressed. Clarissa was bringing out a better side of him. She was so creative and kind-hearted.

He particularly admired her ability to become entrenched in her work as he had observed in her home studio; it was akin to seeing a great artist paint a single brush stroke upon a blank canvas. He didn't have one iota of her creativity.

Patrick's mind spun in the darkness. How could he make up for his faux pas tonight? Could it be combined with her seeing Rainridge? After all the stress of the day, how could he help her relax?

Around four in the morning, Patrick gave up on sleep. He needed a morning ride to settle his mind. Chester likely needed the workout just as much as he did.

Patrick got dressed and was out the door by five. As he approached the stables, sudden inspiration struck Patrick. A goofy grin slid onto his face as he laid eyes on the wedding supply storage area.

This is exactly what we both need.

There was only one way to truly appreciate the scenery of the estate and its surroundings—from up above.

Chapter Thirty

CLARISSA

Clarissa awoke late by her standards. She had spent half the night tossing and turning over her concerns about Patrick, the burglary, the future of her business, and stress over being able to complete Clara's dress on time. Her eyes heavy, she rubbed them, hoping it might assist in the endeavor to leave the warm cocoon of the bed.

In spite of her aching body, she sat up. *There is so much to do and no time to waste. As much as I want to have a lie-in, it is not possible at this stage. We are now seven and a half weeks away from Aurora's big day.*

The aroma of fresh bacon wafted through the air from the nearby kitchen as she made up her bed and began sifting through her hand luggage for her toiletries. She licked her lips.

The bacon will be my reward for getting up. Leave it to Patrick to whip up yet another culinary delight. Paddy has a sixth sense for the foods that bring me comfort and for the foods that he can bribe me with.

He was *always* looking out for her. How could she look out for him? Nothing came to the forefront of her mind. Her shoulders sagged. She sighed and pressed on.

In the daylight, Clarissa was able to fully take in the minimalistic ground floor guest suite. The walls, devoid of decorations, were painted mint green and offered a sense of calm to Clarissa.

The large king-sized bed occupied the center of the room; two large windows encompassed the entirety of the wall opposite the bed. Clarissa drew back the curtains and opened the windows in awe.

The view of the Rainridge grounds provided a piece of living art as the first morning rays of sunlight cascaded over the babbling brook that weaved through the back of the estate. The morning mist floated over the grassy meadow.

Birds chirped, busy at work building nests. An owl hooted off in the distance. In spring, she was willing to wager the grounds were covered in a wide array of flower blooms. The chilly air woke her from the living dream as she prepared for the day.

Morning rituals completed, Clarissa dressed for comfort in denim jeans, a navy-blue button-up silk shirt, and her oatmeal jumper. As she stepped out of the guest suite, she vaguely recalled the layout of the ground floor from Patrick's tour the night before.

She made it two steps before the barking of a dog stopped her in her tracks. Bending down, Clarissa spotted a tan cocker spaniel. It lay sprawled out on the red-carpet runner and perked up in interest as Clarissa approached.

"Good morning to you." She let the dog sniff her hand and scratched its ears. The cocker licked her hand and wagged its tail in excitement. "And just who might you be?" Clarissa read the dog's collar tag. "Guinevere." The dog barked again. "A fitting name for the lady of the house. You don't happen to know where the kitchen is, do you?"

Guinevere barked in acknowledgment and waited, signaling for Clarissa to follow. Guinevere led her past several rooms to the end of the corridor. Outside the kitchen, she heard Patrick whistling as Guinevere nudged the door open with her head.

Clarissa's heart warmed watching Patrick at work upon entering the kitchen. Patrick beamed, showing off to his invisible audience by flipping over a hotcake in the frying pan on the stove. Already, several sat piled up in a neat stack ready to be eaten at the dining table.

Patrick spoke. "Two of my favorite ladies. Excellent timing. Clarissa, help yourself to the fresh jam and tea. The bacon is coming up. How many hotcakes for you? Two? Three?" To Guinevere, he said, "For you, I have a nice juicy rabbit waiting in your bowl. Enjoy girl." Guinevere did not waste any time and barked at Patrick. Clarissa laughed.

Patrick shrugged. "She speaks better English than I do."

Clarissa smiled. "She's lovely. I'm just surprised I didn't see her last night."

Patrick finished making his last hotcake, turned off the stove, and brought the finished lot over to the center of the table. "Oh, my mother brought her down this morning. Here… I have some fresh bacon for us. I'm breaking my own rules this morning by eating meat."

Clarissa's heart pounded. "Your mother! Is she here now? I should have dressed a bit nicer. Should I go and put on some makeup?" Her eyes darted around the kitchen and to the empty doorway.

Patrick helped himself to the orange juice in a relaxed manner. "You are perfect as always. Mother is here, but she went to check on the horses with our head groom. We had a new addition arrive to the stables a few days ago. You'll meet my mother shortly. She will love you as I do." He pecked her cheek.

Clarissa hesitated. "She will?"

I am a bundle of nerves. This is the first time I'll be meeting his family. I want to make a good impression. I should be miffed he didn't warn me, but I'm more curious than anything. What will his mother be like?

Patrick slowly nodded. "Yes. She. Will. Mum turned up this morning, wanting to meet you over seeing her only son. I sent her a text message last night, indicating that we would be in residence for the foreseeable future. She has been splitting time between here and at her new husband's estate, Belshaw Hall, and thought she might introduce herself to you."

Clarissa's stomach tightened. *I suppose it is only fair. Patrick has met my family. I still wish I had more warning.*

"Before I forget, I also wanted to ask you if I might be able to take an hour or two of your precious time this morning to show you the estate in greater detail. I understand you want to establish your workspace, but I thought now might be as good a time as any." Patrick urged her to take some fresh bacon and hotcakes.

"Oh. I would love to see Rainridge. I can put my work off until this afternoon, but after that, I'm afraid I'll have to get down to brass tacks and work straight through to the evening."

Patrick agreed, "Of course."

The back door to the kitchen opened. Guinevere stopped eating and eagerly wagged her tail in anticipation of their guest. A woman with light brown and graying hair pulled into a short ponytail came through and slipped off her muddy Wellington boots.

Pulling a silk headscarf off her head, she changed into a pair of worn house slippers. Patrick made his way over to the woman, who stood a head shorter than he, and greeted her. Clarissa pushed her chair back and stood. She fidgeted with her hands.

"Mother, I am beyond thrilled to finally have the chance to introduce you to Clarissa Lee, my girlfriend." Patrick's eyes lit up. "Clarissa, this is my mother, Lady Lucy Manners formally Nelson."

Instead of the expected handshake, Lady Lucy engulfed Clarissa in a warm embrace. Clarissa stiffened, then relaxed. "So you are responsible for the much-needed change in my Paddy. Words cannot describe how happy I am to *finally* meet the woman that makes his heart sing. Welcome home."

Welcome home? Wow. That was not the type of meeting I was at all expecting. I thought she might be a bit untraditional and relaxed, similar to Princess Charlotte, but not to this extent. Lady Lucy is so warm and bubbly.

"Um… the pleasure is all mine?" Clarissa tripped over her words. "I'm afraid I wasn't aware of your arrival. Please forgive my appearance."

Lady Lucy released Clarissa. "Oh pish posh, you are lovely, my dear. Besides, I'm sure I have scared the wits out of you. Excuse a nosy mum, but I jumped at the chance to meet you the moment I read Paddy's text message. If it is any consolation, Paddy wasn't aware I was coming until he came down from his rooms to make himself breakfast and saw me."

Lady Lucy's hazel eyes sparkled with mirth. "I won't stay long. I promised Alistair I would be back before ten this morning. We are heading up to Saint Andrews for a golfing holiday."

Patrick's eyebrow rose. "I didn't think you played golf?"

Lady Lucy shrugged. "There is always a time to learn. Life is about seeking out new adventures. For the next few Saturdays, you will find me out *clubbing*."

Patrick sighed. "That's *par* for the *course*." They laughed.

Clarissa enjoyed watching mother and son interact. She could tell the two of them shared a strong bond. She hoped, in time, her own bond with her parents would mirror that of Patrick and his mother.

"If you would be so kind as to walk me out, Paddy, I won't

encroach upon you two any longer than necessary. I truly did just want to meet you, Clarissa. Please enjoy the rest of your stay here." Lady Lucy signaled to Guinevere who dutifully followed her out.

"I'll be right back," Patrick promised.

Clarissa sat back down and reviewed her meeting with Lady Lucy. *She is a bit eccentric, to say the least. An interesting contrast to Patrick, who is much more reserved. I wasn't aware she remarried. How long ago did Patrick lose his father? Two years?*

Patrick returned in no time and they finally tucked into their breakfast. Clarissa relaxed for the first time all morning. "I am sorry Mum popped up unannounced."

"Truthfully, I enjoyed her spontaneity."

Patrick said, "Mum has always been the type of person who decides to do things on a whim."

Clarissa bit into one of her hotcakes. "It worked out well. Besides, it was nice to see you two together. Pardon me for asking, but how long has she been remarried?"

Patrick played with his fork and stared off in the distance. "Not overly long. In fact, she only announced it to me the day you and I met one another."

Clarissa sensed there was more to the story. "Patrick?" she asked.

Patrick pushed his plate away. "Lord Greyston, my mother's new husband, is an outstanding gent. He is my godfather and has done so much for us over the years." He took a breath. "This is dumb, but I have only recently come to terms with my mother replacing my father. I am not one who does well with change. The day we met, I ran away from Rainridge. I didn't react to the news well. You're aware of my depression. I have good days and bad. That day, I just could not bring myself to fully accept my mother without my father. I found myself so low."

Clarissa processed the information. Patrick rarely opened up about his depression. She grasped his hand and squeezed. "Change is never easy. No matter what, always remember, I'm here for you too." She did not feel it appropriate to say much more but just to reassure him that she was fully available for him, no matter what he might need.

"Thank you."

The grandfather clock in the entryway struck eight. The sounds reverberated into the kitchen.

"It's eight already?" Patrick abruptly stood and looked at Clarissa. "Time is going by all too quickly this morning. We had better get a move on it if we are to see everything in time."

Just what does he have planned?

Chapter Thirty-One

PATRICK

Giddy with excitement, Patrick had a difficult time not spoiling his surprise as he quickly led Clarissa to the field between the orangery and carriage house outbuildings. Patrick's groundskeeper had promised their transportation would be ready by nine.

Patrick attempted to normalize his voice. "I thought you might enjoy a *unique* perspective of Rainridge and the Cotswold on your very first visit."

Clarissa's eyes locked onto the wicker basket and a team of six people working to fill a hot-air balloon.

She asked uncertainly, "Patrick? Is that a real hot-air balloon?"

Patrick snickered. "If I were to say it was a figment of your imagination from undue stress, would you believe me?"

Clarissa shot back, "If it were about two weeks from now, yes."

They looked on. Patrick brazenly explained, "This is the latest purchase for the estate. Mother and I thought having a hot-air balloon would add to the distinctiveness of Rainridge as a wedding destination."

Clarissa agreed and absorbed the information. "How do you even steer these things?"

Patrick pointed to the burner filling up the balloon. "You add hot air to allow the balloon to rise and stop adding air when the balloon is ready to descend. There is no steering system. Everything is dependent on the wind and what direction it's blowing."

"Wicked." Clarissa's eyes nearly bulged out of their sockets. "How do you know where to land us?"

Patrick left that question to the pilot of the balloon who had taken an active interest in the conversation. He greeted Patrick and Clarissa. "Good morning, miss. Don't mind me if I answer that question. Lord Renbrook has the permission of the local landowners to utilize their properties for landings, depending on where the wind takes us. We always strive for a flat, open patch. Lord Renbrook has a car service following the balloon's path. We stay in contact via radio, and following the ride, it will return you to the manor house."

Clarissa all but ran up to the basket. "Well, what are we waiting for? Can we go now?"

Patrick followed along as the pilot and his copilot performed their safety and radio checks. "You can wait in the basket if you want, Clarissa. It's going to be a few minutes. Our pilot is in charge from here on out."

Clarissa pulled Patrick along with her. "This is the best surprise ever. I'm so happy right now. How did you plan this so fast?"

Patrick was thrilled. "The pilot and crew are always on standby. They live in the area. I was up early and thought it might be prudent to test out the balloon for myself. It's undergone a few test flights, but this is personally my first time out. There is not a single person I'd rather share this experience with."

Clarissa snuggled into Patrick's arms. She rose up onto the

tips of her toes and kissed him. The slight chill he had felt was gone with Clarissa in his arms. She felt so soft. Her hair smelled of roses.

As he kissed her, Patrick tasted the cinnamon and sweet maple syrup from the morning's breakfast upon her lips. He felt a bridge of energy being shared between the two of them. They were connecting on a deeper level.

The pilot spoke, "We're ready when you are, Lord Renbrook."

Chapter Thirty-Two

CLARISSA

T he pilot fired the burner. Propane filled the balloon as it slowly rose off the ground. Clarissa gripped onto Patrick, doubtful of the safety of the wicker basket.

She had been nervous about being a thousand or more feet up in the air, but the gentle drifting motion of the balloon relaxed her. With Patrick, she felt secure. The morning was indeed the best time to fly. The winds were calm.

Patrick largely stayed quiet. "Rainridge is just a dot now, but you can make out where we took off, the stables, and grazing lands. The pond to the east is shared with our nearest neighbors."

Looking out onto the endless, rolling, lush green fields below. The trees appeared so minuscule and mystical with the low hanging fog. Clarissa noticed a handful of streams snaking across the land surrounded by blips of villages—quintessential English countryside. The air was cool but manageable.

What would it be like at sunset up above with Patrick? It would be so romantic! She never wanted to land. Rather, she wanted to stay up in the balloon forever.

"This is so surreal," Clarissa shouted to Patrick. The sound of the burner made it difficult to hear one another. Patrick agreed.

"What inspired you to purchase this?" Clarissa asked as she drew circles on Patrick's arms.

Patrick colored. "I was always inspired by Jules Verne and wondered at what an adventure it would be to truly travel around the world in eighty days."

Clarissa grew sad; she didn't know much about Jules Verne. Patrick was forever mentioning literature and spouting historical facts. She wanted to have a witty reply or be able to banter back, but the truth of the matter was, she had never read the "great works." She smiled at Patrick, but it didn't quite reach her eyes.

Patrick didn't seem to notice her discomfort. "The museum we are constructing is going to have a small-scale balloon experience for visitors to enjoy. I've been working on what types of other exhibits we'll host. The entryway will have a time machine that will transport the visitors back to the Victorian age. As they travel through time, they will learn of inventions from the past and will eventually end up experiencing present-day modern marvels."

Patrick's eyes glowed as he spoke about his project. Clarissa was endeared by his delight. Much like her own project, Clarissa was so proud of what he had accomplished in a short amount of time. There was no doubt of the museum's success.

"I've probably bored you to death with the details. We're not supposed to speak about our work right now. I wanted to show you the Cotswolds and Rainridge. I'm an abysmal host." Patrick frowned.

"No. You're wonderful. Dare I say, nearly perfect. I enjoy hearing what is on your mind. Tell me more about living here." Clarissa didn't have much experience with the southwest part of England. She had grown up in the Midlands.

"The Cotswolds encompasses several counties, from Stratford-upon-Avon to Bath. I believe, in all, it's close to eight hundred square miles. This area has roots dating back to the Stone Age. I'll take you hiking sometime up to the Rollright Stone circle. It's over 5,000 years old." Patrick spoke on and went into more depth than Clarissa could process.

Patrick had promised the balloon ride would only take an hour of her time. Time flew by. She was saddened when the balloon slowly returned to earth. They were about fifteen miles from Rainridge.

Had the ride been shorter, maybe they would've stayed on Rainridge property. As the balloon descended, the empty field below grew increasingly large. Clarissa braced herself unnecessarily for a hard landing.

It never came to pass. As the basket touched the ground, it bounced two or three times as the pilot expertly pulled at the rigging and collapsed the balloon. Clarissa marveled at how rapidly the balloon could inflate and deflate. The entire process was complete in maybe ten minutes.

"Excellent job, mate," Patrick thanked the pilot and copilot. The car following the balloon pulled up along the dirt road not far from the landing site.

Clarissa also gave her thanks to the crew. Exhilarated, she wished to see all of the towns they had flown over in person for herself. However, she also knew she would have to wait until after the royal wedding. They walked over to the car and were driven back to Rainridge.

"That was *quite* an experience today. I will *never* forget it." Clarissa looked through her long lashes at Patrick and parted her lips. Patrick met her halfway, greedily claiming her mouth for himself. Warmth washed over her, and her body tingled in bliss.

When they returned to Rainridge, Clarissa dutifully set her sewing studio up and got to work on Clara's second dress. She felt inspired and was able to make headway on the bodice. Clarissa forced herself to focus.

In just a few weeks you can spend all the time you wish with Patrick.

Chapter Thirty-Three

CLARISSA

C larissa worked late into the night for the next several nights. With Clara due to arrive for a fitting in a week's time, she wanted to complete phase two of the second dress so all that would remain were alterations.

Sewing kit items were spread out in an organized fashion and filled all the available surface spaces. The dress form sat draped with several layers of fabric waiting to be sewn together.

Over by the sewing machine, the finished skirt of Clara Little's wedding dress lay stretched out so it wouldn't wrinkle. At present, she sat embroidering Swarovski crystals onto the neckline.

Clarissa heard a gentle knock on the door. "Come in!" she called out.

Patrick, carrying a late-night snack platter of cheese, crackers, apple slices, and a glass of sparkling water, entered the room. "I thought you might be in need of some fortifications." He placed the items down near her sewing machine.

"Not here!" she exclaimed and quickly moved the light fabric of Clara's dress away from the food.

Patrick opened his mouth into an "O" shape. "I am so sorry, Clarissa. I wasn't thinking."

Clarissa's eyes twitched with fatigue. Her expression softened as Patrick took up one of the empty chairs in the back of the sewing studio. He rubbed his eyes; Clarissa sighed. Each night, Patrick attempted to spend a few minutes of time with her.

The pit of her stomach clenched with guilt. *I haven't made any effort to spend time with him lately. What kind of girlfriend am I?* She set aside her work, stood, and stretched her aching wrists out.

Moving across from Patrick, she helped herself to the items on the plate and gave him her full attention. "Tell me about your day."

Patrick leaned back in the chair. His fingers played with the signet ring on his pinky. "My day wasn't too exciting. I rode out, examined the grounds, and supervised some of the plantings for the gardens. We just received some new fruit trees and rose bushes. I hope in time these will grow, making the estate more self-sustaining. Our events manager, Kelly, is delighted to finally have flowers available in-house for the many arrangements and bouquets. Fresh flowers are one of the more expensive costs of the events business."

Clarissa closed her eyes. "That sounds nice. You will have to show me the flowers sometime. If I had a greenhouse, I might never leave. That is part of the reason I constantly visit Kew Gardens. Flowers and plant life calms and relaxes me." Patrick moved to massage her shoulders.

"Now I am aware of how to tempt you away from here. I have a few plants that may interest you by the orangery." Patrick worked his fingers into one of the tender spots by the base of her neck. "There isn't a chance I could persuade you to take a day off tomorrow, is there? I would love to take you into one of the surrounding villages. I can promise there will be many cottage gardens and floralscapes to see."

Clarissa tensed and slowly removed Patrick's hands, not meeting his eyes. "I'm afraid not. As much as I would love to, Clara will be here next week, and if I stop, I won't have the top of her gown ready for her to try on."

Patrick sighed. "Alright. It was worth a try. Please try to sleep a full eight hours. Clara and I need you to be healthy. I'll see you in the morning." Just as quietly as he entered the room, he slipped out.

Clarissa stared at the nearly-empty plate and placed a hand on her shoulder; it was still warm from Patrick's touch.

Patrick knows the deadline I am under. Am I wrong to want to finish the dress? Clara is my priority right now.

Clarissa pondered over Patrick and finished her snack. Drawing upon her ever-dwindling reserves of energy, she continued her work.

∼

Clara arrived for her fitting two weeks into Clarissa's stay at Rainridge. Light rain fell atop Clarissa's umbrella as they walked together from the front drive up to the changing area.

Clarissa asked, "How has it been learning to drive on what you Americans call 'the other side of the road?'"

Clara laughed. "Now that I've had a few months to acclimate to it, not bad at all. It's taken some getting used to, but I haven't made any wrong turns in the last two weeks. That's progress right?"

They entered the sewing room. "Absolutely." Behind them, Clarissa closed the door. They shrugged off their outerwear and enjoyed a round of refreshments.

"I owe you a debt of gratitude for coming all the way out here from London for the fitting. I had hoped to catch a ride with Patrick to the city, but he required an extra early start," Clarissa explained.

Clara nodded in understanding. "Actually, coming out to Gloucestershire is the perfect excuse to leave the chaos of London behind. Princess Charlotte is driving nearly everyone in her vicinity mad. I have two full days off from the theater, which for me is rare, and I intend to make full use of it by playing tourist with Amanda. I have always wanted to see the city of Oxford and its beautiful architecture. There is a pub there called the Eagle and Child where the Inklings used to meet."

Clarissa gave Clara a blank stare. Clara laughed. "The Inklings were a literary discussion group at Oxford that included JRR Tolkien and CS Lewis. I promised Amanda after a pub lunch we could check out the designer outlet shops at Bicester Village."

Clarissa offered, "Oxford is certainly a fun place. Patrick has told me the best places to see are Christ Church and Trinity Colleges. The landscaping is wonderful. Bicester Village is an experience in itself. There are so many shops to see."

Clara deadpanned. "That's what I'm afraid of." Clara laughed. "No... actually, Amanda isn't as much of a shopaholic as she used to be. She's changed her ways since meeting Eddie. With the amount of time she's put into work, school, and assisting with keeping Charlotte at bay, she deserves to shop until she drops." They chatted for a few more minutes.

Clarissa's stomach flip-flopped. Her breathing quickened. "I have your second dress ready for a fitting. Are you ready to see it?"

Wordlessly, Clarissa passed Clara a pair of white gloves. "I suppose I should preface that this dress has evolved and taken on a life of its own since the sketch consultation. I've completely scrapped that original dress for the one you are about to see."

Clara calmly placed a hand on Clarissa's shoulder. "No matter how it looks, I'm sure it's perfect. You have my full trust. I still can't believe that in just six weeks, David and I will be officially official. Time has gone at warp speed since the beginning of the year."

Clarissa's heart fluttered at Clara's reassurance. From the dress form in the center of the room, Clarissa slowly pulled off the white cloth hiding Clara's reception dress. "I call this the 'Second Act' dress. I was trying too hard to tell the world two different stories about you. Seeing a videoed performance of you as Sleeping Beauty, I realized I needed to change the second dress. Your ceremony dress is more of the fantasized and whimsical version of the dancer side of you. In contrast, this dress is the more adult, sophisticated person you are outside of the theater. I modified Audrey Hepburn's *Breakfast at Tiffany's* classic black dress."

Clarissa had designed a rather bold, fitted, halter-neck, flowing sheath dress out of blush pink fabric, complete with a flowing skirt. The color was pinker than the champagne color of the ceremony dress. Swarovski crystals adorned the neckline and waist area, giving off the illusion of a diamond collar necklace and belt.

Clara breathed in and circled the dress. Her large hazel eyes glistened with a faraway expression. "David's nickname for me is Aurora. It couldn't be more fitting to have dresses modeled after Act I and Act II of *The Sleeping Beauty*."

A few goosebumps caused Clarissa to shiver in delight. Clara exhibited an inner radiance as she caressed the shimmering crystal detailing.

We've both come a long way from our first meeting until now. She let out a breath. *She found her prince and I found Patrick. It is scary to think how connected our two worlds are.*

"I don't think I can wait a moment longer. Can I try this baby on?"

Clara impatiently slipped her shoes off and pulled her medium-length hair up onto a bun with the speed of practiced hands. They moved in front of a full-length looking glass Patrick had brought up from the bridal dressing suites. Clarissa diligently assisted Clara as she changed into the gown.

Clara waltzed from side to side. "The fabric is very light and airy. Is it chiffon?" Clara asked.

Clarissa nodded. "Excellent eye." Clarissa straightened the skirt and checked the fit of the top. "The initial fit is solid. How does it feel? Are you able to move? Any areas of discomfort?"

Clara twirled. "No, everything is sublime. As if I danced 'once upon a dream.'" She hummed to herself.

Clarissa laughed. "While I am ecstatic to have your seal of approval, I implore you to please be as particular as you can with any feedback. Do you find the back too open? I wasn't certain how you might feel with bare arms."

Clara turned to the side and glanced at the back of the dress. "I dance with bare arms every day. It doesn't bother me, but maybe we could have a wrap made just in case. Our reception is going to be outside in covered tents at the Windsor Palace gardens. At night, it can be chilly."

Perfect. I wasn't sure about the wrap, but she definitely wants it. I can start on it straightaway.

"Let me just find a pencil and some paper to sketch on."

Supplies in hand, they collaborated and came up with a wrap design that satisfied both women.

Just as the two were in the midst of wrapping up their consultation, Clarissa's mobile rang. She ignored it and frantically tried to silence it. Twice more it vibrated.

Clara said, "Somebody is desperately trying to ring you.

You should probably answer it. Don't worry about me. I'm just going to text Amanda."

Clarissa apologized for the disruption, stepped into the hall, and unlocked her phone to see a message from the detective working on her case. With shaky hands, Clarissa returned the detective's call.

What is going to happen next?

"Hello, Detective Wade? This is Clarissa Lee. I'm sorry I wasn't available until now. How can I be of assistance?"

The Scottish detective answered. "Miss Lee! Thank you for ringing me! I have news for you. After failing to have an update for you last week, we've had a major break in the case. Three men have just been apprehended, attempting to force their way into your Portobello Road boutique. It was a sheer coincidence that I happened to be in the area and stopped by to check in with Miss Morozova about a neighboring boutique that was ransacked two days ago. The assailant's van is quite full of many of your personal belongings. We need you to identify the intellectual property in person at your earliest convenience. With any luck, we can have these three in front of a magistrate by the end of the week."

Clarissa paced the hall. "You've arrested the burglars? Forcing their way into my Portobello boutique?"

"That's correct, Miss Lee. We now know that these three henchmen were hired by one of the tattlers to obtain any information pertaining to the wedding of Miss Clara Little and His Highness the Duke of Leeds for just shy of four million pounds. We have a confession and so much evidence it should be a fairly easy case to prosecute."

Clarissa glanced at her watch. It was ten-thirty. "I'm in Gloucestershire right now, but I will be on the next train to London and ring you as soon as I am in town." Clarissa confirmed a few more details and disconnected the call.

Clara, having heard some of the call, immediately asked if

she could offer any assistance. "I can't believe how low some people will sink to. I shoulder much of the blame."

"No, this is all on the tattlers. I am just relieved this is almost over. They've caused me so much stress over the past weeks. I am so sorry to have to rush out, but I need to head down to the train station as soon as possible." Clarissa searched the room for her coat. Her mobile beeped, indicating a low battery.

"I'll do you one better; I'll take you down to London myself."

Clarissa shook her head. "No. You already have plans. I will not let you ruin your only two days off to shuttle me around. It would be as if the burglars had won. I will not let them have even the smallest of victories."

Clara bit her lip. "I don't feel it's right to let you take the train. What if Amanda let you take the car she's driving up here? Our security team can ride with us."

Once again, Clarissa refused. "No, I am too on edge to drive. The train is the fastest option and gives me time to think."

Clara sighed. "You are certainly stubborn. Can we at least drop you off at the station?"

Clarissa hesitated, then reluctantly agreed. "Thank you."

Chapter Thirty-Four

PATRICK

Patrick glanced at the clock on his dashboard. Six in the evening. Turning into Rainridge, Patrick parked the car and turned off the engine. Tiredly, he closed his eyes and sat in the driver's seat in contemplation.

After meeting with several contractors, it was clear that updating the roof and plumbing for Rainridge would cost just under seven hundred and fifty thousand pounds. Their budget had only allocated half a million.

With a leak in the orangery, how long before it required a new roof too? To add to his woes, the museum project hit a snafu; the limestone needed for part of the museum's exterior was stuck in transit, adding a delay of three weeks to the project.

Patrick pinched the bridge of his nose. At least he was home and could relax over dinner with Clarissa.

I hope her fitting with Clara went well. She might even be willing to go for an evening stroll and have some much-needed free time. He breathed deeply. *There is no need to stress Clarissa out with my problems.*

Stepping out of the car, Patrick picked up his work bag

and headed inside. Opening the door, he was surprised to find the home inordinately dark. *Is the power out?* Frowning, he tested the closest light switch. The surge of electricity whined as the lights came to life. *Alright. That's been sorted out, but why is it so dark?*

Patrick investigated and found the remainder of the home dark and eerily quiet. Patrick walked up the stairs to the first floor. He clicked on the lights, stood in front of Clarissa's workroom, and knocked in quick succession. No answer. His heart thumped wildly.

He knocked again. "Clarissa?" he called out. No answer.

I promised to respect her space, but this is not like her.

He wrestled with himself. His breathing grew tense. He anxiously waited with bated breath and finally turned the knob and opened the door to a cold, empty workroom. The tidy room revealed nothing out of the ordinary.

Worried, Patrick rushed from the room and proceeded to check all the other rooms of the house. Clarissa was nowhere to be found. Where was she? There was no note... all of her belongings appeared to be there, including Clara's dress. Patrick frantically opened his phone and tried ringing her. Her mobile went straight to voicemail.

Think. Who else can I reach out to?

Patrick attempted to dial her shops, and finally, Sonya. Not a single person answered their phone. He left voicemails.

David is out of the country, and I don't have Clara's number. There isn't a way to reach him until he lands. Where else could Clarissa be?

Beyond worried, Patrick decided his next course of action would be to search the grounds. *She isn't as familiar with Rainridge as me.*

His mind jumped from one horrible thought to another. Though it was nearly pitch-black outside, Patrick enlisted the help of his groundskeeper, and together they scoured the estate grounds.

Two hours later, their results yielded nothing. Patrick's chest ached. He stared into the fire of the study. His hands gripped his phone in a death grip, willing it to ring.

What if she's hurt and I have missed her? Or was she kidnapped? Of course, there was another alternative—what if Clarissa had left him? What would happen if she *was* out of love with him? Mary had certainly cast him aside without any qualms.

I thought our relationship was on solid ground. Did I drive her away with being the man who is always reviewing ledgers, invoices, and stooping over a book? Am I not exciting enough? Have I not changed as I thought I had?

Patrick's mind relived painful memories of the past with Mary. He wallowed in pity. He hadn't realized she never loved him until it was too late. Had he done the same with Clarissa? Could he trust himself to know anything?

I thought she was the perfect woman for me. Do I truly even know her? The room grew colder as the fire went out. Patrick sat in darkness.

No, she would never willingly leave the wedding dress. If I do not have any news by morning, I will ring the police. He had no notion of how long he sat alone.

"Patrick?" A familiar voice called out into the darkness.

Is that Clarissa? Afraid to raise his hopes, he waited until Clarissa repeated, "Patrick?"

His voice flat and devoid of emotion, he answered, "In the library."

The door opened, revealing a glowing halo of light and Clarissa. She rubbed her arms and shivered. "Paddy, it's cold in here. Why are you sitting in the dark?" Clarissa turned the lights on.

Patrick blinked a few times as his eyes adjusted to the light.

Unmoving from his spot on the couch, he whispered, "Where have you been?"

Clarissa dropped the blanket she had started to pick up. "Excuse me?"

He repeated, "Where have you been?" Patrick slowly stood. "Do you have any idea how worried I've been about you?" The emotions of the day caught up with him, and Patrick could not hold himself in check. "I came home and found a dark, foreboding, empty home. No note. I called everyone I could think of to see if you had been kidnapped or worse! I searched the grounds and nothing." Patrick paced the room.

Clarissa's hair was thrown up in a messy, slightly damp bun. Patrick's eyes probed over Clarissa. Her defining brown eyes widened in confusion. She stood rigid, tension clearly being held up in her shoulders. She stammered, "I've been in London all afternoon and into the evening…"

Patrick threw his hands up in the air with disbelief. "She went to London. Why did you not travel down with me this morning? I thought you were supposed to be working with Clara Little. Or have you been lying to me?"

Clarissa's eyes flashed in anger. "I would *never* lie to you! Do you not know me well enough to even be asking a question like that? You need to calm yourself before we can chat. You are not the only one who has had a long day."

Without waiting for any word, Clarissa swept out of the room. The echo of her feet running away from him caused Patrick to punch a pillow in frustration.

Calm down? How did she think I would respond to her being gone? How can she think I don't know her as I do? Patrick sank down and held his head in his hands. *What reason could she have possibly had to go to London?*

His mobile vibrated on the cushion next to him. *Who is calling me now?*

"Yes, hello?" he barked into his mobile.

Sonya's panicked voice came onto the line. "Patrick? I left my mobile at the Portobello boutique, and I only just retrieved my phone. I didn't fully understand your message. It came across garbled. It's been a frantic afternoon. Is Clarissa alright? Her train left London two and a half hours ago. She should be there by now."

Patrick stiffened. "She arrived just fine."

Sonya prompted him for more information, unsatisfied with his response. "And? Is she alright? Clarissa spent just over four hours at the police station. She held herself together so well. I was worried it might have been too much for her and begged her to spend the night at my flat, but she insisted on being stubborn and returning back to Gloucestershire tonight."

Police station? Four hours? Too much? A sense of dread washed over Patrick.

Wearily, he said, "Sonya, you had better start from the beginning. What happened this afternoon? There is a lot of information I am missing. Clarissa and I had a dreadful row when she arrived home. I have majorly screwed up, but in order to fix my mistakes, I need to understand the entire story."

Sonya huffed. "If you have done *anything* to hurt her, so help me I will…"

"You may do whatever you deem necessary to me as soon as I have seen to Clarissa's well-being. Now, what happened?"

Sonya recounted their afternoon. The more he heard, the more Patrick wished to sink into a black hole. Patrick took a moment to recover his wits.

"Thank you for bringing me up to speed. Clarissa is a remarkable woman I in no way deserve. I *have* to go and find her and set everything right."

Sonya's voice softened at hearing Patrick's sincerity. "Don't linger on the phone with me. Go."

Patrick resisted every instinct to go after her the moment he disconnected the phone. He gave himself a few minutes to get into the right head space and to figure out exactly how he might make amends with the only woman he had ever deeply loved.

Chapter Thirty-Five
CLARISSA

Salty tears flowed down Clarissa's cheeks. Her lips quivered. Once in her room, Clarissa firmly shut the door behind her and sank down onto her bed, crying into her pillow.

He's not Mark. He loves you.

She repeated it to herself a few times. Pulling her knees up to her chest, Clarissa rocked back and forth. She hit her breaking point and sobbed into her knees.

The stress of the royal wedding, the burglaries, and the confusion over her relationship with Patrick took hold. For so long, she hid all of her anxiety and pent-up emotions behind a mask.

I can't do it anymore. It's too much. I'm not strong enough. I'm not the person everybody thinks I am. I'm just Clarissa. Nobody else. She could not stand to be indoors any longer.

There was only one balm she could trust to soothe her broken spirit—nature. Not caring how she appeared, or what time of the evening it was, Clarissa slipped a jacket over her attire and slipped out into the cold, wet, inky night.

Around her, trees rustled their leaves as the wind whispered through their tops. She remembered seeing the estate's greenhouse outbuilding from the balloon ride, yet had not found time to view it in person. Walking quickly, Clarissa found small lanterns illuminating the pathway to the building, seemingly inviting her inside.

The door opened without any problems. Upon entering the facility and turning the lights on, Clarissa did not expect to find such a vast collection of pots in varying shapes and sizes scattered atop every flat surface.

Clarissa's eyes spied six hanging petunia pots of striped pink, white, and purple flowers suspended overhead. She recognized the orange and yellow dahlias, white freesias, and blue hydrangeas, but could not identify many of the other variants.

She inspected the label of each plant closely. *Leave it to Patrick to write the scientific and common name of each plant, the date it was planted, and the last watering on it. He leaves the plants arranged in no particular order, yet takes the time to meticulously label them.* Everywhere she looked, she found herself reminded of Patrick.

It took me so long to learn to trust again after everything I had experienced with Mark. I have been so afraid to become close to anyone. The way Patrick reacted tonight scared me. Have I made a mistake?

For all of his faults, as she reflected on the past months, he stood by her every step of the way. He was the man who fixed her flat's door handle, left her meals, swept up broken glass in her shop, and who worried so much about her safety, he opened his family estate to her.

Clarissa pondered the thoughts as she inspected all the plants. Many flowerpots contained buds waiting for the signal from nature to open. Very soon, this greenhouse would be an explosion of colors.

Paddy is the only man I can picture in my life. I love him so much. Despite what may have transpired, I trust him. I did run off to London suddenly, and Patrick has opened up to me about his depression.

Clarissa's eyes teared up again. *I never wanted to hurt him.* Was that why he reacted as he had? Was Patrick afraid of being hurt again?

Chapter Thirty-Six

PATRICK

Patrick's attempts to play a game of chess against himself failed. He could only focus upon his conversation with Clarissa.

There is nothing I can do except apologize to her and explain what made me snap. I just hope she can forgive me. Our problem was our lack of communication. This entire episode is just one giant misunderstanding. I'll go insane if I sit here any longer.

Judging that enough time had passed, Patrick started toward Clarissa's guest suite. After knocking carefully several times, he placed an ear to the door. He couldn't discern any noise.

Was she in her room? Patrick considered opening the door, but instead smacked himself on the forehead.

If I were Clarissa, I would need an area to disassociate myself from the world. Kew Gardens is her favorite in the world. There is only one location on the estate I can think of her seeking refuge in.

Taking off at a jog, Patrick opened the front door and sprinted down to the greenhouse. From the outside, Patrick watched with fascination as Clarissa soaked in each and every plant growing inside the greenhouse.

He slowed his pace. Thousands of insects and crickets buzzed, filling the night with sound. He hesitated outside the doorway. Nervously, he let himself inside.

The greenhouse atmosphere trapped the heat of the day, creating the ideal growing conditions for plants. "Be careful, Clarissa, that is a juvenile bougainvillea that has rather sharp thorns. It may appear innocent, but it hides a rather nasty secret."

Clarissa briefly looked up with interest. "The bougainvillea has among the tenderest roots of any plant. I have had a wickedly difficult time transplanting them. I thought perhaps a biodegradable nursery pot might serve me well this year. We have a trellis set for it to climb near the outdoor wedding space."

Clarissa replied, "I've never seen one so small. I know just how large they can become."

Patrick took several tentative steps in Clarissa's direction. When she didn't retreat, he placed his hands behind his back, waiting for a signal from her.

Clarissa initiated the conversation. "I realized, being in the greenhouse, that every direction I turn, I see you. You are such an important person in my life, but today when you accused me of lying to you, it broke me in ways I am still trying to decipher."

Softly he said, "I overreacted today and was petrified at what finding an empty home might mean. I worried so much about your safety. If you had been kidnapped or missing, I don't know what I would have done."

Patrick stared at the ground. "After I spoke with Sonya, I felt haunted by our conversation. I *do* know you well enough to know I should not have jumped to my own conclusions. I let my emotions take over. I will never truly be able to fully apologize to you. I realized only after the fact I may have come across as controlling."

Clarissa grabbed Patrick's hand and squeezed it. Clarissa spoke next. "I needed time to process my own emotions, but I *do* understand you worried about me out of love. The fact that you are here now speaks volumes about you. I have only just now realized how the situation from your perspective may have appeared. We are both at fault. I never thought to leave a note or to ring you. My focus was entirely on reaching London. I thought I might be strong enough to close this chapter out on my own, but I am ashamed to say I hit my breaking point. I need my support system. I need you."

Patrick guided them over to his workbench. He rearranged a few pots so they could sit. "I was terrified today that I might lose you. Being alone also triggered memories of abandonment from Mary and a return to the darkest of places I have tried so desperately to put behind me. My worst fears became a reality. I know that I am a far cry from being the type of man you deserve, but..."

"Patrick what nonsense are you babbling on about? It is *me* who is the one who brings the baggage and inadequacy to this relationship. I can never measure up to being a *lady* of high society. You require a woman who can match your intellect, assist you with all those ledgers you are forever pouring over, and..."

Patrick could not believe what he was hearing. "What *ever* gave you the impression you had to be someone other than yourself? Have I ever cared as to what anyone else thinks? No."

Patrick spoke into her hair. "I love you because you're so different from anyone. You stand out as my fierce dragon. I love the way you create with your hands and find a way to succeed no matter what. I love your drive, your determination, and your passion. I love you for being you. Not anyone else. You."

Chapter Thirty-Seven

CLARISSA

Clarissa's fingers traveled up the scratchy woolen sleeves of his jumper. Her stomach was tied up in knots. Her heart warmed. "There was a part of myself that has been missing for so long. A void that yearned to be filled. I love you so very much. You have captured my heart."

Patrick wrapped his arms around Clarissa. She buried her face into his chest. She needed to show Patrick just how much he was loved. She didn't delay but slammed her lips into his.

Patrick let out a small growl from his throat. Clarissa liked this side of him. She stopped thinking and ran her hands through his hair. The rush of feelings that bolted through her body made her feel so alive, so breathless.

She whispered his name. He squeezed her a little harder. Her heart was ready to burst. "I've waited so long to kiss you like that." She wanted to prolong the moment and seal it into her memory for all time.

Patrick panted as he pulled away from her. "You're so beautiful. I never knew you had such a wild side."

Clarissa felt as if her heart was running along a racecourse. She felt dazed and hypnotized by him. "Never doubt me, Paddy," she whispered.

"I won't. So long as you never doubt me, my love," Patrick breathed.

They kissed again, and at that moment, Clarissa knew they would be able to move past this bump in the road. It came along with the territory of being human. That night, Clarissa and Patrick learned much about one another and stayed up late into the night discussing everything that popped into their minds.

Just before sunrise, Patrick guided them to his favorite view of the estate. Patrick whispered into her ear, "This is one of the most amazing places to see the sun return from her slumber and conquer the darkness. I am honored to be able to share it with you."

Chester snorted and proceeded to eat the long grass, impervious to the two humans.

Clarissa snuggled into Patrick's chest as they sat atop Chester's saddle blanket, waiting for the magic to happen. "Thank you."

Silently they watched the sun climb, its rays highlighting the estate's manor home, rolling fields, and unyielding stream.

Clarissa smiled. "Simply perfect."

"Indeed," Patrick replied.

Another three weeks at Rainridge passed in the blink of an eye. Falling into a comfortable rhythm, Clarissa and Patrick found the perfect balance of work and leisure. In exploring the small villages and wildness of the Cotswold, Clarissa questioned if she ever wanted to return to London.

But with the royal wedding only three weeks away, she could no longer delay her departure. Despite her reluctance in returning to London, Patrick reassured her Rainridge had waited for the Nelson family since the nineteenth century; it could wait for them a few more weeks.

Chapter Thirty-Eight

CLARISSA

The streets of Windsor were packed two days before the royal wedding was set to take place. A sense of national pride and royal fever spread out across the United Kingdom. Members of the media from around the world camped themselves outside of Buckingham Palace, Kensington Palace, and Windsor Castle in anticipation of capturing the royal bride-to-be unaware.

Clarissa was back in London and staying at Kensington Palace in her own little bubble. She had nearly the entire east wing of the palace at her disposal. Despite being a guest the day of the wedding, she remained on pins and needles until the moment her duty to Clara was discharged.

Each detail of the bridesmaid dresses, maid of honor dress, and both of Clara's dresses needed one final review. Clarissa had to admit that her team had come through and did an excellent job with the garments.

Clara arrived at eleven in the morning tired, yet over-the-moon excited. She chatted animatedly with the members of her bridal party.

Outside of Mrs. Collins and Amanda, Clarissa enjoyed

having the opportunity to meet the women who Clara claimed were the most important in her life: Princess Alice, the bubbly sister of the Prince of Wales, Jenna Evans, the shy daughter of Doctor Evans, and Olive Nakamura, a former roommate from Seattle. Today, the plan was for Clara to model the entire wedding look from head to toe. Clarissa didn't want to leave anything to chance.

At the same time, the closer they came to the finish line, the more Clarissa couldn't wait until life returned to relative normal. She was ready for her extended vacation with Patrick. The tickets were booked. They would spend a whole two weeks lost to the wilds of the Hawaiian Islands, America's fiftieth state.

Olive, a native of Hawaii, had quite a bit of wisdom to share. Clarissa soon found herself invited to dinner with the Nakamura family when she and Patrick visited.

"The only thing I need to warn you about is that my mom is a bit of a tennis fanatic. Next week is the big Honolulu Tennis Open tournament, and for the duration of the event, nothing else in our household matters."

Clarissa tilted her head to the side. "Hm... I wonder if that's where my brother is playing. He mentioned a short jaunt in the States. I hadn't thought to connect the dots."

"Your brother plays pro tennis?" Olive asked.

Clarissa's cheeks flushed. "Yes. His name is Henry Lee..."

Olive laughed. "Ranked number eighteen in the world. Made the third round of Wimbledon last year. Oh, I'm well aware of who he is, and yes, he's playing. He is invited to dinner, too, if he doesn't mind my mom."

"I shall extend the invitation his way." Olive's easy-going nature immediately drew Clarissa in.

"Henry mentioned something about a new doubles partner too... Alex something or other. I can't recall his name." Clarissa's thoughts were interrupted by Sonya who signaled she was ready for Olive.

The large banquet room the women were in now was transformed into an area akin to a fashion show with dedicated stations for each member of the bridal party. Sonya oversaw the bridesmaids so that Clarissa might focus on Clara.

Directly after the fitting and any alterations, the dresses and accessories would be driven via armed guard to Windsor Castle. Sonya joked that the dress had more security than the jewels.

From her own makeup station, Clara floated over to Clarissa. As a ballerina, Clara carried herself in a different manner from the rest of the populace. Every movement she made appeared so graceful. Well versed in putting together a performance look, Clara opted to do her own wedding hair and makeup.

For her ceremony, Clara's hair remained down with curls cascading down her back. A few stray tears escaped Clarissa's eyes. She sniffled and took a moment to compose herself. Butterflies formed in Clarissa's stomach.

Clara looks so regal, and she doesn't even have a dress on yet!

"If you start crying, *I* am going to start. I mean, it just hits you all at once. I know that once the dress is on, I'm going to lose it myself." Clara accepted the box of tissues from Clarissa.

Clarissa helped herself to one, then slipped on her white gloves. "Shall we start with the ceremony dress then?"

Clara nodded. Clarissa assisted Clara as she stepped into the dress. Clarissa slid the delicate lace sleeves over Clara's arms before buttoning up the skirt and bodice. Amanda Collins had her phone clicking away, much to the annoyance of Clara.

"Really, Amanda? Won't there be a zillion photographers out there?" Clara huffed.

Amanda brushed off her bestie. "You'll thank me when

you have time to step back and say, 'Hey, I'm so happy I had a picture of the moment I saw myself in the dress all jacked up.'"

Clarissa wanted to laugh but was too full of nervous energy to do so. Everything today had been going too smoothly. She was paranoid that something was bound to go wrong. Sonya appeared next to Clarissa and smoothed out the edge of the train and the skirt. Amanda snapped away in the background.

Dress fully in place, Clarissa said, "Now all we need are the veil and tiara."

"They are on the table behind…" As Clara turned, the sound of fabric ripping reverberated across the staging room.

Clarissa froze, ready to faint. She shut her eyes and held her breath. What had just happened? What part of the dress had ripped? Was it repairable? When she opened her eyes, Amanda and Clara's faces were ghostly white. Clara stood stiff and in shock. Clarissa's heart skipped a beat, veil and tiara forgotten.

"Oh… my… gawd! The dress is ruined!" Clara's body shook.

Clarissa had never seen the dancing duchess in such an emotional state. Ecstatic one moment, traumatized the next. Sonya carefully held Clara in place until Clarissa was able to assess the damage. She breathed a sigh of relief. The rip was on the back seam of one of the skirt panels. Some of the delicate work on the overskirt had been stepped on as Clara put her shoes on.

"I can fix it. It'll take me some time, but it's not a huge problem." Clarissa had no idea where the miscalculation had been. Clara had already tried the dress on with shoes during the second fitting, unless they were not the shoes from the last fitting!

"Are these shoes the same ones you had on the last time you were with me?" Clarissa's gut told her no.

Clara's face slowly began to regain its color. She held herself still to avoid any more damage to the dress. "No." She sniffled. "David gave me these this morning. He made them for the wedding for me. I didn't think it would be a major problem."

Mystery solved. Clarissa gazed down at the white satin shoes carefully decorated with the royal monogram Clara would adopt upon marriage. "That's very sweet. I only ask because I want to reexamine the hem. That's why you may have trod on the skirt. I allowed it for heels, not flats.

Clara winced. "I should have told you. I'm sorry, Clarissa."

Clarissa had already pinned the panel back in place and was now working on the bottom of the dress. She was going to need to do a lot more work to fix the dainty flowers at the base of the dress. What was another sleepless night or two for a happy bride?

"Better to happen now than on your big day." Clarissa triple-checked the placement of her pins and stood up. "Let's see how the full ensemble comes together with the veil and tiara."

Disaster averted, Sonya and Clarissa assisted with setting the English rose tiara and veil upon Clara's head. The tiara shimmered from each angle, enthralling the members of the bridal party. Gingerly, Clarissa straightened the veil and placed it behind Clara just over the train of the skirt. Clarissa stepped back.

Clara stared at herself in the mirror for several long moments. She smiled, flashing her pearly whites. Her eyes glimmered, and at the moment, Clarissa grew three inches taller. In seeing such a jubilant bride, Clarissa felt a sense of fulfillment and purpose.

This was the reason Clarissa pushed herself as hard as she did. Designing was not about the money or the fame, but about making dreams come true. *I've worked so hard the last few months. This is everything to me. Just seeing Clara so exhila-rated is all I need to know that I am doing what I am meant to do.*

Sonya hugged Clarissa tightly. "You've done it, Clarissa, and I couldn't be any prouder of you."

"Let's hear three cheers for Clarissa's brilliant work!" Amanda called out.

Clarissa's cheeks burned. "And you haven't even seen the finished ceremony dress yet!"

~

Clarissa let out a deep breath. Patrick held her arm as they walked up the steps to the clamor of the massive crowds outside the chapel of St. George at Windsor Castle. Photographers clicked away at some of the other arriving guests.

Patrick whispered into her ear, "Just wait until they find out *you* designed Clara's dresses. You will not receive a moment's peace. I will be more than happy when we arrive in Hawaii."

Clarissa giggled. "I cannot wait."

She soaked in the sight of Patrick in his morning dress. He appeared so dapper in his white shirt, gray trousers, gray waistcoat, tie, and black tailcoat. All he was missing was a top hat. His amethyst pocket square matched the dress she had designed for herself.

Patrick and Clarissa took their seats. "How was Clara when you left her?" Patrick asked.

Clarissa shrugged. "Nervous, terrified, and beyond happy all at once. I have a few photos of her in the carriage if you want to see her."

Patrick shook his head. "No. I can wait to see the dress you designed when Clara arrives."

The chapel held eight hundred guests varying from other

members of the British royal family to heads of state, friends, and well-wishers. Clarissa recognized a few faces from the Westminster Ballet. Patrick indicated the mutual friends he and David shared from their school days in attendance. Today, Clarissa sat on the bride's side of the chapel, near Mrs. Collins.

Clarissa asked, "Did David mention how many guests would be attending the reception?"

Patrick answered, "No, but he had spoken of it being smaller and more intimate than the ceremony. I would wager perhaps only two or three hundred guests."

"That is still a lot." Clarissa grimaced. "But I can understand. Between my own mama and baba, they had close to three hundred guests at their own wedding. Mama had four different wedding dresses. Thank goodness I was not asked to design so many."

Patrick grinned. "Nevertheless, you would nail them all." He kissed her on the cheek.

The choir and chapel organist provided soft background music. Above them hung the banners of the British royal orders of chivalry. Pink, white, and orange blooms decorated the interior of the chapel and framed the altar.

The music changed. The crowds cheered loudly as the groom and best man arrived, causing the waiting guests inside to buzz in excitement. Princes David and Eddie both wore royal dress uniforms of the British Army's Household Cavalry Mounted Regiment. David's navy-blue officer uniform of the Blues and Royals division stood out in contrast to the red of the enlisted Life Guards uniform worn by Eddie.

Princess Charlotte, in the front of the groom's side of the church, had tissues out to dry her eyes and a large green hat. The princes made their way up to the front. David had difficulty focusing on his music sheet. He pulled at his glasses several times. Eddie whispered into David's ear, Clarissa assumed, to relax his cousin.

King Reginald and Queen Angus were the last guests to arrive. Everyone stood as *God Save the King* played. The king and queen took the place of prominence in the front pew reserved solely for them. Clarissa's heart picked up its pace.

Anticipation built as the level of cheers outside resounded to their highest level yet. A few moments thereafter, the doors to the chapel opened. Clarissa caught a glimpse of Clara ascending from a gold carriage. Clara's bridesmaids, arriving in a separate carriage, each slowly walked down the aisle toward the altar in satin dresses accompanied by a pageboy or girl.

Amanda sauntered by in a stunning periwinkle blue. Prince Edmund's eyes were glued to his girlfriend as she stood across from him and winked. Clarissa was fairly certain the television cameras hidden to the side of the chapel had caught that.

Clarissa was surprised in a way that Clara had allowed the bridal party to precede her. In a typical English wedding, the bridal party followed the bride. Everyone in the church rose. The bridal march played.

Several audible gasps came from the crowd. Chills ran through Clarissa's body upon hearing the reaction to the dress.

Patrick squeezed her hand. "You've done brilliantly. Listen to how much buzz *your* design is creating. Clara is almost as stunning as you."

On the arm of Mr. Collins in a dove gray morning suit, Clara drifted up the aisle. Clara's eye's glittered, her cheeks were rosy and her smile infectious. Clara's attention was focused on one person, David. His eyes locked in on Clara. They were lost to their own world.

As Clara moved past, the full effect of the gown was on display. The hundreds of hand-detailed flower appliques on the skirt almost appeared to have their own LED lights. Clarissa was glad Clara had opted for a short train.

She couldn't tell where the tear had been just two days before. In exchanging vows, rings, and finally their first kiss as husband and wife, Clarissa could not help but notice the amount of love and admiration David and Clara shared with one another in each and every gesture.

The guests of the wedding enjoyed several special musical performances by the Westminster Ballet's first violinist, first cellist, and harpist. The ceremony lasted just forty minutes, presided over by the Dean of Windsor and Archbishop of Canterbury.

After the newlyweds disappeared for a few minutes to sign the wedding registry and wedding license, Clarissa took several photos of the beautifully decorated chapel on her phone. To her amusement, she noticed several text messages from her family. *I'll look at those later.*

As the new bride and groom and royal family departed, Clarissa relaxed, enjoying the ability to be an observer to the pageantry on display. She would meet Clara just before the reception to assist with changing into her second dress. With the doors wide open, David and Clara were ushered into an open carriage drawn by a team of four white horses and liveried servants.

They waved to the crowds. Images from the day would pop up on the internet and over all types of media across the world. Clarissa imagined Clara and David would be exhausted by the time she was ushered into a car and taken back to the reception venue on the other side of Windsor Castle.

Patrick pulled Clarissa aside just as the crush of guests began to depart the church. "I am so utterly amazed and humbled by the sheer amount of talent you possess. The dress you created for Clara is a true work of art. I am so incredibly lucky to have such an artist as my girlfriend."

Clarissa's eyes watered. "Hearing that from you makes my heart sing."

They kissed. Patrick sighed. "I suppose we had best make our way to the reception. I dread having to share you with the rest of the world."

Clarissa's cheeks flushed. "Do you think news travels that quickly?"

Patrick offered his arm to Clarissa. "Would you like to make a small wager?"

Clarissa considered the offer. "No. I have learned I make my own odds."

They stepped out into the sun as someone cried, "That's Clarissa Lee! The dress designer."

They looked at one another and laughed.

Later that evening, Clara and Clarissa privately met together. "Thank you for everything you have done, Clarissa. This truly has been the best day of my life, and it is in many ways all thanks to you." They hugged tightly. "David is enraptured by the dress. I have never received so many compliments."

Clarissa grinned. "I owe you a debt of gratitude too. Without you, I would never have met the man of my dreams."

"I hope you are taking some much-deserved time off after this," Clara stated.

Clarissa responded, "Absolutely. Two entire weeks!"

Clara lifted her brows. "That's it? I suppose I shouldn't be one to speak. David talked me into taking a month off. That is the longest I will have ever gone without dancing." They laughed. "When you return from break, I am going to need an entirely new wardrobe."

Clarissa winked. "I will be ready for the challenge. There is nothing better than designing for a royal."

Epilogue

CLARISSA

TWO YEARS LATER

Kew Gardens was a popular tourist destination in the summer months. The gardens displayed their full glory. The air was pleasantly warm. Patrick and Clarissa strolled along one of their favorite pathways.

Each time they went, there was always something new to discover. No two trips were ever the same. It was rare to be able to coordinate their schedules to have the same time off on a weekday.

In the days following the royal wedding, the number of orders placed on the Clarissa Lee website crashed the system. Clarissa could not possibly have fathomed how popular her dresses might become. Business never slowed and now, two years later, she had shops located in Paris, Rome, New York, LA, Hong Kong, and Toronto. Though, designing for Clara was still a top priority.

Patrick remained in high demand and was asked to consult on projects for museums in and around London after the successful launch of the World of Curiosities Museum. He continually worked on finding new ways to innovate and push the boundaries of what exhibits the museum offered to the public. In the year since its inception, the museum had already set the record for attendance.

After a stroll through the Palm House, the Princess of Wales Conservatory and this year's Costa Rican rain forest exhibit had provided a particularly fun look at orchids. Clarissa felt inspired then and there to begin sketching her next wedding collection on the spot. Patrick, however, had other ideas.

Clarissa pouted as they neared the Waterlily House. "Can't I please have five minutes to jot down what we saw?"

Patrick crossed his arms. "Absolutely not. If I give you five minutes, we'll be here until closing. I know you, Clarissa. You get carried away. Today I'm just saving you the trouble."

She knew Patrick was unlikely to budge. One of the gardeners on the grounds overheard their conversation and chuckled. She had been ready to banter back when she spied a familiar face behind Patrick's shoulder.

She exclaimed, "Old Jim! It's good to see you today. How are your grandchildren?"

Old Jim pocketed his pruning shears, wiped off his brow, and went to greet the couple. He and Clarissa hugged; Old Jim shook hands with Patrick.

"Good to see you, Miss Lee and Mr. Nelson. The grandchildren are well. Did I tell you last time that my Cassie is about to become a mum too? Me and the Misses could not be any prouder. Our brood has certainly grown." Old Jim grinned. "I was hoping to see you today. I have a particularly perfect specimen I came across this morning for you to take with you."

Since their first meeting two years ago, Old Jim had encountered the pair countless times. He always saved Clarissa any flowers he thought may catch her fancy.

He ran off to his cart and returned with a bright orange orchid. "Now, I'm not supposed to offer this to you, but in this case, we can make an exception." Old Jim winked at her. Their conversations always followed along the same lines.

Clarissa's eyes grew. The orange orchid was from the Costa Rica exhibit. It was a stunning mixture of orange and red. She went to sniff it. *This is almost like a Jo Malone fragrance.* She turned to show Patrick, and to her utter shock, Patrick was down on one knee, presenting her with an open ring box.

"Two and a half years ago, you captured my heart. You walked right into me and hit me in the face with a broken doorknob. I've been utterly enchanted with you ever since. We've been through many ups and downs and adventures together. You've seen me in my best and worst of times. There is no other person I could ever imagine spending the rest of my life with. Clarissa, will you marry me?" Patrick choked.

Clarissa nodded as Patrick stood and slipped onto her finger a pink sapphire ring with small diamonds running along the band. She jumped into Patrick's arms, knocking them both over. She kissed him all over his face. "Yes, yes, yes a million and one times over."

Old Jim passed Patrick his phone and winked again. He had filmed the entire scene.

An audience around them clapped and cheered.

"This is for your parents and my mother. I promised both of them I would send it over the moment I popped the question to you. They are expecting us at lunch," Patrick confessed.

Clarissa's relationship with her parents continued to improve. Monthly lunches assisted with bridging the divide between them.

"This ring is stunning!" Clarissa admired the sparkling sapphire ring on her left hand.

Patrick offered a cheesy grin. "It is one of Sonya's designs."

"I should have known." Clarissa's heart swelled with happiness. Her one-time business partner, Sonya, had finally taken the plunge and opened her own jewelry boutique. Sonya, a born businesswoman, was yet another success story.

"I love you, my dragoness."

"I love you too, Lord Renbrook."

They kissed again, a pair of star-crossed lovers, as if not a single other person in the world existed.

Acknowledgments

This book would not be possible without so many members of my amazing team. First off, thank you to Kaylee Baldwin and Ranee Clark of Sweetly Us Press. You ladies have been with me from day one. Thank you for your advice and insight into bringing Clarissa and Patrick's story to life. To Charity Chimni, thank you for your amazing proofreading skills. To Brooke Gilbert, thank you so much for the stunning new cover and for all of your helpful advice and feedback! I could not do this with out you. To my family, thank you for putting up with all of the research that goes into each novel. I appreciate you investing your time watching 'Project Runway' and 'Say Yes to the Dress' with me. To my ARC team and to my readers, I thank you for continuing to support me. I am only able to do this because of you. From the bottom of my heart, thank you.

About the Author

Tomi Tabb writes closed-door romantic comedies filled with heart, hope, and happily-ever-afters. From royalty and bodyguards to engineers, athletes, and performers, her stories celebrate kindness, found family, and the joy of falling in love. Inspired by *Pride and Prejudice*, Tomi writes the  character-driven romances she loves to read—equal parts swoony, hopeful, and satisfying.

A California native, Tomi holds an MA in History and is putting the finishing touches on her doctorate in History, blending her love of research with her passion for storytelling. She lives with her family, one very spoiled cat, and an energetic toddler who keeps life wonderfully unpredictable.

When she isn't writing, you'll likely find her figure skating, watching tennis, or hunting down the newest pumpkin-flavored treat—one of the many reasons fall will always be her favorite season.

Website: TomiTabb.com

Also by Tomi Tabb

The Unexpected Royals

Dancing With a Royal

Jiving With a Royal

Designing for a Royal

Friends of the Unexpected Royals

Designs on Love

Engineering Love

Coasting Into Love

Set to Love

The Skaters of Sequoia Valley

The Rules of the Rink

The Sloth Zone

Caught in a Loop

The Royals of Isola Nostrum

The Great Austen Adventure

For the Love of Dinosaurs

Standalones & Companion Stories

More Than a Passing Shot

Pointe Shoes and Sugar Plums

Jingle Blades

Historical Romance

The Mysterious Mr. Marcellus

9 79898 853017 6